The
Fortune Quilt

Lani Diane Rich

NAL NEW AMERICAN LIBRARY

New American Library
Published by New American Library, a division of
Penguin Group (USA) Inc., 375 Hudson Street,
New York, New York 10014, USA
Penguin Group (Canada), 90 Eglinton Avenue East, Suite 700, Toronto,
Ontario M4P 2Y3, Canada (a division of Pearson Penguin Canada Inc.)
Penguin Books Ltd., 80 Strand, London WC2R 0RL, England
Penguin Ireland, 25 St. Stephen's Green, Dublin 2,
Ireland (a division of Penguin Books Ltd.)
Penguin Group (Australia), 250 Camberwell Road, Camberwell, Victoria 3124,
Australia (a division of Pearson Australia Group Pty. Ltd.)
Penguin Books India Pvt. Ltd., 11 Community Centre, Panchsheel Park,
New Delhi - 110 017, India
Penguin Group (NZ), 67 Apollo Drive, Mairangi Bay,
Auckland 1311, New Zealand (a division of Pearson New Zealand Ltd.)
Penguin Books (South Africa) (Pty.) Ltd., 24 Sturdee Avenue,
Rosebank, Johannesburg 2196, South Africa

Penguin Books Ltd., Registered Offices:
80 Strand, London WC2R 0RL, England

First published by New American Library,
a division of Penguin Group (USA) Inc.

First Printing, March 2007
1 3 5 7 9 10 8 6 4 2

LIBRARY OF CONGRESS CATALOGING-IN-PUBLICATION DATA:
Rich, Lani Diane.
The fortune quilt / Lani Diane Rich.
p. cm.
ISBN-13: 978-0-451-22027-1
ISBN-10: 0-451-22027-7
1. Women television producers and directors—Fiction.   2. Quilts—Fiction.
3. Psychic ability—Fiction.   4. Fate and fatalism—Fiction.   I. Title.
PS3618.I333F67 2007
813'.6—dc22   2006018410

Set in Janson
Designed by Spring Hoteling

Printed in the United States of America

Praise for the novels of Lani Diane Rich

"I love Lani Diane Rich's thirtysomething heroine. . . . Fast, funny, and always true to herself, Wanda is one of those heroines you want to have lunch with."—Jennifer Crusie

"A sparkling debut, full of punch, pace, and wonderfully tender moments."—Sue Margolis

"Terrific and absolutely hilarious . . . with a thoroughly delightful and original heroine."—Melissa Senate

"This effervescent debut novel will strike a chord with every woman who has ever been tempted to give her life an extreme makeover."—Wendy Markham

"A warm and funny story. A perfect read for a rainy day. Or *any* afternoon."—Karen Brichoux

"Rich has managed to skillfully blend serious topics with humor, and readers will love her for it."—*Booklist*

"Sprightly dialogue. . . . A fast, fun read, especially for those who enjoy the quirky characters of authors like Jennifer Crusie and Eileen Rendahl."—*Library Journal*

"Wacky characters, nonstop action, riotous dialogue . . . the merriment keeps the pages turning."—*Publishers Weekly*

To the Hileman-Hastings of Soldotna, Alaska, without whom I would never know how wonderful a big, loud, Catholic family can be. Love you guys.

Acknowledgments

Wow. I made it through another book alive. How unexpected. Following is the list of people without whom this book would have won the death match and swiftly finished me off:

My husband, Fish, and my daughters, Sweetness and Light, who gave me endless love and support even when I was cranky and on deadline and frankly didn't deserve it.

Cindy Barry, who made excessively supportive noises even when we were both sure I would miss my deadline. I didn't, by the way. Thanks, girl.

Robin La Fevers, who continues to be my rock of wisdom and sanity when I possess neither. I hope you don't regret giving me your home number! Well. Too late now.

Whitney Gaskell, Alesia Holliday, Michelle Cunnah, Eileen Rendahl, and Beth Kendrick, who, no matter how crazy or stupid my behavior, always say, "No, you were totally right." You just can't buy friends like that.

My agent, Stephanie Kip Rostan, for her general wonderfulness, and for hooking me up with my editor, the fabulous Kara Cesare, whose fabulousness is so fabulous it's almost blinding. I couldn't have asked for a better team in my corner on this one. Thank you both for your faith and incredible senses of humor.

Chapter One

I shove the heavy red velvet drape to one side and peer out into St. Michael's, watching the guests trickle in as my two sisters chatter behind me. My eyes finally lock on the man I'm searching for, sitting dead center on the bride's side of the church. I let the drapery fall and hand my father a ten-dollar bill.

"I got ten on David," I say. Dad winks at me and tucks the bill into the kitty, a small plastic jar in the shape of a cat with a slit cut into the back of its head. As far back as I can remember, that kitty has been the repository for cash generated by family wagers and fines incurred from breaking family rules, such as listening to boy band music or watching reality television. *The Bachelor* alone has almost doubled the college fund for Five, my youngest sister.

Dad shakes the kitty, although the effect is muted, since there's no change in there. "Okay. Carly's in for ten on David."

"David?" Five rushes to the drapes, her sage green bridesmaid's dress whooshing around her ankles as she pokes her head through the part in the drapes. "Which one's David?"

"Blue suit. Center, bride's side. Kinda hairy." I look out over her shoulder, no easy task considering she's five inches taller than me even without her shoes on.

"*That* guy?" she says, the dismay clear in her voice. "He doesn't look like Ella's type at all."

"He was in high school," I say, shooting a look over my shoulder at Ella, who overplays her dark glare. I lean back toward Five. "He was less hairy then, though."

At that moment, Ella grabs us by our elbows and yanks us back.

"You're horrible and you're going straight to hell," she says as she ducks to look at herself in the mirror. "Would someone help me with my veil, please?" She tries to adjust the mirror to tilt up, then ducks again. "Holy Mother of God, who usually gets married here? Munchkins?"

"Now who's going to hell?" Five asks, leaning over Ella and shifting the veil slightly to the left.

Dad hands me the kitty. "David's a fair bet, but I'm keeping my money on Buddy." He pulls out the sheet he printed up earlier, marking his bet on the grid. I cock my head sideways and watch him with a smile on my face, our ruddy-cheeked, red-haired bookie in a white bow tie. He catches me looking and winks at me.

"His name is *Bradley*, Daddy, not *Buddy*," Ella corrects with a huff, then turns to Five. "And what would *I* be going to hell for? You guys are the ones betting on which of my old boyfriends is going to object to my wedding."

"You made fun of short people," Five says. "You're lucky Carly doesn't give you a good, swift kick in the ankles."

"Hey!" I say, bristling at the comment, although I should be used to this crap by now. While Ella and Five both won the genetic lottery with normal height and thick, wavy red hair demanding its own shampoo commercial, I got a bum ticket. I'm terminally cute: heart-shaped face, Kewpie-doll lips, natural apple cheeks, curly reddish-brown hair that I have to cut short and keep moussed or it'll pull an Einstein, and a voice that's perpetually fifteen years old. When I answer the phone, telemarketers ask if my mom's home. My height, in perspective, is really the least of my problems.

"Short jokes are rude," Five continues, then leans toward Ella. "Little people are the new feminists. Didn't you know?"

"The new what?" Dad says.

"You have to be careful what you say, or you'll offend them," Five goes on, jerking her head toward me.

"I'm five-foot-two," I say. "That's a perfectly respectable height, you freakin' Amazon."

"See?" Five says, giving Ella the told-you-so face.

"Daughters," Dad sighs, raising his eyes to God in the best Tevye impression an Irish Catholic can possibly pull off. He puts his arm around Ella's shoulders. "I'm glad I've got one good one in the bunch."

Ella rests her saintly, veiled head on Dad's shoulder. Dad kisses her on the top of the veil and sneaks a five into the kitty.

"I'm putting five on Will, too," he says. "Hedging my bets."

Five gasps. "Will's here?" She runs to the drapes and sticks her head out. "Where? I can't see him."

I nudge Five to the side with my hip and poke my head out next to hers. "The famous Will? Do I get to finally meet him?"

"Oooh, there he is," Five breathes. "Isn't he beautiful?"

"Where?"

She puts her fingers under my chin and shifts my head to the right. "Bride's side, toward the back, pale gray suit, yellow tie."

I squint. He looks like a young college professor. "*That* guy?"

"Mmmmm," Five says, then giggles.

Well, well, I think. *The famous Will.* I had been in Syracuse attending grad school during the drama that was Will Kelley, but the story went a little something like this: Ella had fallen in love with an artist and brought him home, at which point Five had promptly fallen in love as well. For a long time there was a stable truce; Five's only link to Will was Ella, so she accepted their relationship, limiting the prepubescent handkerchief-rending to the minimal amount required by law. Then Ella had, sadly, fallen out of love. Will was forced unhappily from the family picture, and Five called me crying every night for a week, swearing she would never, *never* speak to Ella ever again. Beyond that, the details of the drama—which had taken a backseat to my broadcast journalism master's work and my own romantic missteps—are pretty fuzzy in my head, but I can tell by the breathlessness in Five's voice that she remembers everything.

Now, watching him, I have to say, I'm a little disappointed. The way Five described him, I expected this Will guy to be the Russell Crowe of ex-boyfriends, with sexual magnetism flowing off him in waves. Not that he's a Quasimodo or anything, just more . . . average than I expected. He's tall and a little on the thin side, with sandy hair that's a touch too long and sticks out at awkward angles—hardly glowing with the aura of a thousand angels the way that Five would have had me believe back in the day. I can't see his face because his head is bent and he seems to be reading something, probably the wedding program, but I don't see anything terribly heart-stopping about him.

He has one thing going for him, though; he appears to be attending his ex's wedding alone, which makes him a braver man than me. I wouldn't attend an ex's wedding with anything less than a Calvin Klein underwear model and a flamethrower, I'll tell you that.

I feel Five drumming out an excited beat on my back with her fingertips, and I pull back in.

"I call dibs," she says, her face glowing.

"He's a little old for you, doncha think, squirt?" I say.

"I'm seventeen." Five pushes her breasts up in her

bridesmaid's dress, a disturbing image on many levels. "And Mark Mahaffey, who sits behind me in trig, says I'm the sexiest girl in the senior class."

"Well . . ." I toss a glance at Dad, who's nonplussed as usual. "Mark Mahaffey oughta know."

"You were twelve when Will knew you, Five," Ella says, her voice all kindness, no condescension. Ella's very good at that. "He's crazy about you, but you'll probably always be twelve to him."

"How do you know?" Five's voice is laced with indignation, but she's seventeen. Indignation with her is less an attitude and more a default setting.

Ella gives Five a kind smile. "That's just how it works, kiddo."

Five huffs and is about to respond, but I put my hand on her shoulder to silence her. "Do me a favor, Fiver, and wait until the reception to jump on Ella's ex. You're giving Dad a case of the sweats."

Five allows a small laugh. Ella tosses me a small, grateful smile, then ducks down to check her veil in the munchkin mirror.

"Well," Dad says, taking advantage of the hole in the conversation, "it looks like Carly and I are the only real players in this pool. If you think David's the guy, Car, put your money where your mouth is."

"I don't know." I raise an eyebrow at Five. "You're not fixing this game, are you, kid? You sure you didn't see his face?"

She releases a long-suffering sigh. "It was just a dream. You guys are the ones making a big deal about it."

Ella angles her head away from the mirror to look at

us. "Yeah, but remember the time she dreamed about Dad's car accident before it happened?"

"And don't forget about that incident with Ella and the horse," Dad says.

Five lowers her eyes beatifically. "I'm just a messenger."

I poke my head out through the drapes again. Dr. Greg, the lucky groom, shuffles nervously from foot to foot, consulting occasionally with his best man, whose name I think might be Tim. I make a mental note to ask Ella before I have to dance with him at the reception.

I scan the crowd and count no fewer than five of Ella's exes. She's that kind of girl; the kind who has amicable breakups and maintains friendships. It worries me a bit, her way of living life. No conflict, no fighting; just constant, smooth-running perfection. Seems unnatural to me.

I direct my focus to the contenders for the lead role in Five's predicted wedding objection. There's Bradley the Exterminator, Gabe the High School Teacher, Keith the Man of Indeterminate Occupation and Seemingly Unlimited Funds, David the Radio DJ. And, of course, Will the Artist, the official fantasy man of the youngest McKay sister. I lean out and squint to get a better look. He isn't reading anymore, and seems to be checking out the stained-glass window of the Ascension on the east wall of the church. I can see his face now. He's got about two days of stubble that he's pulling off effectively, and somehow his hair seems less awkward now, but it's something in his expression as he stares at the stained glass that keeps me watching. There's genuine wonder there, appreciation, contentment, like he's just so comfortable in his own skin that he can take a moment out from his ex's wedding to appreciate the simple beauty of a church window.

Hmmmm. I'm beginning to see Five's point about Will. And he *is* here alone. I wonder if the rule about sisters and exes is still in effect if one of the sisters is married. . . .

Suddenly, Will shifts his gaze in my direction, as though he can hear me thinking about him. I freeze. He seems to be staring right at me. We hold eye contact for a moment as I wonder whether he's really seeing me from that distance, or just looking in my general direction. I can see a smile quirk on his lips and then he gives a small wave in my direction. I yank myself back from the drapes.

"Spaz," Five remarks, one eyebrow quirked up at me.

"Bee," I say, and swipe at the empty air for good measure. Based on Five's expression, however, I'm fairly sure she feels confident in her initial spaz assessment.

Dad holds his hands out, and we gather around him, left to right, oldest to youngest, the way we always do. He smiles at each of us.

"I can't believe it," he says, his voice catching slightly as his chest heaves a touch. "One of my girls is getting married."

Ella releases Five's hand and wipes her eyes. Yeesh. Just the hint of a Dad speech and she's history. I laugh on an exhale and she sticks her tongue out at me. Dad squeezes my hand.

"Ella, when you were seven years old, you were playing

in a softball game, and some bruiser of a kid threw a bum pitch and knocked you in the head, and you went down." Dad pauses, and we all go quiet; this is a new story.

Dad has stories for each of us, the classics he repeats at family get-togethers and Christmas mornings. But there are a few that he holds back, saving them for a special moment. We get them on prom nights, at graduations and, apparently, on wedding days.

"I hopped up out of my seat, having no idea what I intended to do—grab you or knock out the bruiser. But your mother put her hand on my arm and said, 'Don't worry about it, Declan. It's Ella. She'll get up. She always does.'"

I feel a tightness in my shoulders, which happens whenever Dad mentions Mom. I learned a long time ago that it's best to swallow my annoyance and let him remember her fondly if he wants to, so I look down at the sage green toes of my maid-of-honor shoes and concentrate on the way the satin shimmers.

"She was right," he says after a moment. "You got up. And you played the rest of that game with all your heart, even though your team was losing. You put everything you had into every swing, every pitch, no matter how hopeless the situation seemed."

"Did her team win?" Five asks, her voice tremulous.

Dad smiles. "They got whomped. And that bruiser kid went home with a trophy, but Ella was the one who stole the show, because she got up."

He and Ella exchange smiles, and I see a tear stroll down her cheek. Dad goes on.

"That's why I know you're going to be great at marriage, Ella, because marriage requires a lot of getting up. Not that it won't be wonderful, because it will. But it will also be hard, and you're each probably going to get hit by a lot of bum pitches."

He pauses, watching Ella, his eyes beaming with pride and just a touch of the Jameson's he'd downed before we left for the church. He releases my hand, and Five's, and moves forward, holding both hands out to Ella. He leans over, kisses her on each cheek, and then puts one hand on her face.

"Ella, honey, if anyone can keep getting up, day after day, I know it's you. You have a beautiful future ahead of you, and I know you'll meet it with courage and faith. I'm so proud of you, sweetheart."

Both Five and Ella go down on that one, sniffling and weeping. Ella swipes at her face and kisses Dad on the cheek with trembling lips. "Thanks, Daddy."

Five ducks around Ella and bends over to check herself in the mirror.

"Goddamn it, Dad, couldn't you have saved that until after the wedding?" she sniffs, running her fingers under her eyes. "I don't have a heart of stone like Carly. You've totally ruined my makeup."

"I don't have a heart of stone. I just have some self-control. And don't say 'goddamn it' in church." I walk over to Dad and put my arm around his shoulders, stuffing another ten into his hand.

"Definitely David," I whisper. He kisses me on the cheek and swipes his fingers over his eyes as the church organ starts playing "Holy, Holy, Holy."

"That's our cue, girls," he says. "Let's get this show on the road."

For the most part, Ella's wedding goes off without a hitch. Five and I exchange a smile as Father Lucey asks if there are any objections. Of course, there aren't. None of us really thought there would be, and the kitty has already been tucked away into Ella's bags, to be found later on her honeymoon in Maui. By the time Father Lucey has gotten to, "you may kiss the bride," my most pressing concern is getting out of my misogynistic shoes before I sustain permanent nerve damage, so when the doors fly open at the back of the church, I am as surprised as anyone.

"I object!"

Heads swish to face the back of the church. I glance at Five, who laughs in shock and then covers her mouth.

"I object!" the voice says again, and I look up, trying to figure out which one of the exes it is. I glance through the crowd and do a mental count; they are all in their seats. I blink, unsure of what's going on, until I feel Five nudge me.

"Oh my God. Is that . . . Seth?" she whispers.

My heart booms in my chest. I squint.

Oh, shit.

It's Seth. *My* Seth. I look at Ella, who is staring at me, wide-eyed. Greg leans toward her, his face grave.

"Ella?" he says tentatively, looking worried, which is a big deal for him. As a plastic surgeon, Greg tries to avoid creasing his brow, as he doesn't ever want to be in need of his own services.

Yes, he actually said that once. Hand to God.

"It's for me." I step away from the altar, my face blazing. My pinched feet stumble on the first of the altar steps, and two pairs of McKay-sister hands are on me, steadying me as a soft shuffle of suppressed snickers rumbles through a section of teenage kids on the groom's side. Brats. I smooth my dress and walk carefully down the aisle with two hundred and seventeen sets of eyes following my every step.

"Seth," I hiss as I reach him at the back of the church. "What are you doing here?"

He blinks at me and cocks his head to the side, his dark brown eyes looking slightly bewildered and not a little bloodshot. I can smell the single malt on him and my heart plummets as I realize what has happened.

"Carly," he whispers, almost to himself, as if he's trying to wrap his mind around the fact that I'm not wearing a wedding dress. His focus trails up the aisle to Ella, then slowly homes back on me. "But . . ."

"It was a misprint, Seth. I gave the newspaper the information, and they must have gotten confused. A correction ran the following Sunday. The picture was of Ella." I clear my throat as the panic closes in. "Couldn't you tell?"

He shakes his head. "But . . ."

"It was a misprint," I repeat. I am speaking quietly, but the silence is so thick that it carries my voice to every corner of the church.

"Oh, God." Seth's face goes white as he looks at Ella. "Oh, man. Ella, and . . . Guy Who's Marrying Ella—I'm so sorry. I thought . . . pfffffeeewww . . ." He exhales roughly and gestures toward me. "I thought . . ."

He turns to me and puts his hands on either side of my face, squeezing my cheeks until I have to work to keep my lips from puckering out. "Jesus, I thought it was you."

I pull his hands away from my face. "Can we talk about this later, maybe?"

He starts to nod, but then his eyes darken, and my breathing grows shallow with tension.

"No," he says. I close my eyes. When he speaks again, I can feel the anger in his voice. "How are we supposed to talk when you won't return my phone calls?"

"I'll call you, I swear." I open my eyes wide and give him my most earnest look. "Just go. Please."

He shakes his head. "No. I'm not afraid to talk in front of these people. I have nothing to hide."

"Fine, I'll talk to you now, but can we at least take it outside, please?" I whisper harshly. "This is my sister's wedding."

"Yeah, and what do you think is going to happen once you shuffle me out of here?" he says, his voice so loud that there's an echo. "You're gonna promise to call me, and then I'll never hear from you again. No, if it takes humiliating myself in front of all these people to get you to talk to me, then let's do it. Right here."

I freeze as it occurs to me that there will be no getting out of this gracefully. My drunk ex-fiancé is ruining my sister's wedding and I am powerless to stop it. Panic clutches my abdomen and the nausea begins to intensify.

I feel a hand brush the small of my back as someone

sidles up beside me. Gratitude rushes through me and I turn, expecting to see Dad, who will fix everything, the way he always does.

But it isn't Dad. It's Will. He steps closer to Seth and locks eyes with him.

"Hey, man." Will's voice is soft and sandpapery and kind, and I feel a lump of affection forming in my throat. "You look like you could use a drink."

The affection wanes. *What?*

Seth runs his fingers through his hair. "Yeah, no shit."

Will smiles, keeping his eyes on Seth. "I've got some Jim Beam in my car. Why don't we all go out and get it, and then maybe you two can talk?"

I blink, staring at Will. What the hell does he think he's doing, offering Seth a drink? Can't he see the man is already drunk? Is he *crazy*? But before I can tell him to mind his own damn business, he's escorting Seth peaceably out the door. I shoot Ella a helpless look, and she blows me a kiss and waves me on. I blow one back, mouth an "I'm sorry," and stumble again as I turn and stalk out of the church, my focus on my feet and my mind on murder.

"I can't believe you did that," I say to Seth when I catch up to them outside.

"I'm sorry, Car," he says, although he doesn't sound sorry. He sounds angry. "I thought you were getting married."

I shake my head and sigh. "And how is that an excuse? Interrupting weddings is what crazy people do. Sane people make a phone call."

We stare at each other in icy silence.

"Hey, you two talk," Will says, stepping back away from us. "I'll just . . ."

He ducks off toward the parking lot, disappearing behind the church. Seth turns to me, his face cold with anger. I clench and unclench my fists, trying to control the shaking in my hands.

"Seth . . ." I begin, but I don't know where to go with the conversation, a conversation I've been trying to finish for eight months, with limited success.

Seth holds up his hands and lets them fall. "Forget it, Carly. Just forget it. Tell Ella I'm sorry and just forget it, okay?"

I sigh. "Seth, you have to get past this—"

"You know what your problem is, Carly?" he says, his voice harsh.

"I have an idea," I say, staring him down.

He leans forward, his eyes flitting over mine. "You have no faith."

I'm thrown for a moment. Where the hell did that come from?

"Okay, Seth," I say. "Well, gee, it's been great to see you—"

"You had no faith in me," he says. "You had no faith in us. We hit a rough spot. Lots of couples do. That's what marriage is, seeing through the rough spots."

My stomach is heaving like a ship at sea. I don't know what to say, but I have to say something. "Isn't it better to know now that I can't do that? That I'm not ready?"

"Ready has nothing to do with it," he says. "No one's

ever ready. You either love someone enough, or you don't. So, you don't. Maybe you never did. Maybe I'm just an idiot to have ever believed you."

A sharp pain stabs through my stomach. "No. Seth—"

"I don't understand, Car," he says. "I never lied to you. I never cheated. I didn't even used to drink—"

He lets out an ironic huff of laughter. I take a deep breath to fight the stabbing sensation that has moved into my chest.

"Seth, I said I'm sorry a thousand times. I can't say it anymore. You just have to accept it and move on."

Seth glances up at the church, and I can see the hurt on his face, as fresh as it was eight months ago, on the night I moved my stuff out of his house and back into my old room at home.

"That should have been us in there today," he says. "We were happy. Weren't we happy?"

"Yeah," I say weakly. "Sure." *I thought we were. Maybe. I don't know.* God, I'm so bad at this. Answers keep running through my head, and yet none of them seem quite right, and obviously none of them will be good enough for Seth. I don't know what he wants from me, but I'm pretty damn sure that whatever it is, I don't have it. Guilt, anger, and frustration all circle around me, tightening and intensifying, making it hard to breathe.

"I don't know what else to say, Seth," I say flatly. I force myself to look him in the eye, but I can't hold the contact, so I stare at the church. "I'm sorry."

"Yeah," he says. "I know. And if 'sorry' answered any questions, we might not be here, again, having this same damn discussion."

He throws his arm out in frustration and I flinch away instinctively, even though I know Seth would never lay a hand on me. I hear soft footsteps to my left and I turn to see Will moving silently into position beside me. Either he was watching us from the side of the church or he has the best timing in the world. I don't really care; I'm just relieved to have him there.

"Who the hell *are* you, anyway?" Seth asks as Will situates himself slightly in front of me, his stance protective yet not aggressive.

"I'm a friend," Will says, his voice calm and even. "You're obviously having a bad day, man. Maybe it's time to go home and sleep it off."

Seth's eyes narrow and he steps back. He looks from me to Will and then back at me. I can tell he's adding up two and two in his mind, and I'm not the least bit inclined to correct the wrong impression he's getting.

"A friend, huh?" He lets out a bitter laugh, and anger flashes over his face. "Best of luck to you, man. You're gonna fucking need it."

Will steps directly between us then, which is brave. He's a bit taller than Seth, but Seth easily has twenty pounds on Will. And Will doesn't look like much of a fighter. But still, he stands firmly there between us, and if I were Seth, I wouldn't try to move him.

"I can call you a cab." Will's tone is kind, but there's an edge in his words that says he means business. Seth stares at him, and for a moment I'm horrified by the idea that they might actually start fighting right there in front of St. Michael's. Finally, Seth takes a step back, and I start to breathe again.

"Whatever," he says, glancing away toward the road. "She's all yours, man. I'm done."

He stuffs his hands in his pockets and starts off down the street, heading toward the bus stop a block and a half away. I step out from behind Will and watch as Seth veers down the sidewalk, head down and shoulders hunched.

"You weren't actually going to hit him, were you?"

Will shrugs. "I think there's a chance I would have gotten in a swing or two before he pummeled me, sure."

I let out a small laugh. "You didn't have any booze in your car, did you?"

His eyes meet mine, and there's a twinkle of a smile there. "There's some Nyquil in the glove compartment, but I think it's expired."

I laugh again, and then my smile fades as my eyes trail after Seth.

"Thank you," I say quietly.

I feel a light touch on my elbow. I turn my head to see Will staring down at me, his face full of kindness and concern.

"You okay?"

"Oh, yeah," I say quickly. "I'm fine."

"I know we don't know each other very well," he says gently, "but if you want to talk . . ."

His eyes are a crystalline blue, and in the sun they seem to sparkle on their own power. They're exactly the eyes you want to pour your soul out to. Soft. Kind. Smiling. Nice eyes.

I look away. There will be no soul-pouring today. I'm just not that kind of girl.

"You know what I don't get?" I say to fill the silence. "What I don't get is why people even get married in the first place. I mean, it can only end in one of two ways, right? Death or divorce. That's it. Why do that to yourself?"

Will chuckles. "That's quite an attitude to have on the day of your sister's wedding."

I allow a small smile. "Believe it or not, this is my sunny side."

Dimples show through his light stubble as he smiles back at me. "I don't believe it."

"You calling me a liar?" I ask in mock offense.

"Yeah," he says, a chuckle in his voice. "I guess I am."

I feel my cheeks start to warm, which means I've already started blushing, so I look away just in time to catch the show as Seth bangs his fist against the *Tucson Citizen* ad on the side of the sun shelter down the street. My shoulders flinch as the sound shoots through the air. Will's hand touches my arm again and I turn to see him holding out an unopened travel package of Kleenex to me. I stare at him.

"Where'd that come from?"

"Boy Scout." He shrugs. "I'm always prepared."

"Thanks. But I'm okay. Really."

He nods, tucks the Kleenex back into his breast pocket. We're silent for a beat. I switch my focus to the heavy cathedral doors and decide not to go back in; the wedding's almost over, anyway. And it's lovely outside, the October sun bright but not blistering. If I wasn't coming off one of the most humiliating experiences of my life, standing here with Will might even be kinda nice.

On that thought, I glance back at Will. Our eyes meet, and he seems about to say something when the church doors open. The guests fly out, parting like the Red Sea to allow Ella and Greg passage to their limo, a rain of birdseed bouncing off their wedding finery. Will and I watch from the edge of the revelry. Ella pauses and looks around before getting in the limo, stopping when her eyes fall on me. She gives a small wave, and I can see the concern in her face. I blow her a kiss to show her all is well. She catches it in the air, her face once again beaming with happiness, and climbs into the limo.

A fresh wave of confusion, anger, and embarrassment washes over me, and I have a sudden and overwhelming need to escape. I drop my head and duck behind the church, making my way to the parking lot, cursing as the heels of my sage pumps flip under me, making me stumble like a drunk. *I'm not supposed to be doing that until the reception*, I joke to myself, but it doesn't relieve any of the bad I'm feeling.

"Carly?" I hear a voice call from behind me. I stop next to a palo verde tree and shade my eyes for a moment to see Will heading toward me. I'm grateful for his help and all, but I'm in no mood to play hunky-dory for a stranger.

"I'm fine," I say. "Really, thanks, but—"

He catches up and ducks his head down a bit to level our eyelines, his concerned expression only intensifying my humiliation.

"I just want to make sure you get to your car okay," he says, pulling back. "Looks like your shoes are staging a coup."

I stop walking and turn to face him. "It's not the shoes. It's me. I stumble barefoot. It's just . . ." I huff, the air from my mouth shooting hair up from my forehead. "It's me."

His eyes narrow a bit in concern. "Are sure you're okay?"

"Why do people ask if you're okay? I mean, if they have to ask, you're obviously not okay, right?" I stare at him. "Right?"

He squints in the sun. "There's no right answer to that question, is there?"

"Fine," I say. "No. I'm not okay. My sister's wedding has just been ruined. I've been thoroughly humiliated in front of two hundred and seventeen people. Two hundred and eighteen, if you include Father Lucey. And then there's Seth . . ." I trail off and sigh. It's no use trying to explain Seth and me to Will. I don't have a solid grasp on it myself. I shake my head and feel a sudden wave of despair, and I am speaking before I can censor myself.

"I gave him his ring back. Why can't he just get over it?"

Will takes an obvious moment forming his response. Jeez. I must really be scary right now.

"Sometimes . . ." he begins, then pauses. "I don't know. Sometimes people have a hard time getting over things they don't understand."

"So, what?" I say. "Now it's my fault because he doesn't understand?"

"No. I just . . . No." He clears his throat. "Hey, want some Nyquil?"

I stare at him for a moment, then break into a sudden laugh. He really is a nice guy. And cute. And funny. And . . .

. . . and it's then that I realize I've been none of those things.

"Wow," I say. "Call Ripley. I believe I've just made the worst first impression ever. Can we start over?"

His smile quirks. "I'd like that."

I hold out my hand. "Hi. I'm Carly McKay."

"I know." He takes my hand in his. His touch is warm and soft and oddly comforting, which makes me oddly uncomfortable. "I'm Will Kelley."

"Yeah. I know."

We release hands after a moment, keeping our eyes on each other. People begin to filter into the parking lot, seeming not to notice us standing in the scanty shade of the palo verde.

"Well." I gesture feebly toward my car. "I'm gonna find Five and . . . Are you going to the reception?"

He shakes his head. "I can't. I'm on my way out of town. I've got an assignment tonight."

"Really? What do you do?"

"I'm a photographer." He glances at a little blue sedan driving past us, then looks back to me. "Mostly catalogs, some magazine work, that kind of thing."

"A photographer," I say. "Nice job."

"It's not as glamorous as it sounds," he says, then gestures toward me. "Hey, Ella said that you're a producer on *Tucson Today*. That's pretty exciting, right?"

"*Associate* producer." I smile. "It's not as glamorous as it sounds."

"It's a good show. I try to watch it when I can."

"Thanks. We're pretty happy with it." I pause, not sure where to take the conversation next as I marvel again at how very blue his eyes are. "So, you're not an artist anymore?"

"Hmm?"

"Ella told me you were an artist."

"Oh." He smiles. "Yeah, I paint a bit. But the photography pays the bills."

I smile, and feel a sudden surge of affection for Will Kelley. "So, what's your assignment?"

He blinks, as though he'd been thinking about something else and has to now get back on track. "Oh. Yeah. I'm heading out to Denver to—"

"Will!" Five calls, rushing toward us. Will laughs and catches her in a hug, lifting her off the ground.

"Fiver!" he says, putting her down and giving her hair a playful ruffle. "How you doing, kid?"

Five steps back from him and smooths her hair, then gives him her best come-hither. "Not a kid anymore."

Will laughs and raises his eyebrows at me. "I stand corrected."

"You'll dance with me at the reception, right?" Five asks, tucking her arm in his.

"Sorry, Fiver," he says, patting her tiny hand in the crook of his elbow and giving her a brotherly peck on the top of her head. "I've got a flight to catch. Rain check?"

Five gives a small pout. "I'm gonna hold you to that."

"I'd expect nothing less." He winks at Five, then gives me a small nod. "It was nice meeting you, Carly. Pass my congratulations on to Ella?"

I nod. Will smiles, then walks away. As soon as he's out of earshot, Five sighs and leans against me.

"Oh, I love that man," she breathes.

"He's nice."

"Did you see his eyes?" she asks, still entranced.

"Yeah," I say. Suddenly, Five returns to the moment and pops off me.

"Oh. My. God. Carly! I can't believe what happened with Seth! I had no idea it was gonna be him, or I so totally would have told you. Are you okay?"

I give her a bright smile and put my arm around her shoulders, guiding her toward my car.

"Now that my designated driver is here, I'm doing much better." I toss my keys to her and she catches them without missing a beat. "Get me to the reception, kiddo. I need a drink."

Chapter Two

"It's not that I don't believe in the possibility of psychic ability. Anything's *possible*." I sip my Circle K soda and lean back in the van, which Christopher and I had long ago nicknamed the Blueberry for its overwhelming blueness, inside and out.

"*You* believe in psychics?" Christopher says, shooting a sideways smile at me. "*You*, who thinks the Easter Bunny is a sinister creation of the jelly bean conglomerate?"

I shoot a smile back at him and slide my sunglasses on. "I never said *sinister*. But, yes, I believe there are things in this world that I cannot explain. My sister has precognitive dreams, and I believe her." I stare out the window and think, for the thousandth time in the past week, of Seth at the wedding. "More now than I used to."

Christopher keeps his eyes on the pale, dusty stretch

of road that will soon be delivering us to the small artist community of Bilby, Arizona, and the home of one
Brandywine Seaver, psychic quiltmaker.

"Which sister?"

"Hmmm?" I say, distracted by a hand-painted roadside
sign that reads HANDMADE EXOTIC UNDERWEAR FOR SALE.

"Which sister has the dreams?"

"Oh. Five."

"Ah. Should have guessed. And what has she predicted?"

"Dad's car accident. The horse that fell on Ella."

"A horse fell on Ella? When did a horse fall on Ella?"

"When she was seventeen. Toy horse. Doesn't matter. My point is, I'm not saying people can't have psychic
ability. But in general, anyone who takes money from the
sad and desperate is inherently suspect." I flip through
my notebook, glancing again at the newspaper article
about a spinster and her psychic quilt, which she was
convinced was her road map to love. "And this particular
instance of psychic hoo-hah is very obviously a big steam-
ing crock of—"

"All right," Christopher says. "I get it. Whatever
happened to objectivity in journalism, anyway?"

"Like government intelligence, baby." I give him a
sideways glance over the top of my sunglasses. "Contra-
diction in terms."

"*Ba-doo-boom-chaaa.*" Christopher smirks as he delivers the comedy rim-shot sound effect that marks all our
age-worn routines. He pulls the Blueberry to a stop in
the driveway at 442 Copper Trail. I check it against the

address on my clipboard. This is Brandywine Seaver's house.

"Brandywine," I say, flipping the papers back down. "What kind of name is that, anyway?"

Christopher pivots toward me in his seat, which ain't easy for a guy his size. He's not fat, but he's got some bulk to him, and when he turns on me, I feel like a kid about to be scolded.

"Look, cut the smart-ass shit. I'm tired of playing the nice guy while you cut people to shreds."

"I don't cut people—" I say, about to once again defend myself on the incident with that shyster malpractice attorney—who deserved everything he got, by the way—but Christopher holds up a hand to silence me.

"Be nice."

"I'm always nice," I huff, and hop out of the Blueberry, stumbling a bit as my Keds connect with the gravel driveway. I hear Christopher chuckling behind me, following up with his standard, "For someone so close to the ground, you sure have a lot of gravity issues, McKay."

"*Ba-doo-boom-chaaa*," I mutter, slamming the door behind me as I regain my balance. I tuck the sunglasses up on top of my head and check out our location. It's a medium-sized two-story log cabin set into the base of the foothills, which rise up behind it like bodyguards. The property is marked by a white picket fence surrounding a rock lawn painted green. The rock lawn itself isn't that unusual in Arizona, where water conservation is always an issue. The green paint, however, is a little too precious for my taste. There are two walkways laid out with flat, white rocks—one leading from the driveway to the house, and the other winding around to the back, where it cuts a path through a mass of palo verde and creosote, and heads for the foothills. There's a sign at the corner of the picket fence that reads RENTALS AVAILABLE; INQUIRE INSIDE.

"If she's so psychic, shouldn't she know where the prospective renters are?" I mutter.

I catch Christopher giving me a warning look as he hoists the tripod bag over one burly shoulder, so I shoot him my toothiest I'll-be-good smile, carefully climb the three steps to the porch, and get zapped as I hit the buzzer. I yelp, then put my fingertip in my mouth to soothe the pain. I can hear Christopher chuckling behind me.

"You're the reason they upped the insurance rates at work, aren't you?"

"Bite me," I shoot at him over my shoulder. I'll own that I have a tendency toward the klutzy, but I can hardly be blamed for faulty electrical wiring. I am internally forming a wittier follow-up when a tall woman wearing jeans and a white button-down shirt steps out onto the porch, letting the screen door slam behind her as she holds out her hand to me.

"You must be Carly," she says.

I pause. I'd been expecting flowing crepe dresses, long, straggly Woodstock hair, eau de patchouli, and costume jewelry. Instead, with a light touch of makeup and graying blond hair pulled back in a thick braid,

Brandywine Seaver looks very much like a bank teller on Casual Friday.

"Hi, Ms. Seaver. Thanks for having us."

Brandywine Seaver takes my hand in both of hers and smiles. "I'm glad you could make it. And, please, call me Brandy."

"This is my videographer, Christopher Evans," I say as Christopher steps up behind me. He puts the light kit down and holds his hand out to Brandy.

"Good to meet you, Christopher," Brandy says as she shakes his hand. She holds eye contact with him for a second, exuding warmth, then looks at me. "My client will be here at about one o'clock, so you're in plenty of time. Shall we get started?"

We follow Brandy into the cabin, which smells of wood, oranges, and cinnamon. The ground level is a big expanse of space. Against one wall are a sofa, chair, coffee table, and a bookcase. Crawling up the opposite wall is a stairwell leading to a loft, which I assume serves as Brandywine Seaver's bedroom. There's a large stone fireplace that goes all the way up into the ceiling; behind it are the kitchen and dining areas. But mostly, the space is about the quilts. An L-shaped workstation takes over one corner, harboring three mismatched sewing machines and what looks like a half dozen different quilts in progress. Everywhere you look, there're fabric, batting, finished quilts folded in piles and hanging on stands. It looks like a Jo-Ann Fabrics in desperate need of a clearance sale.

"Forgive the mess," she says with an easy smile. "The

quilts are an entity all their own, and they tend to take over."

Brandy motions for me to sit on the couch as she settles into an easy chair. Christopher floats around us, setting up lights, framing his shot, hooking Brandy up with a wireless lav mic, doing his camera guy thing. I flip through my notes and scan my questions so we can wrap quickly and get out, which is my producer thing. The locations and the stories change, but the routine never does. Producing for television is just another widget-making job, no matter how you slice it.

"This should be fairly painless," I say, launching into the standard spiel I perform for interview subjects unused to being on television. "Just a few basic questions. Answer naturally, like we're just two people having a conversation."

Her grin widens. "Which is exactly what we are."

I smile back. "Right. Try to look at me and forget the camera. Christopher won't be offended."

She nods and winks at Christopher. Christopher tucks himself behind the camera and gives me a quick wave. "Ready. Rolling. Shake your groove thang."

I look at Brandy and reference my notebook, starting off with the standard softballs to put her at ease. Where is she from, how did she end up in Arizona, how did she get started quilting, blah blah blah. She answers all the questions affably, naturally comfortable in front of the camera. I lean forward.

"So, how does the whole thing work, exactly?"

"Well," she says, hesitating as she constructs her answer. "I make the quilts without knowing who they're for. Sometimes a quilt will only have been done for an hour when the client who owns it calls. Sometimes I'll have a quilt for years before the owner shows up."

I nod and keep quiet. Brandy pauses, and then jumps in to fill the empty conversational space, the way they all do if you wait long enough.

"See, I get the images, a sense of the fabrics and stitches, but I have no idea what it all means. I finish the quilt, and put it away. When a client calls, I go through the quilts until I find the one that belongs to that client."

"And how do you know which one belongs to which client?"

She shrugs, smiles. "I just . . . know."

Ahhhh. I see. "And how much do you charge for these quilts?"

"Well, it varies, but a quilt with a reading typically runs between twelve and fifteen hundred dollars."

Ka-ching. "And how many of these do you sell in an average month?"

Brandy grins. "Depends on the month."

"Do you keep in touch with clients? Do you know how many of your predictions have actually come true?"

Brandy's head tilts a bit. Her smile remains relaxed, but something clicks in her eyes. "I hear from clients every now and again. I haven't done a scientific survey of my accuracy, if that's what you're asking." She leans forward. "But, you know, it's not like I'm giving them lottery numbers or anything. The quilt gives them the information they need at that point in time. It's about their path, you know?"

I smile and think, *No.* Christopher clears his throat,

a warning. I glance at my watch. "Well, that's about all I've got—"

"You don't believe me, do you?" she asks suddenly.

Christopher clears his throat again, and is undoubtedly relieved when the doorbell rings. He undocks the camera and gets some handheld b-roll as Brandy greets her client, a middle-aged woman named Alice who didn't mention when we spoke for the preinterview that she would be wearing an "I (heart) my Schnauzer" sweatshirt. Brandy lays Alice's quilt out on the floor, puts a tape in a recorder, and hits the red button. The reading is your standard psychic con job—a series of vague references from which anyone with sufficient motivation could construe meaning if they try hard enough.

And fifteen hundred bucks is one hell of a motivation.

Close-ups of the quilt. Quick interview with Alice. Exteriors of the house. The widget is made.

"I'm gonna go back in and say good-bye," I say to Christopher as he finishes packing the camera and related detritus into the Blueberry.

"Behave yourself," Christopher warns as I go inside, where I find Brandy rummaging through a pile of quilts under a table in one corner of the house.

"Hey," I say. "We're just about done here, so . . ."

She holds up her hand, telling me to wait. I hug my notebook to my chest and look at my watch.

"Ah! Here it is!" She pushes some stray strands of hair away from her face and reaches her arm way back into a large box. She looks like she's birthing a calf. When she pulls her arms out, she's holding a quilt. She snaps it out and lays it on the floor. The base of it is white, with shimmery blue fabric running around the edges like a wavy ribbon. The ribbon double-helixes through the middle, too, broken up by little blue boxes with images inside. One box holds a book, another holds a frog. A third has what looks like a tin can holding three paintbrushes. It's funky, pretty, unique. I like it.

I wouldn't pay fifteen hundred bucks for it, though.

I glance up and see that Brandy is silently watching me. I jump in to fill the conversational gap.

"Pretty," I say.

"Can I ask you a question?"

I shrug. "Sure."

"What do you think about all this? I mean, really."

I pause, constructing an answer. Brandy leans forward, her hands on her knees, her expression friendly. "Don't worry. You won't offend me."

I raise my eyebrows. "Are you sure?"

She smiles. "I'm tougher than I look."

I glance out the window. Christopher is loading the Blueberry and way out of earshot. I turn my focus back to Brandy.

"I think it's a brilliant hook to move your product." I gesture toward the multitude of quilts surrounding us. "Of which you have quite a lot. Do I believe that the quilts are imbued with a mystical quality that allows you to tell the future? No. Do I think it's a little unethical and a lot immoral to take fifteen hundred bucks out of the mouths of schnauzers to move your stock? Sure. But, you know, it's a capitalist society and it's not your fault there's a sucker born every minute so . . . God bless, I guess."

I surf the momentary high that always comes from saying exactly what I'm thinking, but Brandy's prolonged, silent stare dulls the rush. Most people get offended, or think it's funny, or . . . something. Brandy just stares.

I shrug away an uncomfortable feeling in my shoulders. "You asked."

"That I did." She kneels down at the edge of the quilt, pulling the tape recorder from a shelf and setting it beside her. "And now I'm sure."

"Hmm? Sure of what?"

"That this one is yours."

"Sorry?"

"The reading should only take a few minutes." She gestures toward the floor. "Have a seat."

This is definitely the weirdest bribe attempt I've ever seen, and I once came home to fifty pounds of frozen rib-eye steaks from a meatpacking plant on my doorstep.

"Look, you don't have to sell me on anything. It's a feature story. Total softball. I won't make you look bad, I swear."

"Oh, I'm not worried about that. You may not believe in this process, but I do, and I'm absolutely certain this quilt is yours. It's been here waiting for you for, gosh . . . when did I make this?" She rolls her eyes up toward the ceiling and her lips move as she whispers to herself. Then her eyes descend back to me. "Twelve years."

I stare, expressionless, for a moment. Does she really expect me to believe this quilt has been waiting for me for twelve years? Please. But, since I'm pretty sure I can smell crazy cooking on the back burner and I make it a rule not to mess with crazy, I play along.

"Twelve years. Wow."

She grins up at me, earnest in the extreme. I smile lightly. "Thanks, really, that's nice, but I can't afford . . ."

She laughs, and I trail off. It's a brilliant, tinkling laugh, like crystallized sunlight.

Yep. Definitely crazy.

"Oh, don't worry about that," she says. "People come to me however they come to me. Some are clients. They want to pay for the quilts, and typically they can afford to. But if you show up here, and I have your quilt, then it's yours. No charge."

I glance out the window. Christopher's leaning on the Blueberry, having a smoke. I look down at the quilt and decide it can't hurt to humor her. I kneel on the floor. She hits the record button and closes her eyes. We sit there in total silence for what feels like a very long time but in reality is maybe a minute or so. Then she hums lightly and opens her eyes, looking down at the quilt.

"Your world. It's very structured. That's what the boxes mean. You like to keep things separated, under control."

Just nod and smile, I think, and that's exactly what I do. As she talks, Brandy moves her hands over the various areas of the quilt, her palms down but never actually touching the fabric, always hovering just above as she makes her astounding pronouncements about my life.

My career is in the middle of an upheaval. (Um, not really. If anything, it's in a rut.) Something about South

America. (Hah. I've never been south of Rocky Point.) My emotional center is jagged. (I have no idea what this means.) I have to pay attention to the paintbrushes. (I fight a laugh on this one, as the extent of my artistic ability is limited to stick figures and the occasional smiley face.)

"Return the frog," she says.

"Um. What?"

"Accept the book with the amber spine. Take the cab."

"Is that like 'Leave the gun, take the cannoli?' " I say before I can stop myself. There is a long silence and I wonder if I've offended her, although I'm starting not to care. My knees are uncomfortable from kneeling and I'm debating over whether I should move or not when I hear her say the name, "Mary."

My eyes widen and my breath catches in my chest. "What did you say?"

She raises her eyes and focuses on me. "Does that name have meaning for you?"

No. Lots of women are named Mary. That doesn't mean anything. Still, I can't seem to stop myself from saying, "My mother's name was Mary."

Brandy nods, looks down at the quilt. "Ah. Well. That makes sense."

"Why?" I look down at the quilt as well, as though it would suddenly become something other than a funky jumble of boxes and ribbons. "What about her?"

Brandy watches me for a while, her eyes trying to read mine, I guess. It makes me uncomfortable, and angry, and I'm just about to get up and leave when she speaks again.

"She's not dead." Brandy tilts her head slightly to the side, and while she's looking at me, I get a strong feeling that I'm not what she's seeing.

"No." I feel my throat tighten. "We don't know."

Brandy watches me for a moment; then her face relaxes in understanding. "She's just gone."

"We haven't heard from her since I was twelve," I say, wondering why I'm talking about this with the crazy quilt lady. I don't talk to anyone about this.

"You're angry," Brandy announces, her eyes narrowing as she watches me. "Your aura just turned red around your chest and shoulders."

Oh, you've gotta be kidding me.

I push myself up to a standing position. "I'm not angry, and I don't have an aura, but I am running up against a deadline, so . . ."

She looks up at me. "Everything's about to change."

"What?" Now I'm annoyed. Although I don't know why. I don't believe in this stuff.

"Oh," she says, her voice compassionate and her eyes slightly off focus, like she's staring at something a few feet behind me. "It's going to be all right, but you have to pay attention."

"It's all right now," I say. "Pay attention to what?"

And then she blinks, shakes her head, and appears to snap out of it. She shuts off the recorder and starts folding the quilt. I guess today's crazy quota has been met.

I hold out my hand to stop her. "Look, thanks, Brandy, but—"

"Stop arguing, please," she says, her voice tinged with weariness. She holds the folded quilt and the tape out to me. "It belongs to you, and even if you don't believe in the rest of it, you got a pretty blanket out of the deal, right?"

Excuses about perceived conflict of interest and journalistic integrity flash through my mind, but they fade fast. Even though the Mary thing is exactly the kind of vague coincidence that makes ladies who heart schnauzers pony up the big bucks for this kind of stuff, I can't shake the sense that this quilt is somehow connected to my mother, and despite all reason I am suddenly overwhelmed with wanting it. I reach for it, and feel an instant sense of calm when I hold it in my arms.

"Thank you."

She smiles and cocks her head to the side. "Call me if you have any questions."

I nod and find my way out. When I reach the Blueberry, Christopher tosses his cigarette butt on the ground and chuckles, eyes on the quilt.

"You've got to be shitting me."

"Shut up." I toss the quilt into the back of the Blueberry. "Let's go make some widgets."

The most persistent memory I have of my mother is from when she brought Five home from the hospital. She looked like she hadn't showered in days, which was unusual for her. She was the kind of woman who never left the house without makeup. I didn't make too much of it at the time, figuring this was just the way it was when there was a new baby in the house. I was four when Ella was born, and couldn't remember the aftermath of that for comparison, but to my twelve-year-old brain, it made sense. I helped Mom up to her room while Dad tended to Five. It was when my mother looked down at me, her eyes distant and strange, that I had the first inkling something was really wrong. She didn't say anything to me, just headed into the bedroom, where she stayed for the next six weeks.

Whenever I wasn't in school, I took care of Five. I sterilized her bottles. I mixed her formula and left it, ready to warm, in the fridge. I bathed her at night. I gave her midnight feedings. I failed my pre-algebra exam.

I remember Dad telling me that Mom was just tired and overwhelmed, and that he was proud of how much I was helping out. Then one day I came home from school and found Five sitting in her crib, screaming, her diaper brimming with yuck. I went into the bedroom and yelled at my mother, told her to get up off her ass and take care of the baby. I had never spoken to my mother like that before, and it worked. Her eyes cleared, and for the first time since coming home from the hospital, she was actually able to focus on me. It only lasted long enough for her to scream at me to get the hell out of her room, but at least it was something.

She left the next day while Ella and I were at school. We came home to a note and a neighbor, who handed Five over to us and left.

Dad held it together pretty well, but he never got over it. It was like one of those cartoon characters, running through a wall and leaving a bunny-shaped hole behind. One look at Dad, and you could see the Mary-shaped hole left there. He never even filed for divorce. Technically, if she's alive, they're still married.

I don't think about my mother very much. There's no reason to. But on the day that Brandywine Seaver gives me the quilt, I find I can think of little else. When I get home that night, I sneak the quilt up into my room and tuck it under my bed, as though it's some sort of contraband. I don't know why, though. If Dad saw it, he wouldn't think twice about it. As well he shouldn't.

It's just a quilt.

"So, tell us about the quilt," Lindsay says three days later, leaning over Christopher to refill my glass of wine. It's our weekly Friday-night get-together, in which Lindsay—Christopher's roommate and certifiably the coolest girl on the planet—cooks us a lovely roast with garlic mashed potatoes and I bring something from the Albertson's bakery for dessert. We are nibbling on caramel brownies and drinking red wine, and I feel relaxed and happy. Christopher sits on the couch between the two of us and shakes his head.

"Lindsay wants a quilt now," Christopher says. "Tell her it's a load of crap or I'm gonna have to cover her rent next month."

I look at Lindsay, ignoring Christopher and waving my wineglass lazily in the air as I talk. "She didn't say anything of substance. It was all just random stuff about South America and paintbrushes and a book with an amber spine . . ."

Christopher raises one eyebrow. "A what?"

"And, you know, I don't believe in that stuff anyway."

"You didn't mention the book with the amber spine before." Christopher's voice is tight and strange, and his cheeks are red. For such a big guy, he really can't hold his drink.

"Of course I didn't, because it doesn't mean anything," I say. Lindsay reaches for another brownie.

"Well, now that we've taken care of the softball questions," she says, setting the brownie down on the plate in her lap without taking a bite, "there's something we need to talk about."

"No," Christopher says, warning deep in his tone, and Lindsay rolls her eyes. I can't help but smile. They act like such a married couple sometimes, and I'm ninety percent sure Lindsay's in love with him. Sadly, Christopher's too thick to know a good thing when it's making him garlic mashed potatoes, and I'm sure as hell not gonna be the one to tell him.

"She's a *girl*," Lindsay says, shooting a look of pure, loving evil at Christopher. "She needs to talk about this stuff."

"Not all girls need to talk everything to death," Christopher says, grabbing his beer bottle off the coffee table.

"*Yes*. They *do*. Ella's still on her honeymoon, so who is Carly going to talk to if not you and me?" She leans forward to build a direct eyeline between us that excludes Christopher. "The thing with Seth at the wedding. How are you doing?"

I take a deep gulp of wine, then wince as I swallow. "I'm fine. It's no big deal. He's just . . . you know . . . still having a hard time. I guess."

Christopher snorts. "You're making excuses for him? He got drunk and made you miss your sister's wedding."

I pat his hand. "Take it down a notch, there, Bulldog. I was there for most of the wedding, and Seth . . . you know. He's still adjusting."

"He's an asshole." Christopher takes a swig of his beer.

Lindsay nibbles her lip. "Are you sure you're okay? I mean, that had to be tough. And you know, we've never really talked about why you guys broke up in the first place. Did he . . ." She pauses, and a look passes between her and Christopher. "Did he do something . . . bad to you?"

"What?" I laugh, then stop when I see how intently Christopher is watching for my answer. "This is what you think? You guys have been talking about this?"

Christopher picks at his beer label, not looking at me. "Not us. Her."

"He just seemed to love you so much," Lindsay said. "And then, suddenly, poof. Gone. I was just worried—"

"He didn't do anything wrong." My throat feels dry and I grab for my wineglass. "He was great. I just wasn't ready, I guess, and he couldn't accept that. When I gave the ring back, he kinda freaked out." I see Christopher tense next to me, and I backtrack. "Not in a bad way, just . . . he started drinking, he wouldn't stop bugging me about it, and it just got to be too much. So I ended it for good and moved back to Dad's."

Lindsay nodded, her face full of sympathy and understanding. "And how's that going, being back home?"

I shrug. "It's okay. I mean, at first, it was really comforting, you know, being Daddy's little girl again after going through all that crap with Seth. Then there was the preparation for Ella's wedding, and Five really seems to like having me around. I'm probably going to get my own place again after November sweeps, when things calm down." I stare down at the wineglass in my hand, and feel a little shaky from thinking about Seth. See, this is why I don't like talking about this kind of stuff. It doesn't do any good, it just upsets me, and who needs that? I down the last of my wine. "And that's it."

Lindsay watches me expectantly, and I see a slight expression of disappointment seep over her face as she realizes that's the end of the conversation. But still, she smiles, because Lindsay, as previously stated, is the coolest girl on the planet. I aspire to be Lindsay someday, with her long blond hair that does what it's told and her great cooking and her ability to always be kind no matter how bad a verbal ass-kicking someone desperately needs. Lindsay never says the wrong thing. Lindsay would have taken the quilt graciously, sent a thank-you note exactly three days later, then called Brandywine Seaver to report every instance in which one of the predictions might possibly be coming true.

I hope Lindsay never gets a thing for schnauzers, I think, and the thought makes me laugh a little.

"Well," Christopher says, standing up and grabbing the empty bottle of wine, "I'm ready to kick both your asses at Scrabble. Who's up for an ass-kicking?"

Lindsay and I share a smile as we follow Christopher to the table, where we proceed to annihilate him at Scrabble, the way we do every Friday night.

November sweeps starts, ironically, on October 26, and Christopher and I are plunged into the insanity. We

work long days, drink loads of coffee, and spend count-
less hours trying to soothe our boss, Victor. He's perpetually convinced that *Tucson Today* is on the verge of
being canceled, which it never is, and the paranoia gets
ten times worse during sweeps, when ratings are actually
measured. And every sweeps, *Tucson Today* performs con-
sistently, and there's nothing to worry about, a fact that
doesn't so much as make a dent in Victor's neurosis. He's
like one of those elderly aunts who insists she's about to
die every day and ends up outliving everyone else in the
family. Sadly, though, Victor's freak-outs tend to be in-
fectious to the less hardy on the show.

"So, this psychic quiltmaker story," Eloise Tucker,
the show's host, says as we huddle in the tiny sound
booth, reviewing the voice-over script she needs to read
for the story. "Do you really think it's, you know, sweeps
material? I mean, I'm not going to win a regional Emmy
with something this fluffy, am I?"

I keep my smile on. Eloise Tucker is never going to
win a regional Emmy, because she's never investigated,
produced, or written a story. She just looks pretty, reads
the VOs, introduces the stories on air, and has to have
Tucson spelled phonetically on every script lest she call it
Tuckson. Somehow she has managed to misinterpret Victor's obsession with the *show* winning a regional Emmy
as being an obsession that *she* win a regional Emmy.

And I have no intention of being the person to dis-
abuse her of this notion. I have to admit, though, it's
tempting every time she calls one of my stories "fluffy."
Especially when, as is the case with the psychic quiltmaker,
I was assigned the story and had no choice in the matter.

"I wouldn't worry about it," I say diplomatically, then spell out both *Brandywine* and *Seaver* for her phonetically at the top of the script.

BRAN-dee-wine.

SEE-ver.

"But shouldn't we be out interviewing the family of that kid who got bit by the snake?" she asks.

No, I think, *because: (a) the snake wasn't even poisonous, and (b) we're a newsmagazine, covering human-interest stories with depth and intelligence, not a bunch of news idiots who think the only path to good ratings is to terrify everyone that there's a snake in their backyard waiting to gobble their children whole.*

I don't say this out loud, though, because we share editing facilities with the news people.

"Mmmm," I say noncommittally. "Maybe."

Eloise's eyebrows knit as she looks at the script.

"Yeah. Okay. And how do you pronounce Bilby?" she asks as I'm about to hand her the script. I smile, take the script back, and scribble again.

BILL-bee.

There's a *tap-tap* at the door, which is slightly ajar. Christopher pokes his head in and grins at me.

"Victor's on a tear again," he says, his voice thick with laughter. "He wants us to do something on the snakebite kid."

I look to Eloise, who's standing a bit straighter, no doubt patting herself on the back internally for having such great television instincts.

I swap a look with Christopher, and tell him I'll be there in a minute. He ducks out, shutting the door behind him, leaving Eloise and me in total sound seclusion.

"God, he's so cute," she says, sighing like a teenager.

"What? Who? Christopher?"

"No worries," she says. "I'm not going to steal him from you."

This takes me a moment to process. "What?"

"Oh, come on," she says, leaning closer and speaking to me as though we're girlfriends having a bathroom confab. "Everyone knows about you two."

I laugh outright. I can't help it.

Eloise raises a skeptical eyebrow. "You are sleeping together, aren't you?"

"No! He's my best friend. That'd just be . . . wrong." I am suddenly beset by a mental image of Christopher lounging naked in my bed. "Oh, God. Wrong."

"Seriously?" She doesn't believe me. I can hear it in her voice.

Puppies. Think of puppies. Cute little puppies . . . jumping all over Christopher naked in my bed.

"Gah!" I say, swatting at her with the script. "Yes, seriously. No."

"Oh." Her face brightens. "So you wouldn't mind if I asked him out, then?"

"No," I say, but in that moment I realize I do mind. The idea of Christopher ending up with someone as plastic as Eloise bugs me. Besides, Christopher is Lindsay's, even if neither one of them knows it yet. So, I throw in a little lie. "But his girlfriend might."

"Girlfriend? Really?" Eloise's eyebrows knit together. "Well, poop."

———

"Agh!" Five says as she checks herself out in the hall mirror. "I look like I've been puked up by Mother Goose."

She turns to face me and Dad, her tremendous, hooped Little Bo Peep skirt rustling around her as she stabs the tremendous staff into the ground.

"It's a Halloween dance," I say. "You're supposed to look ridiculous."

"I look *ridiculous*?" Five wails. Dad steps forward and puts both hands on her shoulders.

"You look beautiful, baby," he says. She smiles gratefully at him. "And knowing it took two of us to get you all fastened up in it makes me feel much less antagonistic toward your little boyfriend Bobo there."

Five rolls her eyes. "His name is Bo. Just Bo."

"Wasn't Bobo the dog-faced boy?" I ask.

"No," Dad says. "That was Jojo."

"*Bo*," Five continues. "Not Bobo, not Botox, not Daddy's Little Heart Attack. Just *Bo*."

A horn honks outside, and Five grabs her little white string-drawn satchel.

"I'll be home by one," she says, kissing Dad on the cheek.

"Eleven-thirty, or I send the cops out for you," Dad yells out the door. He waves to both of them, muttering through his smile, "Touch my baby girl, Botox, and I'll castrate you, you little bastard."

He closes the door and puts one arm around my shoulder, guiding me toward the liquor cabinet that sits innocently in the corner of our living room.

"Drink some scotch with your old man, Carly. I need

something to make me forget my baby's out with that little tattooed good-for-nothing."

"Give the kid a break. He got the tattoo with the entire swim team when they won the championship. And it's not like it's in a place where anyone can see it, anyway."

"Exactly!" Dad says, raising one glass with a flourish and handing it to me. "How many nights do you think I'm up wondering how my little Fiver knows that boy has a dolphin on his left buttock?"

"It was in the school paper, Dad. She showed me the article."

Dad raises his eyebrows. "Really?"

I clink my glass with his. "Really."

"They write about buttocks in the school papers now?"

I take a drink. "Your taxes at work."

He lets out a huge sigh. "I swear that child is trying to kill me."

"You survived me and Ella; you'll get through this."

We head down the hallway, settling on the big black leather couch in Dad's office. The walls are lined with Dad's architecture books, and blueprints of his latest project obscure the surface of the desk. The old-world–style globe sits in the corner with Ireland facing out. Just like always.

"So, how are things going with that new building you guys are doing down on Tanque Verde?" I ask.

"Do you think she's happy?" Dad asks.

I think about this for a moment, and shrug. "As long as she doesn't sit down too fast and get hit in the face with the skirt, yeah, I think she'll have a good time."

"Ella," he says. "I was just wondering. I haven't

heard from her much since she came back from her honeymoon."

"She's married now," I say. "She has to dote on Dr. Greg for a while."

"I know," he says. "I was just wondering if you'd heard from her."

I shake my head. "I talked to her for a minute on the phone last week. But she seemed fine. And when's our next Girl's Night? A week from Sunday? She'll be here for that."

"Yeah," Dad says, then takes a deep breath and looks at me. "He's good enough for her. Greg? Right?"

I stare at him for a minute, wondering what's puttering around under that fringe of red hair. "Yeah. I think so. What's with the worry?"

Dad nods and stares down into his glass. "Ah, nothing. I'm just an old man not wanting to accept that his baby girls are no longer baby girls." He smiles and claps a hand down over mine. "And how are you? Have you talked to that Seth since the wedding?"

That Seth. "No. No, I haven't."

"Good," he says, and takes a sip of his drink. "He was never good enough for you."

"Of course not," I say. "No one ever is."

He raises his drink and we clink on it. Poor Botox. He doesn't stand a chance.

Chapter Three

The following week, on a Thursday afternoon, my mother returns.

There are no letters announcing her return. No phone calls to soften the blow. I simply come home from work and there she is, sitting on the couch with Dad, both of them holding drinks. His is the standard scotch on ice. Hers is clear. It could be gin. It could be 7UP. I really can't tell, and I have to wonder why I'm focusing on the drink she's holding rather than the fact that my mother is in our living room.

I am standing in the foyer, my beat-up messenger bag hanging heavily over my left shoulder as I stare at a woman I haven't seen in seventeen years. I still can't believe it's her, but at the same time, I know that it is. It is from her that I get my height, my looks, my terminal cuteness. She is me, plus thirty years. Hopefully without the abandonment of my family, but otherwise we're dead ringers.

After a long silence with a side of staring, Dad pushes himself up from the couch.

"Carly." He says my name just as though he's stating a fact, not like he's talking to me. "I wasn't expecting you home this early."

"I . . . uh . . . I left a tape. In my room." My eyes are still focused on my mother. I don't feel anything yet, but I know it's coming, like those tense moments of calm after the flash of lightning when there's nothing to do but wait for the ground-shaking thunder.

My mother stands up. Her hair is like mine when I don't mousse it—wild and directionless. Her eyes are red-rimmed and wide.

"Carly." Her lips tremble and her voice cracks, and I realize with a powerful certainty that I do not want to speak to her.

"I can't do this now," I say. "I have to go back to work and I can't do this right now."

I look at Dad. He looks shell-shocked as well. I don't want to leave him here to deal with her alone, but he's a grown man. He can handle this. He'll have to.

"Carly," she says again. My throat tightens and I hold up my hand.

"Not now," I say. I turn around, go up to my room, and search for the tape I couldn't find at work. Perfunctorily, I scrounge through my room, focusing my entire existence on finding the tape. Not on my desk. Not on my dresser. I get down on my hands and knees and feel under my bed. The tape is underneath the quilt. There's a stab of panic as I think about Brandy's words.

Everything's about to change.

Total vague pseudopsychic crap, and yet the panic escalates, moving from my chest into my throat. I squelch it under a heavy sense of professional duty. I don't have time for this. It's sweeps, for Christ's sake.

I don't have time for this.

I pad down the stairs and slip out the back. By the time I get to work, I have myself half convinced that she was just a figment of my imagination. It's the desert heat giving me hallucinations, although, in November, it's really not that hot.

LSD. Someone laced my morning coffee with—

Brain tumor. Brain tumors cause hallucinations, don't they? I know they make people smell toast when there's no toast. Right? Something like that.

"Carly?" I look up and see Christopher in the parking lot, having a smoke. He really needs to quit smoking. If Lindsay finds out he's smoking again, she's going to kick his ass.

"Do brain tumors make you smell toast?" I ask as I walk toward the front door. Christopher tosses his cigarette to the side.

"I don't know. Why? Do you smell toast?"

"No." I reach for the door handle, but Christopher puts his hand on mine, stopping me from opening the door.

"What's going on?" His eyes search my face, and his eyebrows are knit.

"Nothing. I'm fine. Just tired. I think I need some

coffee, or something." I hold up the tape and lamely add, "I got the tape."

"Are you sure you're okay?" He looks worried. Christopher doesn't get worried easily. I must look like hell.

I pull on a bright smile. "I'm fine. Now get your ass in there and let's get this bastard edited."

When I return home, Dad is there. My mother is not. My theories about hallucinations and brain tumors are beginning to hold water. I'm relieved.

Until I see that Dad's bottle of scotch is empty. I walk into the living room and lean against the wall.

"Dad?"

He raises his head, a look of mild surprise on his face, as though he didn't hear me come in. He probably didn't. He looks a lot like he did in the months after she left, distracted and shell-shocked.

"She's staying at the Sheraton," he says. "She likes the beds there." He offers a weak smile. "Apparently they have good beds."

I take a deep breath. I'm amazed and impressed that my shock has lasted as long as it has. I feel oddly calm and in control as I stare down at my old Keds. They're dirty and there's a hole forming over my left big toe.

"Where has she been?" I ask finally.

"New Mexico," he says. "She had a lump on her breast."

"Oh. God." My mind swims for a moment before Dad speaks again.

"It was nothing. Turned out to be nothing, but for a

while she thought maybe it was something, and . . ." He stares down into his glass, his expression confused. "So I guess that's why she's back. I guess she realized . . ."

He trails off. I feel as though I've been jerked on the end of an unforgiving tether. I can't imagine how Dad must be feeling.

"What are you going to do?" I ask.

He releases a heavy sigh. "Can I answer that question tomorrow?"

"Yeah." My heart tugs slightly to see him sitting there, slumped over a glass of scotch, staring into its depths. I am momentarily angry with him for letting her do this to him again, but I shut it down. "Where's Five?"

"Staying at Rebecca's tonight," he says. "She's going on that weekend trip to Flagstaff, remember?"

I nod, although I don't remember.

"She'll be back on Monday. It's a good thing. I don't know how I would have explained it to her." He pauses for a moment. "I'm not sure how I feel about it myself."

I get up, grab a glass from the liquor cabinet, and pour myself two fingers of scotch. I take one fiery sip, then turn to face Dad.

"How long was she here for?"

Dad shakes his head. "I don't know."

"What did she want?"

He looks up at me. "She wants to come back."

"Well, she can't," I snap. My father's face flashes disappointment, then falls into an expression of resignation.

"No," he says finally. "I guess not."

He doesn't sound sure. I take another swig of scotch.

"What are we going to tell Five?" I ask.

He sighs, puts his glass down on the coffee table, and pushes himself up off the couch.

"I need some time by myself," he says. He runs his hands over what hair he's got left, then looks at me. "I'm sorry, Carly. I just need . . ."

"Of course."

He kisses me on the cheek, and finally meets my eyes.

"Look, don't say anything to Five or Ella," he says. "Not yet. Let me do that, okay?"

I nod and listen as he thumps steadily up the stairs. The living room is quiet, and the longer I stand there staring at the bottle of scotch, the more suffocating it feels. I have to move. I have to do something. I have to . . . I have to . . .

I put down my glass, which is still mostly full. I grab my keys out of my pocket, then dump them on the coffee table. It's nine o'clock on a Thursday night. Where am I going to go? What am I going to do?

I think about going to the Sheraton, locating my mother, and telling her to get the hell out. She has no right to come back. Not now. It's too late.

Then the realization hits me like a dope slap to the side of the head; they're not divorced.

He's going to take her back, I think, but then scrub the thought. Dad and I argued about the divorce exactly once, and it was the most bitter—the *only* bitter—argument we'd ever had. He was such a good Catholic that he didn't even think seventeen years of abandonment was a good enough reason to drop the deadweight.

Only it wasn't about being Catholic, and we both knew it. It was the Mary-shaped hole.

And now she's here. Is he really going to forgive her? Take her back?

I realize I'm pacing the room, my hands clenching and unclenching. That's crazy behavior. One more minute alone in this living room and I'll be muttering to myself about the government.

I grab my purse and keys.

I call Christopher on my cell phone. Lindsay is in Tempe visiting her mom, so it's just him meeting me at Flamingo Cove, a huge pool hall in which beer is served by girls wearing fishnet stockings and not much else. But the tables are pink and the beer is cheap. Everything in life is a trade-off.

"You really do suck at this game," Christopher says as he lines up his shot. He's stripes, I'm solids, and I've only sunk one ball. He's going for the eight ball.

He's right. I do suck. But I've had two beers and I feel pretty good. Considering.

"So, you gonna tell me what's going on?" he asks. He shoots. He scores. I'm racking.

"No," I say. "I don't want to talk about it. I want to be distracted."

"Does getting your ass kicked in pool distract you?" he asks, a wry grin on his face. "Because if that's the case, I'm definitely your guy."

"Heh, you're funny," I say, racking the balls. I may not be able to shoot worth a damn, but I rack like a pro. When I finish, I look up to find Christopher's focus on me, his face suddenly serious.

"Just tell me one thing," he says, his eyes dark and unreadable. "This isn't about Seth, is it?"

I shake my head no. Christopher nods, but there's tension in his face.

"Winner breaks," I say.

"Is it someone else?" he asks, his eyes fixed on me.

I laugh. "It's sweeps, Christopher. I have no time for men during sweeps. You know that. Now break."

He lays his cue down on the table and walks over to stand next to me. "You gonna answer my question or not? Is it a guy?"

I stare at him, irritation mixing with affection. While the overprotective-brother routine can sometimes be a bit much, it's comforting, knowing I've got a big, strong guy like Christopher ready to beat the crap out of any guy should I say the word. Not that I ever would. It's just nice to know.

"No," I say. "There's no guy. Trust me; if I was having sex on anything approaching a regular basis, I'd be in a much better mood."

Christopher nods, looks down at the pool table, but doesn't move to pick up his cue. I watch him, and for the first time I really notice that he seems almost nervous.

Christopher's never nervous. Something's not right.

"Christopher?" I say slowly. "You okay?"

"Yeah. No. I'm fine," he says. He runs his hand over his face and shrugs the tension out of his shoulders. "I'm fine."

Something's going on. It occurs to me that maybe something has happened with him and Lindsay. Maybe they are sleeping together. Oh—and she's at her mom's. What if . . . ?

"Did you and Lindsay have a fight?" I ask suddenly, my imagination having connected dots that apparently aren't there, as Christopher looks at me like I'm totally nuts.

"No," he says. "Why would we fight?"

"I dunno." I take a sip of my beer, playing it cool just in case I'm right and Lindsay is in love with Christopher. I don't want to be the one to blow her cover.

I realize that Christopher is staring at me, and I lower my beer. "What?"

"Come on." He grabs my hand and leads me through the pool hall.

"My beer . . ." I say, glancing back at my half-full bottle, sitting on the edge of the pool table. It'll be gone before we get back; those fishnet waitresses are barracudas.

Christopher pushes through the doors and pulls me with him through the parking lot. I ask where we're going, and he doesn't answer. After a few moments, I see we're headed toward his truck. He opens the passenger-side door, grabs something off the dash, and hands it to me.

It's a book.

"Christopher?" I turn the book over in my hands, flip it open to the copyright page. It's a familiar-looking hardcover copy of *Jane Eyre*, and I'm momentarily distracted from his weirdness.

"Oh, my God," I say. "This is just like the one I lost in college. Remember?"

"Do I remember?" He laughs. "You made me search every used bookstore with you for three weeks."

I glance at the title page. "Nineteen fifty-three. With the Eichenberg engravings." I shut the book and look up at him. "This is it. It's just like mine."

He pauses before speaking. "I know."

"How did you find it?"

"It's a long story."

I close it and run my fingers over the cover. "Oh, my God. I can't believe you found one." I tear my eyes away from the book and look up at him. "I can't believe you remembered this after all this time. Where did you find it?"

He swallows. Hard. And he still looks nervous. Over an old copy of *Jane Eyre*? I don't get it.

"Look at the spine," he says.

I turn the book over in my hand. "It says 'Jane Eyre.' "

"What color is it?"

I give him a strange look, then check out the spine. "Um. I don't know. Kind of orangey-yellow?"

"*Amber.*" He gives the word such weight that I'm beginning to wonder if maybe it's Christopher who has a brain tumor. He releases a deep breath and leans back against the truck, staring at me as though waiting for me to get it. I'm flummoxed. Then I pull some pieces together from the cobwebbed corners of my brain, and laugh.

"Oh," I say. "What? You think this has something to do with the psychic quilt?"

There's a long moment of silence, and then he pushes himself up from the truck, putting his hands on either side of my face.

And he kisses me.

Christopher *kisses* me.

Christopher kisses me.

I am stiff. I am shocked. I am . . .

Holy God, there's tongue.

He releases me. I blink.

"What . . . what . . . what . . . ?" I blink again.

He steps back from me and stares, looking almost as shocked as I feel. After a moment, he leans back against the truck and nods toward the book.

"I, uh, I found it at a sidewalk sale seven years ago." He's staring at the book, avoiding eye contact. "Right before you left for grad school. I was going to give it to you then. Tell you . . ."

He trails off.

"Tell me? Tell me what?" My brain feels like a tiny goldfish in a great big bowl. I just can't circle it fast enough, and by the time I get to the other side, I've lost track of where I've been.

"But I didn't, and then you went to Syracuse and you were with that guy—"

Guy? What guy? Syracuse . . . "Oh. What? Mike Bergen?"

His words are rushing out, all over me, landing in messy piles at my feet. "—and you just never seemed to see me that way, so I gave it up. It didn't seem . . . I don't know. Meant to be, I guess. When you were available I was with someone, and when I was available, you weren't." He pauses, his eyes locked tight on mine. "But it's never gone away, Carly. I've never gotten over it. And

I've kept that book all these years. Just in case the right time came."

He finally stops. I stare at the book in my hands, and I still can't process the fact that Christopher has kissed me. He puts his hands on my shoulders and it feels really weird to have his face so close to mine.

"I've always thought we were . . . special. I felt it. I knew it. But it wasn't until you told me about the quilt, that I thought . . . maybe . . ." His hands trail down my arms, and he takes my hands in his. "Lindsay's out of town. I've got the place to myself. Seemed kind of like the right time."

Oh. My. God. Lindsay. My mind is whirling. I'm not certain Lindsay is in love with Christopher, but I kinda think so, and why oh why didn't I ever just be a girl and ask her and stick my nose in the middle of it and get them together because if I had this would never, ever, ever have happened and . . .

Christopher drops my hands. "Okay. Well. I guess the sheer terror on your face is my answer."

I blink and look up at him. "Oh. God. No. I just . . . I wasn't expecting . . ."

"Hey, no big deal," he says, clearing his throat. "Let's just forget it, okay?"

"Christopher . . ."

"Come on," he says, forcing a smile. "I'll kick your ass in pool."

I glance down at the book, then back up at him. "Christopher."

He takes the book from my hands, tosses it back onto

the front seat of his truck, and slams the door shut. "It's okay. I get it. I'm just not up for the I-love-you-as-a-friend speech right now, Car, I'm sorry. You coming or not?"

He looks very much like he does not want me to go with him, so I slowly shake my head. His expression ices over.

"See you at work, then." He turns and goes back inside, and I watch him, frozen where I stand. Part of me wants to run after him, and part of me wants to run away. Part of me feels like I was just hit over the head with a big rubber mallet. I'm not sure that I've drunk too much to drive home, but between the beer and the surprise kiss, I'm not taking any chances. I head toward the closest bus stop. I'll have Dad drop me off here in the morning before work.

Twenty minutes later, I'm home. I sneak into my room and pull my head under the covers, insisting that when I wake up in the morning, it will have all been a very strange, totally surreal dream.

Or maybe I have that brain tumor.

But I don't smell any toast.

Work the next day is relatively normal, if I ignore the fact that Christopher and I can't look at each other. Which I manage to do, fairly well, until we get in the Blueberry to go interview the Snakebite Kid. Victor wants the story put together by Monday, which means that I'll be spending a good portion of my weekend logging tapes and writing the script, and then, Monday morning, it'll be me and Christopher in the editing booth all day while he puts it together. For once, I envy the news people. Their camerapeople are just camera-people. Editors are an entirely separate group of people. But for *Tucson Today*, no such luck. We're more expensive to produce, and we make less money.

The ride to Snakebite Kid's house is quiet. Deathly quiet. Christopher asks me if I want anything from the Circle K when we stop for gas, and I say no. That's it for conversation, until we get to I-10, when twenty minutes of uneventful highway driving looming before us forces Christopher to speak.

"So. Um. Maybe we should talk?" Christopher asks. He sounds very much like he does not want to talk.

This is Lindsay's work, I think. *She probably spent half of last night on the phone with him. Poor Lindsay.*

"Um . . ." I'm usually more articulate. Today, not so much.

"Well," he says after a long silence. "I've completely fucked everything up, haven't I?"

"No. Christopher, it's just . . ." I exhale a deep breath. "My mother came back yesterday."

Christopher nearly veers off into the next lane of traffic. "What?"

"She was there when I stopped by home yesterday, to get that tape? And my dad is . . . I don't know. Talking to her. I'm just . . ."

I swallow hard and shake my head, and feel like I'm about to burst into either tears or hysterical laughter.

"Jesus, Carly," Christopher says after a moment. "Are you okay?"

"Yeah," I say instinctively. "I'm fine. Really. It's just . . . my head's all a big mess, you know?"

"Wow. How's your dad handling it?"

I shrug. "He left for work early this morning. I didn't see him. Last night he seemed pretty shook."

"I imagine." Christopher pauses. "How about Ella? Five?"

"I haven't talked to Ella yet," I say. "Five's on a weekend trip."

"So it's just you," he says, his voice tight. "Handling this on your own."

"There's not much to handle," I say. "She's been gone seventeen years. Now she's back. She'll be gone again soon. It's not a big deal."

"Carly," Christopher says, but then stops himself from saying whatever he was going to say. I feel trapped. I want to avoid both the topics of Christopher's feelings and my mother's return, but I have to talk about one or the other. I cannot get by with a comment about the weather.

"I am worried about Dad, though," I say. "It was so hard on him, the first time she left. Turning her away now is going to kill him."

There's a slight pause. "Are you sure he's going to turn her away? I mean, aren't they still married?"

"Yeah, but . . ." I trail off. Deep down, I am worried that Dad will want to mend things with her, but I don't want to admit that. Instead, I stare out the window, and allow myself to be silent, to disconnect. Finally, we stop at our destination, and Christopher shuts off the engine and turns to face me.

"Look," he says, "I acted like a big asshole last night.

But I want you to know that I'm still me. I'm still your friend. No matter what."

I smile at him. That's such a Christopher thing to do, to put his own feelings aside and think of me first. In the back of my head, I know that I've got to be crazy not to grab hold of this very good thing. Any smart girl would. Then there's a moment when we're sitting there, smiling at each other, and he starts to lean forward, and it freaks me out.

"Snakebite's waiting," I say, pulling back a bit.

Christopher smiles, reaches over, and gives my hand a quick squeeze. "Okay. Let's get moving, then."

I follow behind him up to the house, watching him move with that big-guy grace, wondering if there's really much of a difference between loving someone as a friend and being in love with them, and getting the distinct feeling that I'm about to find out.

It is amazingly easy for me to go on with life as though my mother had never shown up. I spend most of the weekend working on the Snakebite Kid story, and when I'm home, things are normal. Dad seems okay, even chipper. On Sunday night, Ella comes over for dinner and we all eat lasagna and drink wine and speculate over Five's relationship with Botox. Dad makes no mention of Mary, and I follow his lead. I wonder if she's left already, if he sent her packing and is quietly moving on. Maybe he's finally gained closure. Maybe her coming back, however briefly, was a good thing for him. I don't ask him about it, though. I figure if he wants to talk, he'll talk. Until then, it suits me just fine to pretend nothing's happened, and by Monday morning I'm feeling almost normal again. When Dad asks me to be home for dinner to celebrate Five's return from Flagstaff, I'm actually looking forward to it.

At work, Christopher and I spend the morning arguing over editing choices, which is typical, and when we break, we decide to go for lunch at the Taco Shack. Things almost feel normal again until we see Eloise rushing down the hallway toward us.

"Oh, thank God I found you guys," she says, breathless. "There's a meeting in the newsroom. Something big."

Christopher and I exchange looks. As we head down the hall, I feel his hand glance the small of my back lightly, and the touch makes my heart rate kick up. At first I feel hopeful that the response is a good sign, and then I wonder if it's a bad sign that I'm so desperately stretching for good signs. I glance up at him and smile, but he's looking at the crowded newsroom, which is humming with people whose expressions range from angry to totally freaked out.

Oh. This can't be good.

"Everyone quiet down!" I hear Clayton Pall, the station's general manager, yell from the corner of the room. He steps up behind the assignment desk, which is on a raised platform in the east corner of the newsroom. His necktie is loose. Clayton's necktie is *never* loose. Christopher and I exchange looks; this is definitely not going to be good. In a few moments the newsroom is deathly quiet, which never happens. It feels eerie.

"I have some news," Clayton says from his perch behind the assignment desk. "Before I tell you what's going on, I want you to know that the management team is all here"—he motions to a Rockette line of suits standing to the right of the desk—"to answer your questions as best we can, but understand that we still don't have all the information at this time."

I hear someone behind me whisper something about Reginald Davies. Reginald is the station owner, and I've seen him exactly twice in the five years I've worked on *Tucson Today*. I wonder briefly if Reginald has died or something.

"It appears that Reginald Davies has left the country," Clayton says, then clears his throat. "And it also appears that he has taken the bulk of the station's assets with him."

"Holy shit," Christopher breathes behind me. I hear someone behind us say something about Buenos Aires.

"People," Clayton says, raising his hands to quiet the rumbling that's running through the floor of employees. "At this point, we don't know exactly what's going to happen—"

"Will there be layoffs?" someone yells from the back.

The answer is clear in Clayton's face: *Yes*.

"We don't have any answers to that at this time," he says.

Christopher and I get our tacos, then hole up in the editing booth and work until six o'clock. When we finally return to the *Tucson Today* office with our finished tape, we find Victor waiting for us. I sit at my desk while Victor takes Christopher into his office, which has an actual door, so I can't hear what's being said, only the tones of their voices, which are grim. Christopher emerges a few minutes later, giving me a hopeful smile, and then Victor calls me in.

"We've been canceled," he says before I'm even settled in his squeaky guest chair.

I don't absorb this right away. "What do you mean?"

"I mean," Victor says, his voice tired, "we're all being laid off. Well, the producers, anyway. News is going to absorb the camera crew starting Monday."

"So," I say, "do you still need me to oversee the show tonight or . . . ?"

Victor shakes his head, and explains that they'll be running canned shows for the rest of the week, then replacing *Tucson Today* with *M*A*S*H* reruns starting next week. No more live episodes. No more hanging out in the control room, giving the director time cues for the segments and taking shit from Billy the graphics guy, who calls up every graphic with, "Are you sure this is spelled right, Car? You're sure? Looks wrong to me."

And, ha, I think, as I recall the rundown for tonight's show, *for all the trouble that quilt has caused me, the stupid story isn't even going to air.*

Victor sits back in his chair and pokes his thumbs into the pudgy center of a stress ball. "Reginald Davies is a fucknut. Clayton was talking about, if the losses are covered by insurance, or whatever, that they might be able to get *Tucson Today* back on the air but . . . pfffft. It was bound to happen anyway. We just don't make enough money." He shakes his head. "I'll give you a good recommendation. Just don't ask until next week. I plan on staying drunk for a while."

I nod, shake Victor's hand, and wander out to the bull pen, which is what we call the conference table in the center of the room where we pitch stories. Correction: where we *used to* pitch stories. All the cubicles lining the walls are empty. Victor gives us a gruff, "Good night," and leaves. Christopher and I are left standing alone in the bull pen, staring at each other in shock.

"I've been laid off."

"Damnit." He plunks back against the conference table. "What, they didn't even try to get you into the newsroom?"

"It's okay."

"No, it's not," he says, his voice hot. I don't entirely understand why he's so upset; at least he still has a job.

I, however, have been laid off.

I start to laugh.

"Carly?" Christopher looks at me with concern.

"I've been laid off," I say, still giggling. "I've been laid off." I stop giggling. "That's never happened to me before."

He puts a hand on my shoulder. "Let me take you home."

"I'm unemployed, not drunk." I feel the heat of his hand on my shoulder, and it's making me a little dizzy. I don't move, though. "Besides, my car's out in the parking lot," I add, my voice weak.

"I know, but . . ." He hesitates, and his face grows serious. "When am I going to see you again?"

I am suddenly very aware of how alone we are in the office. Christopher's hand moves slowly up from my shoulder until his fingers are in my hair. He pulls me closer, and I realize that I'm standing between his open legs as he leans back on the conference table.

Oh, shit, here we go, I think, and then we are kissing. His tongue is grazing mine in questioning caresses, and I'm kissing him back, and it's good. It's good. It's not, you know, earth-shattering, but I'm liking it. His hand trails down to my waist. I run my fingers over the hairs at the back of his neck and he shivers, pulling me tighter against him. The kiss grows more passionate, and then as I'm leaning up against him, I feel something hard against my hip and I realize *it's Christopher* and this is when the abject terror hits. I try to find my way back to where this was good, to really be here with him, but his hard-on is freaking me out and my heart is hammering and I'm suddenly battling an urge to run far, far away. Finally, Christopher breaks the kiss and looks at me.

"Hey," he says, his mouth curling up wryly at one corner. "There's that look of cold terror I know and love."

"I'm sorry," I say. "There's obviously something very wrong with me."

As understatements go, I think that's a pretty fine one.

He takes my hand in his and eyes me with compassion. "Carly, I'm not gonna push myself on you if you're not ready, but I gotta say, the signals you're sending are pretty mixed."

"I know." He's staring at me as though he wants more, and he deserves more, so I keep going. "I'm just confused. It's such a huge change, you know, from how we've always been with each other. I feel like you're gone, and there's this wonderful guy here who likes me but I don't know him, and . . ."

He reaches up and brushes some hair away from my forehead, which stops me talking.

"He doesn't just like you," he says softly. He looks at me with unconditional caring in his eyes, and I feel a sudden and undeniable urge to vomit. "Carly. I love you."

"What about Lindsay?" I blurt out. Christopher's eyebrows knit, and his eyes flash with a touch of anger.

"Lindsay?" he says. "What the hell does Lindsay have to do with anything?"

"I . . . I . . . I . . ." *Mayday. Mayday.* "I think she . . . you know . . . I think maybe she has feelings for you, and . . ."

Oh, man. My hands are starting to sweat. This is bad, bad, bad. Christopher lets out a huff and crosses his arms over his chest.

"Look, Car, if you're looking for an excuse not to let this happen with us, you don't need one. Either you're in or you're out. And if you're bringing up some imaginary crush that Lindsay might have on me, it sounds to me like you're out."

I'm in a nosedive and I can't pull up. Crash, meet burn.

"I've handled this badly," I say, going in once again for understatement. "Forget the Lindsay thing. Strike it from the record. I don't know what I'm talking about. I'm just . . . there's so much going on right now. I can't wrap my mind around this. Can you understand that?"

He nods, but his expression is tight and hard to read. He pushes up off the table and grabs his jacket.

"Yeah," he says. "I understand."

"You're mad."

"I'm not mad." He forces a smile. "I'm not mad. You want to walk with me out to the parking lot?"

I shake my head. "I'm supposed to meet with Cheryl."

"Cheryl?"

"Human Resources. Laid off. Exit interview. She has to make sure I'm not at risk for coming back and slashing the tires on the Live Van. Yadda yadda."

"Oh. Yeah. That." There's a long moment of awkward silence. "Okay." He leans over and kisses me on the forehead, then moves quickly out of the room. I collapse over the bull pen table and bang my forehead against its cool surface.

"I am a whole new strain of stupid," I mutter to myself.

"Carly?"

I push myself up and see Cheryl from Human Resources standing in the doorway. She glances meaningfully at her watch. Poor thing. It's been a busy day of showing her coworkers the door.

"I was supposed to be out of here at five thirty," she says, apparently not the least bit grateful that she still has a job. "Are you ready?"

Just about ready to slash the tires on the Live Van, I think, but I follow her down the hall to her office just the same.

Chapter Four

"Daddy?" I say as I open the door. I am better now, stronger, not as close to total emotional breakdown as I was after kissing Christopher, although my hands are still a little shaky. I need to have a scotch with my Dad. I need a good night's sleep. I need to talk about something that is not *Tucson Today* and is not Christopher. I need to think about something else. Maybe play backgammon.

I find Dad in the dining room. Ella and Five are sitting across the table from him. They look up at me, their eyes red, their faces wet with fresh tears. Sitting next to Dad is my mother and *fuck* if I can't knock her on timing.

She turns and sees me, then stands up. Her eyes are

red. She has a crumpled tissue in one hand. The other hand reaches blindly for Dad, and Dad takes it.

Dad. Takes. It.

"Oh, holy Christ," I mutter. Ella sniffs and grabs from the Kleenex box on the table. Five looks more stunned than anything. Which makes sense. After all, she has no active memories of the desertion, just the cold, dead ache of it. This has to be even more of a shock for her than for the rest of us. At least we have a point of reference.

"Mary," I say. It feels strange to call her Mary, but she hasn't really earned *Mom*. I turn my attention to Dad. "She's coming back?"

He stands up, still holding her hand. His eyes are red, too. Jesus. What's wrong with this family? Does no one have any self-control?

"She's my wife," he says. "And if you'd listen to her—"

"Um, no. I don't think so." I sound like a petulant teenager, and I really don't give a crap. "No. I have had possibly one of the worst days of my young life and this? Is not what I need right now." I lock my eyes on Dad's. "Answer the question. Is she coming back?"

Dad looks at Mary, then back at me. "We're going to try, yes. We're going to go to therapy—"

"Fuck therapy," I spit at him. "There isn't enough therapy in the world to make up for what she did."

Dad looks like he's been slapped, and he reddens.

"Carly Simon McKay—" he begins, but I turn my attention to Mary.

"What the hell do you think you're doing?" I say. "Where do you get the right?"

"Don't you talk to your mother like that," my father

starts, but Mary puts her hand on his arm and says, "Declan."

"I'll talk to her how I want." I look at Mary and point at Five. "Did you know she hated the name you gave her? Van Morrison McKay? What kind of name is that for a baby girl, anyway? Carly Simon and Ella Fitzgerald were bad enough, but Jesus, lady!"

"Carly!" Dad sounds really pissed off. I've never spoken this way in front of him before. It probably doesn't help that I look and sound like I'm a kid, and that fact fills me with additional fury, which I promptly unleash on my mother.

"She watched too much *Sesame Street* as a baby, because she didn't have a mother, and decided her name was Five." The muscles in my legs start to tremble and I know I should leave, but instead I move a step closer to Mary. "Because you weren't here, my sister is named after a fucking number!"

"Go to your room!" Dad says.

I turn to him, and I'm sure I must look as shocked, hurt, and offended as I feel.

"Just to be clear, there's a difference between looking fifteen and being fifteen," I say, his betrayal blowing around me like a minicyclone.

"And there's a difference between being twenty-nine and acting it," he shoots back.

"Go to hell!" I yell at him. I've never said this to my father. *Never.* My legs are full-on shaking now and I feel like I'm going to fall over. Ella starts to weep actively in the background. I am at sea, I have no anchor, I don't know if I'm out of line or not, and I don't really care.

After the moment of shock passes, Dad opens his mouth to speak, but Mary puts her hand on his arm. Again.

"Declan."

Dad's eyes go to her, and he instantly calms. Because she told him to.

Jesus. She's his wife. Seventeen years, and suddenly, she's his wife again. My legs start to shake even more violently.

What the hell is wrong with this family, anyway?

Mary looks at me. "I thought I was doing what was best for you." Her voice is thick, but she's fighting the tears. Good for her. "You remember how I was. I was a mess. The doctor I found in New Mexico said it was postpartum, but by the time I got better . . ." She shakes her head, blinks hard, gathers herself. "It took me seventeen years to get over the guilt, to get the courage to come back, to tell you how much I've regretted not being here with you."

"Should have taken forever," I say.

"Shut up!"

I shift my focus to see Five pushing herself up from the table. She walks toward us and slowly situates herself at Mary's side.

"At least you got a chance to know her," Five says. She seems so mature, suddenly. Much more mature than me. And she's taller than me. And she sounds older than me. I am overwhelmed with sudden bitterness that my baby sister looks more grown-up than I ever will. "I just want to know her. Think about someone besides yourself, Carly. Don't ruin this for me." A fresh tear skips over her cheek. "Don't make her go away again."

Mary strokes Five's hair and places a shaky kiss on the top of her head. "I'm not going anywhere, sweetheart."

Sweetheart. Huh. I turn to Dad. "So, what now?"

His eyes are such a mixture of anger and sadness that I can't look at them.

"Your mother is moving back," he says.

"No," I say.

He has the nerve to look offended. "Excuse me?"

I cross my arms over my stomach. "I said no. If she comes back, then I'm gone."

I instantly regret the ultimatum, because I am against them. I think they're horrible and manipulative, and I can't believe I've just laid one down. I'm about to take it back when Ella stands up.

"Carly," she says, "you can't do that."

Yet I can't go back. Because as much as I despise ultimatums and the people who issue them, I mean it. "It's done."

Dad, Mary, Five, and Ella exchange looks. Then I see Five entwine her fingers with Mary's. Ella sniffles and takes a step toward me. "You can stay with me and Greg."

She puts her hand on my arm and I wrench it out of her grip, my eyes on Mary.

"I was twelve." I point to Ella. "I couldn't go out for field hockey because I had to be here every afternoon when she got home from school." I nod toward Five. "When she was eight months old, she had chicken pox and almost died. I snuck into her room and slept in the chair by her bed every night for two months because I was so terrified she'd stop breathing in the middle of the night. While you were in New Mexico having a good long conference with your inner child, Dad was wandering around this place like a ghost, and I was the one who made sure we had food. And what? You're sorry, so it's suddenly okay?"

Mary looks down at her feet and begins to weep. Five puts one arm around Mary's shoulder and gives me the most blatantly mutinous glare I've ever gotten. I feel Dad-, Ella-, and Five-shaped holes burrowing their ways through me. And that is when everything breaks for me. The emotion is suddenly gone, as though some determined housewife simply swept it away. I am no longer angry. I am no longer hurt. I am cold inside. I am hollowed out. I am relieved.

"I'm gonna go pack," I say.

Dad gives a tired sigh. "Carly—"

"No worries." I allow a tight smile. "I'm fine."

I turn my back on all of them. My legs take over, carrying me out of the kitchen, up to my room. On autopilot, I pack random bits of my stuff and bring it down to my car. I toss my hairbrush in my suitcase, but I forget underwear. The four of them stay in the dining room; I can hear them talking in hushed tones as I pass by with boxes and luggage. I need something to wrap my little thirteen-inch television in and grab the quilt from under my bed. It is my last trip. I shut the door behind me and get in the car, without the slightest fucking clue where I'm going.

I'm halfway to Phoenix when I glance in my rearview mirror, and a swatch of light from a streetlight washes over the quilt-covered television. A sudden realization and a crazy calm come over me.

It's the quilt's fault.

It's the *quilt's* fault.

Before the quilt, everything was fine. Then Brandywine McCrazy gives me this quilt, talking about books
with amber spines and women named Mary and—

"And—oh!" I say, smacking the palm of my hand
down on the steering wheel and accidentally hitting the
horn. "South America!"

Reginald Davies took off for Buenos Aires. That was
the rumor. I heard it.

My life was fine, it was *fine*, before Brandywine
Seaver and her stupid fucking quilt. A part of me—the
sane part, I'm thinking—sits back helplessly and watches
as I take the next exit and trade I-10 West for I-10 East.
This part of me knows I'm completely off my nut, that I
don't believe in quilts or curses, that spending my time
racing to Bilby to confront a quiltmaker when I'm homeless and unemployed is just plain nuts, and yet, this part
doesn't stop me.

Probably because it couldn't if it tried.

It is past ten o'clock by the time I pull up in front of
Brandywine Seaver's artsy little cottage. The green lawn
rocks, the "Rentals Available" sign, the picket fence . . .
all of it is pissing me off. I'm annoyed by the *air* in Bilby.
I'm annoyed by the very *existence* of Bilby. It's a stupid
artsy stupid town with a stupid name and stupid left-
wing nutcases running around being all Bohemian with
their sandals and their recycled toilet paper, and I despise them all.

The sane part of me realizes, of course, that the only

nutcase in the vicinity at the moment is me, but doesn't make a big deal out of it.

I step out of my car and open the back door, yanking the stupid quilt off the television and bundling it in my arms. I slam the door to my car with my hip and march up the path to Brandywine Seaver's house. This time, I wrap my finger in the quilt to protect it from the zapping doorbell of death.

I hope it catches on fire, I think. *I hope this entire town goes down in flames.*

Brandywine Seaver opens the door. She has two pieces of fabric draped over her shoulder and her hair is half in a ponytail, half out. She looks like she's had a long day, but I don't care, because she and her stupid quilt ruined my life.

She stares at me blankly for a second; then her eyes flash surprise and recognition. "Carly?"

"Take it!" I say, shoving the quilt toward her. She makes no move to take it from me, nor does she look at me like I'm insane. Which I clearly am. What the hell is wrong with her, anyway?

She cocks her head slightly to one side and looks at me with kindness and understanding. "Do you want to come inside? I can make us some tea."

"What are you?" I say. "A witch?"

"Well . . ." Her lips twitch in a smile. "Yes, actually. Wiccan, anyway. But what does that have to do with—"

"I knew it!" I say, pointing my finger at her, only it's still wrapped under the quilt from hitting the doorbell, and I look like an insane Martha Stewart wannabe trying to hold up an insane Martha Stewart wannabe. "You did something to me! You gave me this quilt, and you ruined my life. My life? Is ruined. I am homeless, I am jobless, and my best friend is in love with me. What . . . what . . . what . . . ?" I stammer. I am insane. The part of me that is sane enough to recognize this sighs and gives up. I narrow my eyes at Brandywine Seaver. "What did you do to me?"

Brandy watches me for a moment, her face showing no sign of irritation. She is sympathetic, and yet not pitying. I get the feeling that somehow she knows what's going on without my having to tell her, which I guess would make sense, seeing as how she put the damn curse on me in the first place.

Brandy steps out of her home and puts her hand gently on my shoulder.

"I think you might benefit from a cup of chamomile tea," she says gently. "It's very calming."

I am about to refuse, but then it starts to rain. The thing about storms in the Southwest is that, on the rare occasions when the skies allow them, they really mean it. Within seconds there are big, fat droplets attacking me from all sides.

I am homeless. I am unemployed. And a witch who has cursed my life is offering me sanctuary.

Suddenly, I feel nine years old. Suddenly, I am craving comfort, from any source. I don't care. I just want to be cut a break. I want to be taken care of.

Suddenly, with a desire so raw I can't fight it, I want chamomile tea.

Well, hell. Any port in a storm, right?

"Do you have honey?" I ask feebly, and let her lead me inside.

I am sitting on Brandywine Seaver's couch, wrapped up in a fleece throw. The Quilt of Evil is slumped on the floor below where I'm sitting, and I have my feet tucked up under my legs so that I don't accidentally make contact with the evil. Brandy comes out from the kitchen carrying a tray with a teapot and two mugs.

"Have you ever had real tea? I mean, loose-leaf brewed?" she asks amiably.

"No," I say. "I don't think so."

She smiles, radiating inner peace. "You'll never go back."

She places the tray on her coffee table, pours us each a cup, hands me one, and sits down on the couch.

"So," she says, sipping her mug. "Tell me what happened."

"I don't know where to start," I say. The sane part of me is gaining ground, and I am starting to amass just enough perspective to be embarrassed by my behavior.

"Well," she says slowly, "how about with your best friend?" Her nose wrinkles slightly as she gives me a look of sympathetic discomfort. "You didn't know she was a lesbian?"

I laugh out loud, and it feels good, but it's followed by a wave of sadness that I don't enjoy so much.

"His name is Christopher."

"Christopher?" Her brow crinkles. "The cameraman?"

I am confused for a moment, then remember, of course, she's met Christopher.

"We've been best friends since college. He bought me a book with an amber spine seven years ago because, as it turns out, he loves me, which, you know, who saw that coming?"

Brandy is silent, looking at me as though I'm stupid.

"What?" I say. "You saw that coming?"

Brandy gives a demure shrug, then nods. "Well. Yeah. You guys were only in my house for an hour, but . . . yeah. I thought you were already dating."

I stare at her. Of course she would claim she knew, or her cover as a psychic is blown. But still. It's kind of obnoxious.

"And you knew, too," she says, taking a sip of her tea.

Okay. *That's* really obnoxious. "I did not."

"Yes, you did."

"No." I clench my teeth. "I didn't."

Brandy makes a face that says, "Did, too," but out loud she only says, "Well."

I keep quiet. It's not worth it. Instead I sigh and say, "Well, if you knew so much, you could have tipped me off that Christopher had the book with the amber spine."

Brandy's face is blank.

"You know," I prod. "The amber spine. The book that Christopher had."

She gives a confused half smile and shakes her head. "What? Is that from the reading?"

"The reading that ruined my life?" I say. "Yeah. You don't remember?"

"No," Brandy says matter-of-factly. "I read the quilts to get them out of my head. Once they're gone, they're gone. Did I say something about a book with an amber spine?"

I sigh. "I don't even know if it was amber. It might have been orange. It was dark when he showed it to me."

She quirks her head to the side and grins. "So, he's in love with you. Is that a bad thing?"

"I don't know," I whine. "I'm thinking maybe."

Brandy looks contemplative for a moment, then leans forward. "There's something you need to understand. You got that quilt because it was time for you to have it. Because these things were coming. Maybe the Universe wanted to give you a heads-up. I don't know. But I didn't curse you. All of this would have happened anyway, with or without the quilt."

I stare at her. This hadn't occurred to me. And it sounds like typical pass-the-buck crap to me.

"But the show got canceled. The story didn't even air."

Brandy smiles knowingly. "Doesn't that tell you something?"

"That I've lost my job?"

"No," she says. "That you were brought here for a purpose, and that purpose was not to put my pretty mug on TV."

She's looking at me expectantly. I got nothing. "I was brought here to fulfill an assignment."

Brandy smiles softly. "I'm sorry things are so hard on you right now. Do you want to hear my theory on times like this?"

No. I sip the tea. She's right. It's good. She's watching me, waiting, and I sigh. "Sure."

"I think that when everything goes wrong, it's because nothing was right in the first place. It's like, when you knit . . . do you knit?"

I stare at her. *Do I look like I knit?* I wonder.

She shrugs acquiescence. "Okay. Well, when you knit, if you get something wrong and keep knitting, then when you discover it, you have to rip out all those rows of stitching to go back and fix it. Life is like that. Sometimes, it has to rip out all the stitches to go back and fix what's wrong."

This sounds ridiculous to me. But the tea is good, so I just give a noncommittal, "Hmmm," and sip some more. And suddenly, I am bone tired.

"Wow," I say, yawning. "Sorry. I don't know what's—" I yawn again and can't finish the sentence.

"Oh, yeah," she says. "I should have warned you. Chamomile packs a punch if you're not used to it."

"Oh," I say. *Great. Now I've been cursed* and *drugged.*

Brandy smiles. "Do you have a place to stay tonight?"

I shake my head, staring into my mug. The tea is looking kinda swirly and pretty. I take another sip.

"I'd offer to have you stay here," Brandy says, motioning around, "but the quilts kinda take over all the extra space. I usually need at least a week's notice to have guests." She stands up, smiling. "But I own a cabin, back on the land behind the house. My tenant is a good friend, and he's out of town for the weekend. You can stay in his bed."

Sleep in a strange man's bed? Yuck. "No. That's okay. I'm sure there's a motel around here somewhere."

Brandy looks scandalized. "Motels are where people go to commit suicide. Come on. We can put on fresh sheets. He won't mind."

She starts for the door, and I follow, deliberately stepping around the Quilt of Evil. We walk out to my car and I grab the backpack I filled with a change of clothes and basic toiletries. She leads me down the white rock path that winds to the back of her property. As we get to the side of her house, the foliage takes over, and we're surrounded by creosote and palo verde. The air is fragrant and warm, and the moonlight sprinkles down on us through the trees. The path angles upward toward the foothills, and then opens into a clearing where there are two cabins, each surrounded by so much foliage that they look like they're just wedged into the hills themselves. The closest one is painted yellow; the second one, a little farther down the path, is a robin's-egg blue. Both have small decks that are adorned with wind chimes and mismatched outdoor furniture, ranging from small plastic tables to whitewashed wooden rocking chairs.

"Wow," I say. "How . . . eclectic."

Brandy grins and turns toward the yellow cabin. She pulls a key out of her pocket and turns it in the lock. We go inside and it's . . . interesting. The space is large and open, with white walls and hardwood floors. The cabin is large enough for two, maybe three rooms, but instead it's simply wide open, with a couple of support columns in the middle. A kitchenette lines one wall, with a small table and two chairs nearby. In one corner is a bed, with a slightly ajar door to what I assume is the bathroom.

The other half of the space is taken up by paintings, drop cloths, palettes, paintbrushes. Leaning against the walls, covering the modest sofa and coffee table, are dozens of paintings, some finished and some not. Landscapes, portraits, still lifes. The subjects vary greatly, but the style ties them all together. Everything is painted in little swishes of color, like a bunch of tiny *s*'s, some tightly curled, some relaxed and lazy, all twisting and twirling together to be the parts that create the whole. As I step closer to one, a still life of brightly colored gerbera daisies, the daisies give way to the swishes. When I stand back, the daisies take over again, and I can see the forest for the trees.

"So," I say, "the guy who lives here. He's a painter, huh?"

Brandy sighs. "They're beautiful, aren't they? He hasn't painted in a while, though. I keep bugging him to start up again, but . . ."

She trails off. I don't push. To be honest, I really don't care. All I want from this guy is his bed.

Brandy shows me through the place, pointing out the coffeemaker, the bathroom, the linen closet. I watch her as she puts fresh bedding down, listen as she tells me to help myself to whatever I might need. She seems very familiar with everything, and has no problem offering me this guy's coffee and toothpaste. I wonder briefly if she's sleeping with him or something, but my brain sticks on the word *sleeping*.

I. Am. So.

Tired.

Finally, Brandy leaves. I change into a T-shirt and shorts, brush my teeth, and somehow make it to the bed before passing out completely.

I am staying in a large hotel. Tabitha King is my roommate. She's very nice, and looks a lot like Carrie Fisher. We are drinking tea, but it smells funny.

I open one eye, then squint against the bright sunlight coming in from outside. I blink a few times, glance at the clock next to the bed. It reads 11:04.

Wow.

Something smells good. Coffee brewing.

I rub my eyes, sit up in bed, and see a man in a pair of flannel lounge pants and a paint-streaked T-shirt standing at the kitchen counter, pulling mugs from a cabinet. I scream and pull the blankets up around me. He jumps a bit, as though only slightly startled by my bloodcurdling scream.

And . . . he looks familiar. Am I still dreaming? I rub my eyes. He's still there.

Not dreaming. He must be Brandy's tenant.

And I'm in his bed. Oh, God.

"Hi," I say quickly, hoping I make sense through the sleep haze. "I'm sorry. Brandy said I could stay here. Do you know Brandy? Of course you know Brandy. Anyway, I'm, uh, Carly, and Brandy said it was okay."

I take my hand from my eyes and look at him.

I'm either having wicked déjà vu or I've seen this guy before. Sandy hair, sticking out in a million directions. Dimples. Two-day stubble. Bright blue eyes. My brain shuffles, trying to put him in whatever context he was in when we met the first time. He's giving me a look like his brain is doing the same thing, and then his face brightens and he laughs.

"Oh. Wow. Carly?"

I blink, and a rush of memory comes back at me when I hear his voice, all soft and friendly.

"Oh, my God," I say as the realization hits me. "Will?"

He sets the mugs down on the counter. "That was you under there?"

I sit up a bit, still clutching the blankets to my chest. I'm wearing a big T-shirt, but no bra, and it feels a little intimate to be in a strange man's bed with no bra on. In Will the Artist's bed with no bra on, which feels wrong somehow. Probably because he used to sleep with my sister. Possibly because he might currently be sleeping with Brandy. Or because Five is in love with him.

Pick your complication, folks. Every one's a winner.

I run my hand through my hair, try to wake up a bit. "Yeah. it's me. Brandy didn't tell you she brought me here?"

Will shakes his head. "No. I got in late last night. I saw a tuft of hair sticking out from my covers and crashed on the couch. You know Brandy?"

I glance at the couch. Sure enough, on one end is a pillow and on the other end is a crumpled-up blanket. I look back at Will.

"Wait," I say. "You got in late last night, found a strange person sleeping in your bed, and just, what? Hit the couch? No questions?"

He laughs. "I take it you don't know Brandy very well. Can I get you some coffee?"

"Um." I look around. My bra is on the floor, sitting next to my backpack with my toothbrush.

My bra. Is on the floor. I can feel my face growing hot. Will nods to the coffeemaker and glances back at me.

"Coffee?" he asks again.

"Um," I say. "Yeah. That sounds great." I grab the bra with my toes, swoosh it into my hand, and tuck it under my shirt. Will pretends not to notice, but I can see the small smile he's hiding.

"Just one minute," I say. "Is it okay if I use your bathroom?"

He keeps his eyes on the coffee he's pouring. "Fine by me."

I go into the bathroom, shrug into my bra, replace the T-shirt, give my teeth a quick brush, and run my hands over my hair, which, frankly, is beyond all hope. I step out and Will gives me a quick glance to make sure it's okay to look, then allows himself to make eye contact.

"I took a shot and went with cream and sugar." He walks over, hands me a mug, and sits cross-legged at the edge of the bed. Then he motions toward the head of the bed. "Please. Sit."

I sit. I am in bed with Will the Artist.

Weird.

I sip my coffee.

"So," he says. "Wow. I didn't think I'd ever see you again."

"Yeah." I giggle. God help me, I giggle. "Me, either."

We stare at each other for a moment. The coffeemaker gurgles in the background.

"Well," Will starts. "I have to say, I'm glad—"

The door flies open and Brandy steps inside as though she owns the place. Which, technically, I guess she does, but it's still weird. Her eyes widen as she sees Will.

"Hey, you!" she says. "I didn't think you'd be back until Sunday."

"The shoot was canceled," Will says. "Not that anybody bothered to tell me. I got in at about three in the morning and found Carly here in my bed."

Brandy laughs, like it's no big deal that she and I have completely violated Will's personal space. I deduce that they must be sleeping together.

"I see you two have introduced yourselves," she says. Will and I exchange smiling glances, and he says, "Yep."

Brandy sits on the other side of the bed from Will.

I am in bed with Will and Brandy.

This is definitely weird.

"I think I should . . ." I hook my thumb over my shoulder, motioning vaguely in the direction of elsewhere. "You know."

Brandy looks disappointed. "Oh, do you really have to go?"

"Yeah," I say. "I need to, you know. Find a job. A place to stay. I need to . . ." I feel a heaviness weigh down on me as the events of the last day reappear on my emotional radar. "Get my life together."

Will gives me a concerned look. "What's going on? Something happen?"

"She's been Towered," Brandy says, as though that makes any sense at all.

"Ohhhh," Will says, his face washing over with understanding. I have no freakin' clue what they're talking about. Will gives me a sympathetic look. "Wow. I'm sorry."

"Wait," I say. "What's Towered?"

"It's a Tarot thing," she says. "The Tower. It's when life transitions. You know—rips out the stitches. Brings your tower down and makes you rebuild. Happens to all of us at one time or another. No worries."

I shrug. Whatever. Fine. I've been Towered. When in Rome, just nod and smile.

I grab my bag and look at Will. "Do you mind if I use your shower?"

"Oh, yeah, sure," Will says, motioning toward the bathroom. "The towels hanging on the bar are clean. There's shampoo and stuff in there. Help yourself to anything you need."

"Thanks," I mutter, and duck into the bathroom. I can hear their voices but not what they're saying. Then I turn on the water and all is white noise. I step into Will's small shower booth and the warm water beats down the tension in my shoulders. It isn't until I get out that I realize I have no clean underwear. I turn my old pair inside out and try not to think about it. When I come out, Will is alone, drinking coffee at his little table and reading a paper.

"Well," I say, feeling awkward as hell as he stands up to greet me. "Thanks for everything. I'm sorry for the . . ."

I motion to the bed, mock my own scream of terror from earlier. He laughs.

"No worries," he says. His smile is genuine and his eyes are kind and I want to stay longer, although I know I won't. "Made for an interesting morning."

I smile, take a step to the side while still watching him, and knock over a Chock full o'Nuts coffee can containing a handful of paintbrushes. They roll out over the floor and I shuffle to put them back in while Will rushes over to help.

"Sorry," I say.

"Don't worry about it," Will says, setting the tin upright. "They're just paintbrushes."

I look down in my hand at the paintbrushes, and flash back to Brandy's reading. She said something about paintbrushes, right?

I quickly hand them back to Will, make my exit, and decide that I cannot possibly get out of this town fast enough.

Chapter Five

I am three minutes gone from Brandy's house when I am overcome with a craving for coffee. I am on the main street in Bilby, which—unlike most roads in Arizona, a state of grids—winds lazily through a maze of art galleries, crafty shops, and, as luck would have it, a café called, judging by the hand-painted sign hanging out front, the Café. I pull to the side of the road, run my hands through my still-damp hair, and step out of my car. The air is warm for November and smells faintly floral. I don't smell desert. There are trees. And not an adobe house in sight. There's something about being surrounded by colonial-style buildings all cramped together on a windy street that makes me feel a bit like Dorothy on her first day in Oz.

There are two men sitting outside the Café. They

are on wrought-iron chairs at a tiny circular table with a mosaic surface. They look like they have nowhere in particular to go, which seems odd to me for a Tuesday morning, but then again, this is Bilby. It's another world. They smile at me as I pass them and I smile back.

When in Rome . . .

I push into the café. The walls are a strange cross between lime green and sage, and they are covered with paintings, most of them small, about the size of your standard sheet of copy paper. Next to each is a 3x5 card with the artist's name and the price of the work. A café/gallery. Interesting.

I am about to go to the counter and ask for the biggest, baddest coffee they've got, and then something on the back wall catches my eye. I walk over to it. It's an oil painting on a small square of canvas, a portrait of a woman with swirling dark hair framing her face. Her hands are covering her face, and all you can see are her eyes. She could be laughing, she could be crying, it's not clear. As a matter of fact, from moment to moment, I change my mind as to how she's feeling. One thing I am sure of, once I see all the little swishes of color that make up the painting, is that this was painted by Will. I glance at the 3x5 card next to it.

Untitled
Will Kelley
$40

Damn. I'm good.

"Can I get you something?"

I turn to see a girl with pink hair and an obvious affection for black eyeliner standing next to me, her pen hovering expectantly over her order pad.

"Yes," I say, my eyes automatically floating back to the painting. "I'd like a venti Viennese latte, double the espresso, to go, please."

"Decaf?" she asks.

I turn to her. "No. Definitely not."

"Mmm, hmm." She scribbles. "Skim milk or soy?"

Ummm. "Whole?"

Her eyebrows raise just a smidge, but she scribbles, then grins at me. "Okay. That'll be just a minute."

She walks away, and I turn my attention back to Will's painting. For some reason, I can't tear my eyes away. I am determined to figure out what the subject of the painting is feeling. I look at her hands; they are smallish, delicate. Her left pinky is sticking out a bit, which seems like a whimsical thing, so she must be laughing. But then, in her eyes, there's a slight glistening at the bottom, as though she's about to cry. But then, people do cry with laughter.

I really can't tell.

Minutes must have gone by, because the girl is back with my latte.

"That'll be three ninety-five," she says.

I dig into my purse and hand her my credit card, nodding toward the painting. "And this, please."

She smiles brightly, seemingly thrilled that some art is moving.

"Yeah," she says. "The artist is wonderful, isn't he?"

I nod. He gave me a place to sleep and shower. Buying one little painting is really the least I can do.

When I get to my car, it is ringing. I put the painting (wrapped carefully in blue tissue paper and green ribbon by Black-Eyeliner Girl, otherwise known as Allegra, who is taking a year off before college to help her father keep the Café running—Bilby people don't keep much to themselves, I'm discovering) into the passenger seat and grab my cell phone out of the ashtray. I look at the caller-ID panel on the front of the phone.

It's Christopher.

I put the phone down on the passenger seat.

It rings one more time, then silences. Right now, he is probably leaving me a message on my voice mail, a realization that makes my entire body tighten with tension. The idea of going back to Tucson suddenly fills me with dread, followed by bleak hopelessness.

I flip the phone open and see the little voice-mail icon at the bottom of the screen, under text that announces I have missed five calls.

I sigh. I hit the speed dial for voice mail.

"Carly, it's Dad." My heart seizes at the sound of my father's voice, not a little bit because he sounds so tired. "We just called Christopher's to see how you were and you weren't there. Please call us when you get this message."

Call us. *Us.* My stomach churns. I take a sip of my latte, and my stomach calms. It's a good damn latte.

"Carly." Ella. Her voice is low, almost whispering.

She must have called from the house. "Dad's really upset. I know you're not happy about what's going on, but he's going through a lot. Please, just let him know you're okay. Okay? I love you."

The next is from Christopher. "Car. It's me. Your dad called looking for you and I didn't know where you were. Call me when you get this. Okay? I'll be up."

And then . . . "Carly, it's Lindsay. It's midnight on Monday night, and Christopher and I are a little concerned, because I guess no one knows where you are? Can you call us when you get a chance?" Her tone gets lower. "Christopher's kind of upset. If you can just give him a call, let him know you're okay, it'd really help."

There's a beep, followed by the final message, from Christopher.

"Carly." His voice is tight and he sounds awful. Knife. Through. Heart. "Your dad called me last night looking for you. I told him I was sure you were fine, but I just called him this morning, and I guess no one has heard from you." He releases a heavy breath. "Look, if for some reason you don't want to talk to me, you know, that's okay. Just call someone so at least we know you're okay. I, uh . . . well. You know."

The voice mail bot tells me to press seven to delete all messages. I press seven. Then I put the phone back on the passenger seat. I stare at the winding Bilby main drag ahead of me. I need to follow it to the light, take a right, and go straight for three miles until I catch I-10 back to Tucson. But I don't want to. I want to crawl under something big and fluffy, and sleep. I want to sleep really bad.

I take another sip of my latte.

My phone trills again, and I stare at it. The panel on the front IDs Lindsay's cell phone.

I pick it up and flip it open.

"I'm sorry," I say. "I'm so sorry. I didn't mean to worry you guys. Tell everyone I'm fine, okay?"

"Oh, no, it's okay, I was just going to leave a quick message for you while Christopher was out. Just to, you know, give him a call. He's really upset, Carly."

"I'm so sorry," I say. "I'm really, really, really—"

"Um, Carly?" she says, her voice hesitant. "Did you tell him that I'm in love with him?"

I freeze. Oh, man. Oh, God. I swallow, squinch my eyes shut, and put my hand over them. "I said I thought, maybe—"

"Okay, yeah, that's what he said." There's a long silence, then, "I kinda wish you hadn't done that."

"I'm sorry," I say. "It was just a theory and I don't know why I said it and if it's true, I'm really sorry—"

"Whether it's true or not isn't really the point," Lindsay says, and her voice is uncharacteristically harsh and I know for sure that it's true. "The point is that you're confusing him, and he needs to get an answer from you before he can even think about anything else."

I am struck silent for a moment.

I. Am such. An asshole.

"I'm sorry," she says, and her voice is back to its typical even tone. "I know there's a lot going on with your family right now, and I know things are hard for you. It's just that Christopher is really torn up over this, and I'm a little worried about him. Can you call him on his cell now? He's out looking for you."

"Yeah," I say. "Yeah, absolutely."

"And when you do . . ." she starts, but then stops into a dead silence.

"What?" I say.

"If you love him, tell him," she says quietly. "If you don't love him . . . in that way, I mean . . . then you need to rip off the Band-Aid fast. I know you care about him enough to do that at least."

There's a sharp edge under her sweet tone that makes me feel like total crap. Or *more* like total crap, because I hadn't exactly started out at a high point.

"Yeah. Sure."

She hangs up. I put my hand with the phone in my lap and breathe deeply for a few moments, then dial Christopher's cell phone. He picks up in one ring.

"Carly?" His voice is hoarse. "Are you okay?"

"I'm fine," I say. "I'm so sorry. I didn't mean to make you worry."

"Well, what the fuck did you think was going to happen? You just disappear . . . Wait. I need to pull over." There's a long pause, and I can hear traffic noises in the background. Then, finally, "I'm sorry. I haven't gotten much sleep."

"Christopher . . ."

"Where are you?"

I stare out my windshield at Bilby's main street, winding up into the foothills. "Oz."

"What? Where? Can I come see you?"

"No," I say. "Stay there. Go home. Get some rest."

"Get some . . . what? I need to see you. I need to know you're okay."

"I'm okay."

"You know what was going through my head all night? Do you have any idea—"

"I don't love you back," I blurt out. *Quick and fast, quick and fast, rip off the Band-Aid.* "I mean, I do. I love you so much, but not in the way that I think you want me to. Not in the way that I want to, and I really do want to, Christopher, but I just . . . I don't."

There is his-and-hers silence. I feel as terrible and low and heartbroken as I've ever felt in my life. I take in a deep breath and rip off the rest of the Band-Aid.

"I just think you should know now, you know, before this whole thing gets out of hand."

Ha, ha. Little late for that.

"That's okay," he says, but it's not. I suspect it'll never be okay again. "I just wanted to know you're okay." There's a thick silence, then, "We're still . . . friends, right?"

I swallow against a tremendous knot in my throat that seems bent on choking me. "Oh, yeah. Always."

This is followed by another long, painful silence, and when Christopher speaks again, his voice is strained.

"Okay. Well. I'll see you, then. I guess." The line disconnects. I turn my phone off and flip it shut, tossing it back into the ashtray. Every beat of my heart sends pain shooting through me and I am suddenly overwhelmed with grief. A sob escapes from my throat, and I am on the verge of a nervous breakdown. Here, on the streets of Bilby, Arizona, I'm about to completely lose my shit.

The idea of returning to Tucson fills me with such dread that I can't even entertain the thought of going back. But what else am I going to do?

I sit up straight, white-knuckle the steering wheel, and focus on a sign in a shop window directly in my eye-line. It's a white sign, with hand-painted letters, but I can't read them. I am breathing in, breathing out. I am in control. I am okay.

I am okay.

I exhale a long breath, blink hard a few times, and the letters swimming in my vision settle into a recognizable pattern.

HELP

I squint a bit.

WANTED

I am out of the car and halfway down the street before I even realize what I'm doing. I push into the store and find a tall, gorgeous black woman with fine cornrows of hair cascading down her back over a gorgeous burnt orange African caftan-style dress. She smiles at me. Her teeth are bright and perfect, and she seems so at peace, so comfortable and happy in her environment.

I wonder briefly if she's crazy, too, if the whole town is some kind of free commune for the mentally unbalanced. I haven't met anyone in this town who is bitter or pissed off, and the rule of averages just doesn't support this.

"Can I help you?" she asks.

"Do you have a job opening?" I say, motioning toward the sign in the window.

She gives a gentle laugh. "How old are you, sweetie?"

"Twenty-nine," I say flatly.

Her eyebrows raise a bit and she nods. "Oh. Wow."

"So, do you need help, or what?" This is not my typical job interview game, but then, I've never applied for a job in retail. Very possibly, this could be how it's done.

"Well, yes." She quirks her head a bit to the side and her eyes narrow slightly with concern. "Are you okay?"

I'm about to tell her I'm fine and then a voice in my head says, *Fuck it.*

"No," I say. "My mother has returned from the dead and torn my family apart. The show I was working on got canceled. And . . ." I swallow hard. "My best friend is in love with me."

The woman's face softens. "Oh, honey." She leans forward, and her face crinkles in sympathy. "What's the matter? You didn't know she was a lesbian?"

Wow. People sure love lesbians in this town. "If he is, he hides it well."

"Oh." There is a prolonged silence. One side of her mouth quirks, and I can tell she's trying not to laugh.

"It's not funny," I say, but suddenly, it is. In a moment, we're both laughing. Our eyes are wet with tears, and every time one of us stops, the other one starts it up again. It occurs to me that I am hysterical, and I'm not really bothered by the realization. It's kind of fun. Hysteria is definitely underrated.

We finally settle down, and she smiles at me kindly. She likes me. I can tell. Even though I just dumped my personal life on her and became hysterical in her store, she likes me.

"What's your name?" she asks.

"Carly McKay," I say, holding out my hand. She takes it. Her fingers are rough, but warm.

"I'm Janesse," she says. "Do you have any experience in art supplies, Carly?"

What? I think, then glance around. Hmm. I am surrounded by shelves filled with different kinds of paint, varieties of paintbrushes. Markers. Charcoals. An entire wall dedicated to huge pads of art paper. There's a display of canvases on the back wall. She's right. It's an art supply store.

I hadn't even noticed.

"I'm a television producer," I say.

"I see." She eyes me for a long time, her dark eyes deeply evaluating, before speaking again. "It's mostly just a clerk position. Inventory. Stocking. Register. That sort of thing. It doesn't pay much."

I've been living at home rent-free for the last nine months, I think. *I don't care if it pays at all. Just give me something to do.*

"That's fine."

She nods. "And I'm going to need some references."

A sudden peace washes over me, and I smile. "Do you know Brandywine Seaver?"

"Oh." Her face darkens briefly, and I wonder if I've said something wrong. "Are you a friend of Brandy's?"

"Is that a problem?"

A little visible effort and her face relaxes into a smile. "No. No, not at all. I've known Brandy a long time. She's really great."

"Good," I say, holding up my hand, palm out, index and middle fingers entwined. "Because we're like this."

"Now, it's not much," Brandy says as she fits the key in the lock to the blue cabin, "but it's got all the basics, and it comes furnished, so no worries on that score."

She twists the knob and we go in, and I am surprised that the interior isn't identical to Will's, as I had assumed it would be.

"Like I said," Brandy says, "it's not much."

I step in past her, mesmerized. The walls, like Will's, are simple plaster. Unlike Will's, they're painted. The living room is a bright shade of green. I glance back at Brandy, who is grinning widely at me.

"Pretty cool, huh?"

I glance at the living room and am surprised when I don't hate it. The color is bright, but next to the blue-and-green plaid sofa, it kind of works. There's a simple, bulky, natural wood coffee table that looks handmade. A mismatched yet homey orange easy chair sits out at an angle, facing the fireplace.

I catch my breath and put my hand to my chest. "Oh, it's got a fireplace."

"Mmmm-hmmm," Brandy says apologetically. "That's not a problem, right? I mean, you're not an artist so you're not concerned about stray sparks in the turpentine or the smoke getting into your work, right?"

"No," I say, staring at the fireplace, charmed. "No, I'm not worried about that."

I turn my head. In the back right corner is a tiny

kitchenette; the walls in this area are bright blue. There's a tiny baby sink and a tiny baby stove, with four small gas burners. The table is small, linoleum, functional. The two chairs don't match; one is wooden, the other some chrome number from the fifties. I walk over to the tiny baby fridge and open it.

"That works," Brandy says. "I just haven't turned it on yet."

It isn't much taller than I am, and it's narrow, but how much do I need? I'm only one person.

The cabin is sectioned down the length by a bright pink wall with two doors in it. I motion to the one close to the kitchen.

"That's the bathroom," Brandy says. "It's kinda small."

I walk in. She's right. It is small. But there's a shower stall, a sink, and a toilet. A medicine cabinet with a mirror over the sink. Bright orange walls. All the necessities for the modern, recently Towered girl.

There's another door in the bathroom, and I push through into the bedroom, which has been painted bright yellow. Two large windows grace each outdoor wall, and next to one is a tremendous, tall dresser, which makes me laugh considering the miniature kitchen. In the corner, angled out, is a plain, queen-sized bed on one of those high-set frames. I suddenly feel like Alice in Wonderland. I go and hop up to the edge of the bed, looking down at my feet hanging over the worn but lovely wooden floor, and something clicks in my heart.

I have just fallen in love with this place. I love the

woodsy smell of it. I love the walls, the way they're all funky-colored and they just don't care. I love the mismatched furniture, the tiny kitchen appliances, and the tremendous bed. I love the do-over-ness of this new life.

I am surrounded by possibility. I realize that I am very close to the hysteria I felt earlier at Janesse's, and that this sense of euphoria may be closely linked to mental imbalance, but I don't care. I'm riding it.

I lie back on the bed and stare at the ceiling, which is simply the wood-plank roof of the cabin, reaching upward toward its peak.

Suddenly, I angle up on both elbows.

"Brandy." I laugh. "Why didn't you bring me here last night?"

Brandy blinks like she doesn't understand the question.

"Because," she says as though it's obvious, "nobody lives here."

I sit up. "Well, now they do."

She smiles. "Really?"

I nod. "Really."

She watches me for a moment, cocks her head to the side. "That's very brave of you."

"What, running away from my life?"

"No," she says. "Reimagining your life. Usually when people get Towered, they try to rebuild what they had. It takes a lot of courage to imagine your life might be different."

I think about that for a second. "It's not brave if you have no choice. Then it's just desperately grasping at straws."

"Potato, po-tah-to," she says. I laugh and realize with a splash of surprise that I genuinely like Brandy. Very much.

"So," I say, "where's the closest place a girl can score some underwear?"

Brandy thinks on this for a moment. "Kinja Bale does some cool things with tie-dyed lingerie. She has a store down on Cicada Drive."

"I was thinking something a little more casual," I say. "Hanes Her Way casual. And I'm going to need some basics for this place."

Brandy shrugs. "There's a Wal-Mart in Douglas, but . . ." She scrunches her nose. "It's Wal-Mart."

"Don't knock Wal-Mart," I say, hopping off the bed. "You and me might come to blows."

By late afternoon, I'm all set. I have cheap dishes and cheap silverware, a stocked refrigerator, four bottles of wine (one of which is traveling with me as I move around the cabin, setting up), an alarm clock, underwear, basic lighting, a made bed. I set up my television in the living room, put Will's *She Might Be Crying* painting up on the wall over the fireplace (hey, if he didn't want it named by the new owner, he should have titled it his own damn self) and I sit on my couch, which is pretty comfortable, making up for the fact that it's ugly as a six-pack of sin.

I pick up my glass of wine. *It's just the way I like my men*, I think. *Cheap, red, and Australian.* The joke doesn't make any sense, nor is it particularly funny, but it makes me laugh, because deep, deep down inside, I am panicked and on the verge of hysteria. I comfort myself by channeling Brandy, by telling myself that I have not fucked up everything I've been working toward in the past ten years. Not at all.

I've been *Towered*.

I have *reimagined* my life.

I am a clerk at an art supply store.

I live in a cabin.

In Bilby, Arizona.

I chuckle again. Now *that's* funny.

My cell phone sits on the coffee table, hooked to the charger and blinking green at me, letting me know it's hyped up and ready to go. I shut it off after talking to Christopher, but planned to access my inner grown-up and call everyone this evening. I will tell them I'm okay, let them know that I'll be away for a while, and hang up. I don't want Dad or Ella to worry, but I also don't particularly want to make them feel better, either. I am the injured party here, and eventually they will come to their senses and realize how unfair they've been. I want them to feel bad, but I don't want them to be freaking out about my safety. In my mind, this passes for maturity, and I'm pleased with myself.

Fighting myself every step of the way, I lean forward and snag the phone, unhooking the charge cord as I do so.

Hey, Ella. I've reimagined my life.

No worries, Dad. I'm fine. I've reimagined my life.

Five? Well, you're just gonna love the furry little kittens out of this . . .

I start with Ella's number. Ella will be the easiest. Ella will understand. Ella always understands. Hell, this is the girl who is still friends with every ex-boyfriend who has been remotely willing to stay in touch. If anyone is going to be a soft place to start, it's Ella.

She answers after three rings.

"Ella?" I say. My throat feels tight. "It's Carly."

There's a moment of silence. "Carly? Where are you?"

I chuckle lightly and throw back a glug of wine. "I'm in Bilby."

She pauses for a moment. "Bilby? What the hell are you doing in Bilby?"

"I'm . . ." I can't say the words *reimagining my life*. I just can't. I may have been Towered, but I'm still me. "I got a job. I've . . ." I glance around, and the reality of what I've done hits me fresh, as though it's news. Wow. "I've rented a cabin."

There's a long sigh. "But you're okay?"

"Of course," I say.

"Great," she says, but she doesn't sound like she means it. I'm just about to ask her what's bugging her when she explodes all over me.

"Do you have any idea what you've done?" she says. "You scared us all half to death. Dad was going to call missing persons."

"An adult has to be gone twenty-four hours before you can call missing persons." At least, according to all the TV shows, and why would they lie?

"Christopher has been going crazy. He said you sounded strange when he talked to you this morning. When he called us, I was on the phone with the hospital, asking if anyone matching your description had been admitted."

"You overreacted, then," I say. "I'm a grown-up. I was gone for what, maybe fourteen hours when I talked to Christopher?"

"And let's talk about Christopher," she says. "How could you?"

My head shoots up. Conversational whiplash. "What? What about Christopher?"

"He's a mess. I don't know what finally happened or didn't happen between you two, but you've really wrecked him. God, Car. I can't believe how selfish you're being."

I blink, actually pull the phone away from my face and do a double take. Where's my sweet sister, who's supposed to be on my side in the Christopher thing, even if I'm wrong? When I put the phone back to my ear, the new, angry Ella is still talking.

". . . loves you, and you can't even be bothered to come home and tell him you're alive in person."

"Wait? How do you know Christopher's in love with me?"

"Any idiot can see it, Carly. God. He's been in love with you for years."

I take another gulp of wine. "Gee. Someone could have given me a heads-up, doncha think?"

"And Mom," she says, skidding into another conversational one-eighty. "How could you do that to Mom?"

"How could I . . . ?" This gets me just angry enough that I gain my footing in the conversation. "Are you serious, El? How can *I* do that to *her*? What's up with the selective amnesia, babe? Have you been around for the last seventeen years?"

"She's sorry," Ella says. "If you had stayed around long enough to listen to her, you would have known that."

My throat clenches tight and I swallow against it.

"*I've* been around. *She* hasn't." My voice is shaky. I am on the edge of the great Cavern o' Nervous Breakdown, and my sweet, gentle, forgiving sister is about to push me over.

Something's not right here.

"It's just like you," she goes on, "to blow up like that without listening first, to make a big production over everything, to make things worse when it's already hard enough."

Wait a minute. Ella was supposed to ask me how I am. Ella was supposed to rush down here with a bottle of gin and distract me with honeymoon stories. She was supposed to be comforting me.

I am not comforted.

"You're being selfish," she says. Her voice is sharp and bitter and I hardly recognize it. "You're being terrible and selfish and you can just stay in Bilby for all I care."

And the line disconnects. I pull the phone away from my face and stare at it. The little screen confirms it; my sister has hung up on me. My sister—who once instantly forgave a guy who stole her television, hocked it, and used the money to take a cocktail waitress to Rocky Point for the weekend—*this* girl has hung up on me.

There is a knock at the door. Hands shaking, I get up and answer it.

It's Will, on my doorstep, holding up a small house-plant. He grins.

"Welcome Wagon," he says.

I stare down at the plant. It's one of those impossible-to-kill kinds, with the bright green leaves that look like they're plastic. It looks happy and vibrant. It's in a ceramic pot, painted in swirly images of daisies.

Will is giving me a plant in a pot that he painted himself, I realize, and much to my dismay an awkward sob punches its way out of me as a response to this small kindness.

"Carly?" Will looks concerned, as well he should. My eyes are welling up. I can barely see him. Another sob breaks free and I clamp my hand over my mouth as the tears bounce down my cheeks and over my fingers.

"Oh, hey, I'm sorry," Will says, stepping inside and setting the plant down on the floor before putting both hands on my shoulders. "Do you . . . not like plants?"

I manage a weak laugh and he smiles, a glint of hope in his eyes that this might turn out okay, but then there are so many tears, I can't keep track of them all. It feels like they're falling over me like rain. It's a deluge. I am going to drown. Somehow, I make it to the couch, and Will is next to me with his hand resting on my upper arm. I swipe at my face.

"I'm sorry," I squeak out over the sobs. "I'm not . . . usually . . . like this."

"Can I get you something?" he says. "Some water, some Kleenex?"

"I don't have Kleenex!" I wail, as though I've just realized I don't have a soul.

"Yeah, me either," he says. I look up at him, and he gives me a weak smile. "Yeah, that whole Boy Scout thing was a joke. I'm almost never prepared."

I don't know why, but this brings on a fresh wave of sobs.

"All right, that's okay," he says calmly. He squeezes my arm. "One second, okay?"

"Okay," I say, trying to catch my breath and failing miserably as another round of sobs takes over. "Okay."

It seems like he is instantly gone and instantly back, and he has a roll of toilet paper in his hands. He rips off a section and hands it to me. I swipe it over my face and try to calm down. His hand is running over my shoulder and down my arm in comforting strokes, and my heart cracks right down the middle. I can feel it, I can hear it, and it hurts like a bastard.

"Do you want to talk about it?" he asks after a minute.

I shake my head and there is a long conversational drought. Then, suddenly, for no reason I can understand, I start talking.

"How could she just leave like that?" My voice is scratchy and tired, but I keep going. "If she loved me, she would have stayed. She wouldn't have left me to raise a family at the age of twelve. If she loved me . . ." A fresh wave of pain washes over me, cutting me from the inside. "But she didn't. She just didn't."

"This isn't . . . ?" He sounds unsure as he forms the question. "Are you talking about your mother?"

I nod and sniffle, and his face washes over with understanding. "Oh, man. That's . . . wow. Huge."

"She came back," I say. "Last week. I came home from work and there she was, sitting on the couch, drinking scotch with Dad."

Will is silent, his hand smoothing down over my back. I blow my nose and grab for more toilet paper.

"She and Dad are going to therapy, I guess. Five wants to know her. Ella wants . . . I don't know what Ella wants."

And there's her voice in my head: *You're being terrible and selfish and you can just stay in Bilby for all I care.* I feel the tears sliding down my cheeks, but at least they're relatively calm tears. I simply lack the energy to wail.

"I'm still so angry," I say after a moment. "I can't forgive her. I want to slap her and yell at her, and everyone else wants to sit around a campfire with her, roasting marshmallows and singing freakin' 'Kumbaya,' and what the hell is wrong with them, anyway? Don't they remember what it was like? Don't they care what she did?"

My throat tightens and I can't talk anymore. It seems like there's no space inside me for anything but tears. Will's hand moves around my shoulders and he pulls me against him. I rest my head on his shoulder and another geyser opens, and I feel like I'm never going to do anything but sit here and weep. Will puts his lips to the top of my head and makes shushing sounds into my hair, and eventually I start to come back.

"I'm sorry," I squeak, finally getting the strength to separate myself from him. I snatch some tissue off the roll and resolve to get some Kleenex the next time I'm at the store. "I'm usually tougher than this."

"Oh, hey, no," he says, turning toward me on the couch, his fingers coming up to push my hair away from my face. "I'm amazed at how strong you've been. I don't know how you've gotten through as well as you have."

"I haven't," I say. "Dad can forgive her. Five can. Ella can. I can't. I'm a horrible, terrible, weak, and petty person."

"Carly, come on," he says. "You know that's not true. I've just met you, and I know that's not true."

I look up at him. My eyes are beginning to puff up and I wonder absently if I'm inadvertently squinting. "Wait until you know me better before you make any rash judgments."

He smiles at me. "I think I know enough."

I try to smile back, but end up just taking a deep, stuttering breath.

"Thank you," I say. "I'm sorry."

"Don't be. Everyone has bad days." He reaches up and brushes some of my hair away from my face. I feel a shudder go down my back, and I have a strong urge to curl up in his arms and let him hold me until I feel better. But we hardly know each other, so instead I shift away from him and he drops his hand.

"I'm so tired," I say finally. "I think I might just go to sleep and think about all this again tomorrow. You know, pull a Scarlett O'Hara."

His smile quirks. "That's probably a good idea. I'll let you get to it."

I get up off the couch, and he places his hand gently between my shoulder blades as we walk to the door.

"If you need anything," he says, turning to me and bending his knees to bring his eyeline level with mine, "I'm within shouting distance."

"I'll be fine," I say.

"Yeah, I know you will." He gives me a slight smile,

then opens the door and disappears. I close the door behind him, resting my forehead against it as I stand there, staring at my Keds.

"Hot damn, I'm a basket case," I mutter to myself. Then I go to my new bed, hop on up, and pass out into a black sleep.

It takes me exactly three days to transition from my old life to my new, reimagined one. By the third day into my new existence, I have stopped picking up my cell phone to call Christopher, only to hang up before dialing, and I have mastered the cash register system at Art's Desire. I have stopped dreaming about being back at work on *Tucson Today*, and I have made a friend in Allegra, who forces a new flavor or style of coffee on me every day during my break, refusing to believe that, every day, all I really want is a Viennese latte. I have stopped waiting for my father to contact me to tell me he's sorry, and I have met and been embraced by—in many cases, *literally* so—the vast majority of the people in Bilby.

With the exception, that is, of Mr. Trimble.

Mr. Trimble is a skinny old guy who dresses entirely in black and buys one box of charcoals twice a week, and who, I've discovered, does not respond well to being directly spoken to. As a matter of fact, on my second day at work, when I asked him if he needed anything else, he told me to fuck off.

"Don't worry about Mr. Trimble," Janesse had said. "He's just . . . special. All you have to do is sell him his charcoals and, uh, no eye contact, okay?"

"Special," snorts Allegra now as we sit outside the

Café at the mosaic tables. "That's Bilby-ese for off his nut. How's that peppermint macchiato?"

"Nice," I say, taking a sip. I'm beginning to enjoy her concoctions, for the most part, although I do miss my Viennese lattes. But tomorrow is Friday, and she's promised me that on Fridays I can have whatever I want.

"So, tell me," she says, leaning her elbows over the small table. "You used to live in New York. What's it like?"

"Well, I lived in Syracuse. It's nice, I liked it, but it's not like New York City or anything. And I was only there for a year."

"Who cares? You lived there. That's so exciting." Allegra sits back, leaning her head back and staring at the sky. "I want to go there so bad. I've never been. I've only been out of Arizona three times in my life." She sits up, glances around, then looks at me and whispers as though there are microphones over our heads, "I've applied to go to NYU."

I lean forward, whispering as well. I've found that my when-in-Rome approach to Bilby life has been, generally, working for me. "That's great. Why are we whispering?"

She jerks her head toward the Café. "Sebastian wants me to stay here and run this place."

I stare at her for a minute. Sebastian owns the place, and told me on my second visit to the Café that I should grow my hair long and stop worrying about the kink. I still haven't figured out his relationship with Allegra. He calls her "sweetheart" and ruffles her hair. He's obviously more than a boss, but definitely not a boyfriend. Uncle?

"Sebastian's my dad," she says, as though reading my mind. Which, I guess, she did.

"Why do you call him Sebastian?" I ask. "I mean, is he not your real dad?"

Allegra shakes her head. "No. James is my real dad."

I blink. Hmmm. I haven't met James yet, but it appears Allegra has two daddies. Welcome to Bilby.

Allegra shrugs. "But I call him by his first name, too. It's an equality thing. They want to raise me without authoritarian blah blah blah. And for a couple of gay guys, they're so overprotective. They didn't even let me go to regular high school. I had to be homeschooled. That's why I graduated early and everything, but it would have been nice to have a graduating class bigger than one." She sighs. "There's no way they're going to find Zen with NYU."

"And your . . . do you have a mom? I mean, you . . . you have to have a mom, r-right?"

I'm very unsure of myself in this conversation, and I'm a little embarrassed by it. I don't want it to seem like I'm not open-minded, because I am. But at the same time, I grew up Irish Catholic and have been given very strict rules about what's "normal" and what's not; even though I don't necessarily agree, some of it's just hard-wired in my head. Hell, I think having premarital sex is fine if you're responsible about it, but I still feel guilty whenever I have sex or even think about having sex, which, as I'm twenty-nine and unmarried, accounts for a fair amount of guilt. If you're gonna throw two daddies at a girl like me, you have to allow some latitude for culture shock, right?

Allegra plays absently with her empty coffee cup. "My bio-mom is some surrogate named Safflower. I think she runs a crystal shop up in Sedona. But it was really just a business transaction for her, as far as I can tell." She sighs and stares up at the sky. "I know you didn't live there, but you've been to New York City, right?"

I take a sip of my macchiato. "Yeah. It's nice. Crowded. But everything's there. Plays, shopping—"

"Do you think a person could be spiritually fulfilled being a stockbroker?" she asks suddenly.

"Um," I say. "Sure. I guess. Why?"

She takes a deep breath, and for the first time since I've known her, she actually looks like a kid, her face all hopeful and not bitter. "I was watching this movie on TV and they had this guy and he was a stockbroker and he was in the pit on Wall Street and shouting things like 'Buy!' and 'Sell!' and the numbers were flying by on the ticker and . . ." She exhales, puts her hand to her chest and nibbles her lips. "I got wet."

My eyebrows shoot up before I can stop them. It takes me a second, but I gain control over my face and casually sip my coffee.

I'm beginning to think I don't really belong in Bilby.

"Hmm? Really? Hmm," I murmur into my cup.

Allegra laughs. "Oh, you're not hung up about sex, are you?"

"Who? Me? No." Another sip. "It's just . . . Um, how old are you again?"

Allegra laughs. I know she's seventeen, but she's so . . . comfortable with herself. I've never been that comfortable with myself, ever. And she's only seventeen . . .

With a sudden surge of panic, I remember that Five

is seventeen. Is she talking like this? Is she getting sexually aroused by stockbrokers? Is she doing it with Botox in the back of his mom's SUV?

And then I realize that it's not my concern anymore if she is. That's for Dad and Mary to worry about. The thought leaves me feeling cold and angry, so I take another sip of my coffee to wash it away.

"It just looked like so much fun," Allegra is saying, her voice wistful. "All the activity, all the men running around. Imagine being the only woman on that floor with a bunch of alpha males in thousand-dollar suits acting like primates." She releases a breath and crinkles her nose at me. "Doesn't it get you hot?"

"Um. Well. Not—not—not exactly, but . . ." I'm blushing. I'm blushing. I'm the adult, and I'm the one blushing. This is just sad. "That's not really my thing, though."

Allegra gives me a knowing look. "I didn't think so. You're beta male all the way."

"Beta male?" I ask.

"Yeah." She sips her coffee, and one tight, beaded black braid, formed from the only lock of hair that's not pink, smacks into her latte mug with a plastic *clink*. "You know. The sensitive type with glasses and a tender soul."

"Um . . ." I stammer, and start to get annoyed with myself. I'm an adult and a journalist, for Christ's sake. I can talk about sex. I sit back and try to look casual. "I don't know. My ex-fiancé, Seth, used to have glasses, but then he had that Lasik surgery—"

"Oh, it's nothing to be embarrassed about. Those

types are great in bed." Allegra's face gets more serious. "But, what I was saying was, you don't have to be broke to be happy, right? Rich people can be fulfilled, too, right?"

I think on this for a moment, relieved to be on less sexual, if not firmer, ground. I feel that since I am older, I should have something of value to tell her, some wise words steeped from my experience that will shed light for her. I want to be one of those people, the right person at the right time whose sage words make all the difference.

Unfortunately, I got nothing.

I glance at my watch. "Wow," I say. "Break's over."

Chapter Six

At Brandy's suggestion, I have taken up knitting. She told me that the ritualistic nature of knitting helps align the chakras. I have no idea what that means, but Bilby's at a higher elevation than Tucson, and it's a bit cooler here at night. I could use a warm scarf. Besides, it's either knit with Brandy or spend my evenings alone in my cabin, drinking wine and staring at *She Might Be Crying*, which is what I did last night. Instead, I am sitting in Brandy's house, drinking tea and staring at my scarf.

Which doesn't look quite right. It's a little lumpy on one side, and while I only cast on forty stitches, I have just counted forty-seven. Brandy suggested I use a brighter color to start with because it's easier to see what you're doing, but I insisted I wanted the brown. Once again, my stubbornness is not paying off.

"Oh," Brandy says, checking out my progress. "It's happening when you purl. You see, here?" She points to one edge of my scarf. "You have to pull it between the needles, not over."

"Okay." I start pulling out my stitches. Again. I've started this scarf four times, and have never gotten past seven rows.

"So, um . . ." Brandy pauses and I look up at her. Her face is pensive, her smile seems a little forced, and her hands are white-knuckled around her needles. "How's it going, you know, working at Janesse's?"

"Good." I feel slightly uncomfortable, and start to knit again. "I like her. She's really fun."

"Yeah," Brandy says, picking up her own project. "And she's . . . she's doing okay? I mean, she seems happy?"

"Yeah," I say. Janesse is one of the happiest women I've ever known. The woman hums to herself while doing the books. But Brandy's expression is oddly tight, and I'm not sure if this is the right answer. There's obviously some kind of history between them (lesbians? maybe? estranged best friends?) and I decide it's best to tread carefully.

"She seems happy," I say, then look down at my knitting and realize this row was supposed to be purl, not knit. "Shit." I start to pull out the stitches again.

There's a knock at the door and Brandy gets up.

"You don't always have to pull mistakes out," she says

as she crosses the room. "Sometimes the best work comes out of mistakes."

I don't know whether to take this literally or as a life lesson. With Brandy, you can never be too sure. I choose literally, but still pull the stitches free anyway, as the brown yarn with the lumpy mistakes looks to me like a big piece of knit turd.

Brandy pulls the door open, and Will steps into the room. I glance up at him, trying to play it cool, as though the last time he saw me I hadn't been in the throes of a complete nervous breakdown.

"Here's the rent check for next month," Will says to Brandy. "I've got a job next week, so I wanted to make sure you got it now."

"A job? On Thanksgiving?"

"It's in Canada." There's a slight pause; then I hear, "Hey, Carly."

I look up, supercasual. "Hey, Will. How ya doing?"

"Good. You?"

"Good." I hold up the big pile of yarn in my hand and pull on a deliberately dorky smile. "I'm aligning my chakras."

A smile quirks on his lips and it makes me abnormally happy inside. I turn my attention to my knitting. Brandy picks up a pile of quilts off a chair and motions for Will to sit down. "Well, we'll miss you at Thanksgiving. Won't we, Carly?"

"Hmm?"

Brandy's face falls. "Oh, you're not going away for Thanksgiving, too, are you?"

"I wasn't . . ." I hadn't thought about it, really. Was it Thanksgiving week? Already? "Why?"

"Well, because if you're not going home, you're coming here," Brandy says, her face bright once again.

"I am?"

Will lets out a small snicker. Brandy shoots him a reproachful look as she leans forward and pats me on my knee. "Yes, of course you are. Every year I do a big Thanksgiving meal, and everyone who doesn't have somewhere else to be is invited."

"Oh," I say. "Okay. Well, thank you for inviting me."

"So, you're coming?" Brandy prods. Her face is illuminated and her happiness is tangible and I can't say no, although the idea of going to a Big Bilby Thing kinda makes me want to find a big hole and crawl in it.

"Um, sure. Yeah. I mean, unless . . ." I stop, realizing that if my family was going to ask me to come home, they would probably have done it by now. Thanksgiving is just a few days away. I decide that Reimagined Carly both can and should attend a party, even if it's with strangers who are not bound by the laws of blood to like her. Me.

"Yes." I pull on a Reimagined Carly smile. "Thank you."

Will's eyes meet mine and I can tell he's pleased. My stomach does a little roller-coaster maneuver, and my smile widens. Brandy settles into her chair and I can feel her watching us. I turn my attention back to my knitting.

"So," she says, not indulging even the slightest hint of subtlety. "Will mentioned that you two already knew each other, but he didn't tell me how you met."

"At a wedding, actually," Will says.

Brandy raises one eyebrow and smiles. "Really? What a small world, huh?"

"Yeah, my sister's," I add quickly. "Will and Ella used to date."

"A long time ago." I look up to see Will looking at me. "Centuries, actually."

Our eyes lock for a moment, and I get this weird impression that he's making a point.

"And my littlest sister is totally in love with him," I say. My face is growing warm. This is just stupid.

Will laughs. "Five's a great kid." He puts a slight emphasis on *kid*.

Our eyes meet again, and I accidentally poke myself in the leg with the knitting needle.

"Ow!"

"You okay there?" Will asks.

"Fine," I say, rubbing my leg. "These are dangerous."

"Most things are." Brandy turns her attention to Will. "Can I get you something to drink, Will? I have tea, water, wine . . ."

"Wine sounds great," he says. My face continues to flush, and I hate it. Between Seth and Christopher, I already have enough road kill on my romantic highway. I am in no position to be smitten with my next-door artist.

Brandy smiles at him. "You know where it is."

I glance up. Something passes between them, and I remember how they were when we were all in the bed together the first morning I was here. It occurs to me again that they might be sleeping together, which throws the Janesse-Brandy-Lesbian theory out of the window, along with any other ideas I might be having about Will.

"Ow!" I say again, as I stab the palm of my hand while trying to cast on.

"Maybe you should have some wine, too," Brandy says. "It might relax you."

"I'm relaxed," I say, my voice sounding tense even to my biased ears. Will returns carrying a wine bottle and three glasses. He looks at me and smiles. "Do you like cabernet, Carly?"

Ordinarily, if it's made from grapes and has any sort of alcohol content, I'm in. But at the moment, the thought of staying there drinking wine with them like a big fifth wheel makes me want to run screaming from the place.

"You know what?" I say, standing up. "I just remembered. I've got a thing . . . a book. A phone call. I have to go." I gather up my yarn and needles and stuff them in the small canvas project bag Brandy gave me. "I'll just see myself out."

Brandy stands up. "Are you sure?"

"Yeah." I back toward the door, almost trip over a pile of quilts, then turn and scurry toward my escape, waving at them awkwardly over my shoulder.

"Thanks," I say. "See you tomorrow."

I shoot out the door and almost flip ass over teakettle on Brandy's stoop when I hear the door open behind me. I turn around and there's Will, a bemused half smile on his face as he looks at me.

"Hey, Will." I sound more like a fifteen-year-old than ever, and I clear my throat.

He tucks his hands in his pockets and dances easily down the steps. I'll bet the satanic door buzzer doesn't zap him, either. Psychic's pet.

"Hey," he says. "I was wondering. What are you doing tomorrow?"

"Um, nothing." I have the day off from Janesse's and the only plans I'd really made were to drink some wine and work on my scarf/turd.

"Well, I was wondering if you might want to go on a little hike through the foothills. There's a big, flat rock on the east side with a cool view of the valley. It's the perfect place for a picnic."

"It sounds nice, but . . ." I lean forward a bit and lower my voice. "I don't really hike."

"Well, I have a secret for you." He leans forward and lowers his voice as well. "Hiking is just walking. You can walk, right?"

"That's up for debate."

His smile quirks up one side of his face and I have to stop myself from sighing.

He straightens up. "Pick you up at ten tomorrow morning?"

I nod, my attempt at playing it cool. "Sure. Step out of your front door and take a right. I'll be there."

Will watches me for a moment, and I think he's going to say something, but then he just turns and jaunts back up the steps and into Brandy's place. I stare at her front door as it closes behind him and then turn to walk back to my cabin, only stumbling once on the way.

Yay me.

———

Will, as it turns out, is full of shit. Hiking is not walking. Walking is something you do on a nice, level surface—like a sidewalk, or a path, or a floor—to get from Point A to Point B. If Point A and Point B are too far apart, you get in a car and drive, the way God intended.

Hiking, on the other hand, involves climbing over rocks and stepping through foliage that doesn't particularly want you there. And Point A and Point B? Are very far apart. By the time we get to the big, flat rock, I've swallowed two bugs, ripped a hole in the knee of my jeans while stumbling over a branch, and formed a blister on the heel of my left foot.

Despite this, I'm still having a pretty damn good time. Hiking out here in the wilderness, ingesting bugs, I'm about as happy as I've been in recent weeks, and this is all the proof I need that I have a huge, unwieldy, ill-timed and yet undeniable crush on Will Kelley.

"You doing okay?" he asks as I pull my sad self up onto the rock. He's already unpacked a fleece blanket and laid it out, and is now pulling cheese and crackers out of his big, yellow, outdoorsy-guy backpack.

"Fine," I say. I throw myself down on one edge of the blanket and lie back, face to the sky, dramatically gasping for breath. "You're right. View's gorgeous."

He laughs, sits next to me, and grabs my hand to pull me up to sitting. He motions out toward the valley and I have to admit, it's pretty. It looks almost European, with all the buildings huddled together in the valley, their asymmetric roofs winking in the sunlight between the vibrant red soil of the copper-rich foothills on either side.

"It's beautiful," I say, and mean it. Will grins and dives back into his pack, from which he pulls out two plastic wineglasses, just the cup parts, with tiny plastic screws sticking out of the bottoms. He hands the decapitated glasses to me, then sticks the equally pathetic plastic stems in my hand.

"Make yourself useful," he says. I screw the stems onto the glasses and he pours the wine. I feel positively wooed, and I have to admit, I like it. We clink our plastic glasses and drink, looking out at the scenery. It's beautiful. It's perfect. I grab a cracker and a slice of cheese and chew happily.

"I thought this might cheer you up," he says. "This is where I come when I'm feeling . . . I don't know. Just when I'm not right with the world. It helps give me perspective."

I feel the cracker stick in my throat and wash it down with a bit of wine as I realize that this isn't a date. It's therapy. If this is the case, I'm pretty sure Will hasn't brought enough wine.

"You know, I'm really okay," I say, grasping at the flailing threads of my frayed dignity. "Really. I know I must have seemed like a total basket case the other night, but I'm okay. Really."

He gives me a little smile and nods out to the valley, pointing to a spot off in the distance.

"See those? That's where we live."

I squint. He's right. I can see Brandy's roof at the edge of the valley, where the foothills begin, and then, nestled within the foliage behind her place, are our two smaller rooftops.

"And that," he says, shifting his index finger down and to the left, "is Janesse's art shop. And there's the café."

I stare at it, transfixed with wonder. "It all seems so tiny."

"See?" he says. "Perspective."

I'm fairly sure I've never felt this embarrassed. I try to regroup, appreciate the gesture for what it is—an attempt by a really nice guy to help his total case of a neighbor. I grab another cracker and decide to be gracious and pleasant. And to immediately change the subject.

"So, what's the deal with Brandy and Janesse?"

He gives me a surprised smile. "You don't know?"

I shake my head. "No. But every time I mention one of them to the other, they both get weird."

Will gives a small, sad smile. "They used to be married."

I blink. "Lesbians can get married in Arizona?"

He laughs. "They're not lesbians."

I am silent, drowning in dumbfoundedness. Will leans forward, throws me a bone.

"Janesse used to be Jamal."

I feel like I should be saying, "Ohhhhh," but I still don't get it. And then . . .

"Ohhhhh," I say. "Oh. Oh, man. Wow. Really?"

Will nods. My initial reaction is to be kind of annoyed, because Janesse is a thousand times prettier than me. She's gorgeous. *He's* gorgeous. Wait, no. She.

Yeesh. I'm confused. I can't imagine how Brandy must feel.

"Poor Brandy."

"Yeah." Will brushes some crumbs off his knee. "She took it pretty hard. I think it's still hard for her."

"When did he . . . I mean, she . . . become a she?"

"About three years ago. I moved into the cabin right after the big blowup, so I mostly just witnessed the aftermath."

"Ah, so I guess that's when you and Brandy . . . ?" I start, not sure how to finish the sentence.

"When me and Brandy what?" There's a slight twinkle in his eye, and I get the distinct impression that he's enjoying making me grope around on this one.

I roll my eyes and look out at the horizon. "Nothing. Just . . . you two seem . . . close."

"We are." He leans toward me a bit. "Not like that, though. She needed a shoulder to cry on and I happened to have one available." He smiles at me. "We're just friends."

"Oh, good." *Way to play it cool, Zuko.* "Not that it matters, you know. I mean, it wouldn't bother me or anything if you two were . . ."

Oh, man. This is just sad. I stuff a cracker in my mouth to shut myself up.

"Good crackers," I say, and a few crumbs fly out of my mouth. *I. Am. Smooooooooth.*

"Glad you like them," he says, his voice thick with amusement. I grab my wine and wash down the crackers.

"Did you bring Brandy out here, too?" I ask tentatively. "You know, to cheer her up?"

He keeps his eyes on mine, and a small smile quirks at one edge of his mouth. "No."

I am shamelessly happy to hear this. We sit in companionable silence for a while. I stare out at the valley, and this is when the thinking starts, which is followed soon by the talking.

"I think there's something wrong with me." The words are out before I realize I've said them, and I instantly regret them.

"Just one thing?" Will shakes his head and takes a sip of his wine. "You got me beat, then."

"No, I mean . . ." I sigh, feeling stupid. But then again, I'm not weeping all over him, so yay me. "I don't feel like me anymore."

He looks at me for a moment, his eyebrows knit slightly. "I don't understand."

I swallow hard. I didn't fully realize this until now, and I'm a little nervous sharing it with him, but I keep going anyway. "I used to be confident. Strong. Articulate. I knew what was what and who was who and suddenly, it's like I don't know anything." I close my eyes and blurt out the rest. "The other day, I was watching Oprah and she did one of those long-lost-family reunion shows . . ."

"And what?" he says. "You cried?"

"No," I say. "I *wept*. With blubbering and everything. For an hour."

He seems nonplussed. "Those shows are sad."

"You know the commercial with the talking baby?"

He pauses. "The one for the sub shop?"

I look at him, challenging him to make that redeemable. He grins.

"Okay. You win. You're emotionally unstable."

"Thank you," I say. "And it's not just the crying. Allegra talks about sex and her two daddies and beta males being good in bed, and I get all flustered and awkward and change the subject to the weather."

"Well, I don't think getting flustered around Allegra is all that unusual . . ."

"It is for me. I don't get flustered. Ever."

Will shrugs. "Maybe it's just that you've never had the option."

I look up at him. "Huh?"

He stares off into the sky, his face thoughtful for a moment before he looks back at me.

"When we were dating, Ella talked to me a bit about what happened. How your dad kind of hid in his work after your mother left, really relied on you to take care of Five. You basically became a mother at the age of twelve. That's gotta be hard. Maybe now that you don't have those responsibilities anymore, maybe your emotions are just catching up and it's throwing you off your game."

This is a little too Psych 101 for me, but since it's Will and I'm under the influence of the Big Crush, I try to look as though I'm considering it.

"Maybe. I don't know. All I know is I used to have it together and now I feel like I don't know anything about anything."

"Well," he says with a shrug, as though the answer is obvious. "You've been Towered."

I stare at him, trying to see if he's kidding or not. I can't tell, but my vote would be not. "What the hell does that mean, anyway?"

He laughs. "I don't really know. It's a Brandy-ism; I

usually just nod and smile. As far as I understand it, it just means that your life has been kinda bulldozed, you know? And now you have to rebuild it."

We share a smile. I grab a cracker. "Have you ever been Towered?"

He picks up the wine bottle and refills my glass.

"I'm in Bilby, aren't I?"

At work the next day, Janesse is still prettier than me. I find myself staring at her all day. She's tall for a woman, definitely, and now that I'm looking for it her wrists do seem a bit bigger than those of most of the women I know. Her feet don't look that big, though, but then again, mine are size six and every foot bigger than mine kinda looks the same to me, so . . .

"Who told you?" she asks as she sidles back behind the counter. I realize I've been leaning on the counter and straighten up, wondering if I was too obvious with the staring.

"Who? Told me what? Hmm?" I ask in what I hope passes for casual.

She raises one eyebrow at me. "That I used to have a dick."

"Oh. That." I sigh and relax. Big deal. She used to have a dick. Get used to it. Welcome to Bilby. "Will. I'm sorry. I didn't mean to stare. Was I staring?"

Janesse laughs. "Honey, if staring bothered me I would have ended up like Mr. Trimble a long time ago. I'm used to it." She shoots me a sideways glance and a smile plays on her lips. "But really? You didn't know?"

"No," I say. "I had no idea."

She giggles and turns to me. "No, seriously. Even with these hips?"

"What hips?" I say, rolling my eyes at her.

"Exactly. Real women have hips. And booties." She turns her back to me and shakes what she's got. "I have no ass."

I grin at her. "You are one hundred percent woman, trust me. Men are not insecure about their asses."

She turns back to face me and sighs. "I guess it's just our curse."

"Can I ask you something?" I say.

"Sure."

"Your breasts are gorgeous. Did you have them done?"

She mocks an offended expression. "No way, baby. These are all mine."

"But . . . how?"

"Hormones." She touches her hip. "Little patch, right there."

"Wow." I step back and take a good look. They're not big, but they look great on her, and they're perky as hell. Then again, they're only three years old. "They're beautiful."

Janesse beams and practically dances into the stockroom. The bell on the front door rings and Mr. Trimble comes in. I make no eye contact as I walk to the charcoals, pull out a box for him, ring it up at the register, and accept his ready four dollars and eighty-six cents. He leaves without telling me to fuck off. I consider this a win-win.

A moment later Janesse comes back from the stockroom with a box full of oil paints for me to stock.

"Why doesn't he ever buy paper?" I ask.

"Hmmm?"

"Mr. Trimble. Twice a week, with the charcoals. No paper."

"Baby," Janesse says, "there are some people you just don't ask questions about, and Mr. Trimble is one of them."

I accept this and take the box of oil paints. Janesse and I hum companionably to the Sting song on the radio as we stock the oils and I find myself, for the second time that day, smiling involuntarily. As I stock, I try to recall the last time I caught myself smiling like that. I can't remember.

Janesse closes the shop at seven, and we say good night and head our separate ways. Instead of heading straight back to my cabin, I wander through the winding streets of town. I'm charmed by it, really. In Tucson, everything is laid out on a grid, which makes it easy to find your way around, but that's it. In Bilby, the roads go in the direction they damn well want to. Like it or lump it.

I pass by Miner's Inn, a tremendous red brick structure that was originally built as a boarding house for miners during the heyday of the copper-and-silver boom, before the town got mined out. I continue down the road, winding ever so slowly upward toward the foothills, and realize that everything in Bilby used to be something else. The library used to be a mercantile store. The restaurant used to be a post office. It was like the whole town had been Towered, rebuilding itself into an artsy retirement community after the mines dried up. I wonder if it was an accident that I ended up here, or if I was drawn here by the energy of a place that wouldn't say die.

I turn down the other end of the street and start back toward Art's Desire, where my car is parked. I stop at the town's sole stoplight and look around. Gladys and Mack, the retired couple who own the independent bookshop, the Town Bookie, are standing outside, putting up Christmas lights. Gladys has the lights strung all over her arms and they twinkle as she gestures at Mack, who stands on the ladder and ignores her. I smile as I watch them. Then the light turns green and I continue on my way.

Chapter Seven

Will leaves for Ottawa the next day. He doesn't drop in to say good-bye to me before he leaves, which disappoints me, but which I decide is a good thing. Maybe I misread the whole hike-out-to-the-flat-rock thing. Maybe he was just being friendly. Although, there was this moment when he walked me home where I thought he might have been thinking about kissing me, but that could have been my imagination.

It's definitely a good thing he didn't stop by to say good-bye, I decide. The last thing I need now is another complication. And, if anything did happen with Will, how can I say I wouldn't end up doing exactly the same thing as I did with Christopher? And Seth?

"Do you think people can be . . . broken?" I ask Allegra as I dice shallots on the tiny kitchen island in the apartment over the café that she shares with her two daddies. Allegra invited me over so I could provide moral support when she tells James and Sebastian that she wants to move to New York City and become a stockbroker; I'm beginning to think that was just a ruse to get me to do the dinner prep work.

"You're not broken," Allegra says, biting into a baby carrot as she watches me from her perch on the kitchen counter.

"I didn't ask if I was broken. I asked if you thought people could be broken." I swipe the diced shallots into a small glass dish as instructed by Sebastian before he and James went into the living room to argue over the evening's music selection.

"You're not broken," Allegra repeats. Mozart plays from the other room; Sebastian won the music war. "You're just a little dented." She quirks a brow at me. "Nothing a little hammering won't cure."

I roll my eyes and reach for the garlic. "Do you ever stop thinking about sex?"

She throws up her hands and reaches for another carrot. "Hey, I'm not the one who had the fire dream."

"What fire dream?" James says as he scoots into the room. He's tall, with dark hair and a patrician nose. If Allegra would let the pink grow out of her hair and lighten up on the eyeliner, she'd look just like him.

"Nothing," I say, focusing my energy on the garlic. "Just a dream."

"Who had a dream?" Sebastian says, following James into the crowded kitchen. He looks pointedly at Allegra. "And why is our guest doing all the work?"

Allegra hops off the counter and pivots around me to get plates for the table. "Carly had a dream that her bed was on fire."

Two sets of male eyebrows lift in unison. I chop the garlic.

"It wasn't a big deal." I can feel my face reddening. I reach for my wine and take a big gulp.

"And while her bed was on fire, she was in her living room with a strange man who kept telling her it's going to be just fine," Allegra calls over her shoulder as she sets the table. I take another drink of wine.

It wasn't a strange man. It was Will. And at this moment I am thrilled beyond the telling of it that I didn't share that bit with Allegra.

"Ohhhhh," James says knowingly, and he and Sebastian share a look.

"It was totally a sex dream," Allegra says, then turns to James. "Carly thinks she's broken."

"I didn't say me," I start, but James cuts in.

"No, definitely not broken," he says, cocking his head to the side as he watches me. "Just stalled. How long have you been celibate?"

I turn a look on Allegra.

"Don't blame me," she says, holding up her hands. "I'm just a product of my environment."

James laughs. "Oh, you don't have to tell us. But a bed on fire? That's a been-too-long dream. If you're celibate by choice, maybe you should reconsider. And if you're not, there's a great straight bar in Douglas—"

"You know, I think we should talk about the stock market," I say, and Allegra stops setting the table.

"Okay," she says, straightening her posture. "We can do that."

James gives a little laugh. "What? Talk about the stock market? All those greedy little bastards cutting each other's throats trying to make more money for someone who already has too much?"

Sebastian rolls his eyes and snorts, but they both slowly grow silent as Allegra stays strong and tall.

"I've been accepted to NYU," she says finally. "I start in their business program in the fall, and I want to be a stockbroker."

Both James and Sebastian freeze. I'd crawl under something if there was something to crawl under in their tiny kitchen, but the best I can do is just stay very still. To be honest, I'm not sure they remember I'm there, anyway. Allegra's chin rises a notch, and she looks about as determined as I've ever seen anyone.

"You are two gay men who had to move two thousand miles away from home in order to gain some acceptance. I don't think I need to tell you how important it is to be understanding of alternative life choices."

Allegra is so strong and confident that I can't believe she even needed me here. Until, that is, I see that the hand clutching the forks is shaking a little. When I look up, I catch her eye and smile. She smiles back.

Finally, after what feels like a really long pause, James

walks over to her and puts a hand on her shoulder. "Do you think doing this will make you happy?"

Allegra's smile widens, and she nods. Sebastian joins them and sniffles as he pulls Allegra into a hug.

"They'll make you lose the pink hair," he says mournfully.

"They won't if she's good enough," I say. I don't know what I'm talking about. I don't know anything about Wall Street. But as all three of them look at me, I realize that for possibly the first time in my life, I've said the exact right thing at the exact right time. They share a smile, and then each of them gets back to work. After a long, companionable silence, James is the first to speak.

"So back to Carly's celibacy . . ." he begins, and we all laugh. As I approach the table to take my seat, Allegra reaches out and squeezes my hand, a perma-smile bright in her eyes. For the moment, I think maybe she's right. Maybe I'm not entirely broken.

Just dented is okay. Just dented is workable.

I can be just dented.

Thanksgiving comes quickly, and up until the day, I've managed to not think too much about the fact that my dad hasn't called and invited me home for the holiday. I don't know if I would have accepted, but the fact that he hasn't called is like a splinter burrowed under my skin that I can't get out. It bothers me with every movement I make. I spend the morning being cranky with everything, including both my coffeemaker and toaster, telling each to bite me within the span of ten minutes. Art's Desire is closed, which means there's no Mr. Trimble to

abuse and distract me, no Janesse to compare myself to
and fall short of. I decide to hike out to the Big, Flat
Rock of Perspective, but getting blisters and swallowing
bugs just isn't as much fun without Will, and I only get
about a third of the way there before heading back. I am
restless. I am irritable.

It's only ten in the morning.

On my way back to my little cabin, I stop by
Brandy's. I hold my finger over the doorbell, determined
to try it and see if it doesn't zap me again. But before I
get the chance, Brandy opens the door. She is wearing a
white apron over a long-sleeved red dress. Her hair is
pulled back from her face, and she's wearing makeup. She
smiles when she sees me.

"Hey, Carly," she says. "What's up?"

"I was just, uh, stopping by to let you know that,
uh . . ." I am distracted by the look of the cabin behind her.

It's clean. Nary a quilt anywhere. Wow. I look back at
Brandy.

"I don't think I can come tonight," I say. "I think I'm
coming down with something."

Her smile doesn't so much as flicker. "No, you're not."

I am surprised. I mean, obviously, I'm lying, but you
don't call people on their excuses in polite society. It simply isn't done.

Then again, it'd probably help if I didn't try to lie to
a psychic.

Brandy smiles at me with warmth and compassion.
"It's going to be hard for you today, I know. This is your
first Thanksgiving without your family, right?"

A rush of heat flows into my face, behind my eyes,

and suddenly I really want to cry. I can't believe she's trying to make me cry. That's so mean.

"That's not it," I say, and sniffle. "I think it's really just a cold. I might be running a fever and I don't want to get everyone else sick, so I'm just gonna—"

I am stopped by Brandy reaching out and pulling me to her. She kisses my forehead, and pulls back.

"Ninety-eight point six. You're fine."

"Brandy." I swipe at the lipstick that's surely on my forehead. "I do not feel well. I'm going to go home and rest. Thank you for your invitation, but I just wanted you to know there will be one less guest for you to worry about."

Brandy holds up her finger. "Wait here." She disappears into the house, the screen door banging shut decisively as I stand there, feeling like a child. I tell myself I should just walk away, get up and leave—it'd serve her right, bossy little psychic—but then she returns and stuffs an apron into my hand.

"If you think I'm going to let you go back to that little cabin by yourself and wallow all day when there's a perfectly good party happening here, well, darling, you've got another think coming." She gives me a look of annoyance as I stand there dumbly with the apron in my hand, and finally she grabs it and hooks the neck loop over my head. "What you need is something to do, and as it turns out, I need help. Now go in, get yourself a glass of wine, and let's get to work."

She steps out, holding the screen door open and pointing into the house. For a reason I'll never fully understand, I enter as ordered.

"Wine?" I say over my shoulder to her as I head back toward her kitchen area, which is covered with canvas grocery bags filled to spilling. "It's not even noon."

She eyes me with confusion. "Aren't you Catholic?"

"Yeah," I say. "What's that got to do with anything?"

"Well . . . your people drink at church, right?" She gives a small shrug. "I just didn't think you'd be so provincial about this sort of thing."

"I'm not being provincial—" I begin, but she ignores me, whipping a wineglass from a cabinet with one hand and swooping a bottle of red wine off the counter with the other.

"Sweetheart," Brandy says, "it's Thanksgiving. You'll never get through it unless you start drinking early. But you have to do it right—no more than one glass of wine per hour, and you must have at least eight ounces of water for every glass of wine, no exception. But once dinner's served"—she hands me my glass with a grin—"all bets are off."

We work through the morning, and as much as I don't want to admit it, Brandy is right. Peeling potatoes and drinking wine before noon seem to be just the things to draw me out of my funk. We put some Aretha Franklin on and make a very sad spectacle of ourselves, singing and dancing and drinking and cooking. It is two-thirty when we're done with the prep work, and Brandy leads me outside to her shed to get the extra leaf for her dining table.

"Thank you," I say as I follow behind her on the little stone path that leads to her shed, which is painted red with black dots, and looks quite a bit like an oversized, cubic ladybug.

"For what?" she asks, pulling open the door.

"For not letting me go back and wallow," I say. "This has been fun."

She turns to look at me, her hand over her eyes to shade them from the bright Arizona sun.

"You've got a red blotch over your shoulder," she says. I angle my head and pull at my sweatshirt, looking for the stain, and Brandy laughs.

"No, I mean, in your aura."

I drop the sweatshirt. "Oh."

"I know you don't believe in any of that," she says, "but will you humor me by answering a question?"

"Can I avoid it?"

She grins. "Whatever happened with your best friend? Christopher, right?"

I feel a pain in my ribs and I twist my torso a bit to relieve it. "Nothing. I mean, I talked to him when I first got here, but . . . not since then."

She nods, crosses her arms over her chest. "Weren't you two best friends?"

"We were. Yeah." She continues to just stare at me. I take a deep breath. "I'm not sure what you want me to say, Brandy."

She motions to the allegedly red spot in my alleged aura. "If you don't acknowledge the problem, you'll continue to be blocked."

"I'm not blocked."

And again, with the staring. I shift on both feet and stare back defiantly. Then, I give in with a martyr's sigh.

"Fine. I called him, I ripped off the Band-Aid, and I haven't heard from him since so I assume he hates me, and that pretty much brings us up to date."

Brandy nods. "And how do you feel about that?"

I can tell by the look in her eye that resistance is futile. I close my eyes for a moment and . . . share.

"I miss him." I can feel my eyes heat up a bit under the lids, but keep them closed. "But I don't want to hurt him any more than I already have, so I think it's best just to forget about it." I open my eyes, blink hard once, and motion toward the shed. "Can we get the stuff now?"

Brandy doesn't move. "It's okay to grieve, you know."

"If someone were dead, I would."

"There's a theory that when two people form a relationship, they form a third spiritual entity. When the relationship dies, that entity dies. Grief is a completely natural response, and it's almost impossible to move on if you don't allow yourself to experience it." Her focus goes out to the horizon. "Trust me on this."

"So, what?" I can hear the defensiveness in my voice, but I can't seem to squelch it. "I'm supposed to just sit at home and cry and grieve?"

"No. But I'm pretty sure you're supposed to do something."

Her smile falters a bit, and it's then that I finally realize we're not talking about me. We stand in silence for a while, and I wonder what it must have felt like for Brandy the night Jamal told her he wanted to be Janesse. As heartbreaking as the whole thing with Christopher was, I don't imagine it holds a candle to what Brandy went through.

I am still trying to form something worth saying when Brandy turns and heads into the shed. I follow her, and we silently move cardboard boxes, uncover the additional table leaf, and start back toward the house. We are halfway there when Brandy stops and turns to face me.

"I can take this the rest of the way by myself," she says, her typical bright smile back on full duty as she shifts the leaf out of my grip. "You go get changed."

I glance down at myself. Jeans and a sweatshirt—the height of style for my wardrobe. "Something wrong with this?"

"It's Thanksgiving. It's a holiday. You have to dress. That's part of the fun."

I shake my head. "This is as good as it gets, babe."

Brandy looks me up and down, then jerks her head in the direction of the house. There's a delighted twinkle in her eye that scares me a bit. "Come on."

I follow her. We set the leaf in the hallway and she takes my hand and drags me upstairs to the loft, and I discover where all the quilts, fabric, and supplies went. They are in piles three feet deep around her bed, on her bed, on her dresser, with narrow paths between to allow passage from one area to another. Brandy winds her way to her closet, opens it, and pulls out a flowy orange crepe dress. She holds it up, crinkles her nose, and tosses it on the bed, then dives back into the closet.

"Um, Brandy?" I say. "You're at least six inches taller than me. Nothing you have is going to—"

"Shhhh!"

"Okay." I watch as she tosses out dress after dress, most of them full-length and in which I'd look like a little girl playing dress up. I stand there, staring at the piles of quilts around me, wishing I had my glass of wine with me.

"You know, it's really okay," I try again after a few minutes. "I'm sure I've got a sweater or something. It's just, I worked in television production and I wasn't on-air much, so my wardrobe is kind of late-eighties-teenage-boy antichic."

"Oh, my God. It's perfect!" Her voice travels back at me, muffled from the closet. Then she steps back and holds out a little chocolate-colored number, chiffon over silk, with a halter top that dips down to a ruched Empire waist and . . .

"Where'd you get that?" I ask.

She checks the tag. "I ordered a dress through a catalog like six years ago, and they screwed up my order." She gives a little squeal of excitement and holds it out to me. "It's a petite."

"You kept it for six years?" I take it and check the size, then hand it back. "It's too small."

She pushes it back at me. "Try it on."

"It's. Too. Small."

The doorbell buzzes, and I hear Allegra yelp and curse. Brandy claps her hands together and giggles.

"Showtime!" She runs past me, tossing out, "Just try it on!" over her shoulder as she darts down the stairs. I sigh and grab the dress, holding it up to my body and checking myself out in the sliver of real estate left on the mirror over Brandy's dresser.

It *is* pretty. It'll look terrible on me. I know this as certainly as I know my own name, but I also know that

Brandy won't take no for an answer until I've at least tried it on. If then. I stomp into her bathroom and slam the door, dumping my jeans and sweatshirt and grumbling to myself as I step into it. I've barely got the side zipped when Brandy pushes into the bathroom without knocking.

"Jesus, Brandy!" I say, but am silenced by her expression as she puts her hand over her mouth and her eyes moisten.

"What? What happened? You okay?"

She touches my shoulders and turns me toward the mirror. I stare at myself for a moment. In the last ten years, the only dresses I've worn have been bridesmaid dresses, which are designed to make the bride look good. The chocolate in this dress plays nicely off my hair, and the green in my eyes catches even my attention. The top leaves little to the imagination, and isn't meant to be worn with a bra, but it's pretty. *I'm* pretty.

Wow. Who'da thunk it?

"Why did you keep it?" I ask. "They sent it to you by accident."

"There are no accidents," Brandy says, tugging a bit at the skirt to fluff it out. "Everything happens exactly how and when it's supposed to, and we just say it's accidental because we don't have the patience to wait and find out why things happened that way. The Universe sent this dress to me so I could hold it for you, Carly." She turns me to face the mirror and stands behind me, her face aglow over my shoulder. "How could you imagine that's not the case?"

I have to admit, she makes a good argument. The dress is perfect, and I never would have bought it for myself in a million years.

Brandy gives my shoulders a tender squeeze, then steps toward the door. "I'm going to get Allegra up here; she's a genius with makeup."

"But . . ." I say. "I can't wear this. I . . . I don't have any shoes . . ."

. . . *and I'm half-naked,* I add internally. I'm ready to admit that the dress is perfect. I'm not entirely convinced I'm ready to wear it in front of people.

"You can go barefoot," she says. "And lose the bra. Allegra will be up in a minute."

She shuts the door behind her and I stare at myself in the mirror for a minute before reaching back and unhooking my bra.

Twenty minutes later, Allegra is finished with me. She has moussed my hair and given me a light makeup job, and Brandy was right; Allegra's a genius. My eyes are smoky, and my lips and cheeks are sun-kissed, and I look like a real girl.

Allegra packs her makeup back into her purse and grabs for the bathroom door. "I'm gonna go. Count to twenty and then follow me."

"What? Why?"

"For your dramatic entrance, dummy. It'll be fun." She lets out a little snicker. "Will's gonna totally die when he sees you."

I grab her arm. "What? Will? Will's here?"

She laughs. "Just count to twenty, okay?"

"He's supposed to be in Ottawa until Monday. What's he doing here?"

"I don't know. He showed up right before Brandy sent me up here." She looks down at her arm. "Wow. For someone so tiny, you've got a hell of a grip."

I release her arm, and she laughs and opens the door. "Just count to twenty."

She disappears and I tentatively step out into Brandy's loft. My stomach is full of butterflies and I feel light-headed. I adjust my halter top and feel totally exposed. My back is bare and my breasts are free range under the silk and . . .

Something catches my eye, and the panic in my brain subsides. In the middle of the pile of quilts on Brandy's dresser, I see a familiar pattern. I walk over to the pile and tentatively pull at my quilt, revealing the image of the box with the paintbrushes. I run my hand over it and hear Brandy's voice in my head.

There are no accidents.

Allegra calls my name and I clench my breath in my lungs and start down the stairs as Aretha belts out "Until You Come Back to Me" in the background. I hear the catcalls before I can see who's giving them—mostly, it's Sebastian and James whistling and cheering, but Mack and Gladys from the Town Bookie are making some noise as well. Brandy and Allegra are laughing and sharing knowing looks. The only person who is perfectly still and silent is Will. He is standing at the back of the group with a glass of wine in his hand. He's wearing a light green Aran sweater and a pair of dark jeans and he's . . .

beautiful. Our eyes meet, and slowly he smiles. My heart dances and I smile back. Then on the last step, my right big toe catches on the back of my left ankle and I stumble. James catches me and sets me upright, and I quickly check my breasts to make sure they're still inside the dress. They are. Thank God.

James tells me I'm gorgeous and gives me a kiss on the cheek. Sebastian grabs my hand and spins me twice. Allegra helps herself to a glass of wine and refills mine, handing it to me as Sebastian trades me for Brandy.

"For a gay man, he really loves dancing with women," Allegra says, linking her arm in mine as we watch Sebastian dip Brandy.

"He can dance with me anytime," I say, winking at Sebastian as I sip my wine. Sebastian winks back and laughs.

"Oh, gross," Allegra says, moving toward the kitchen. I glance up and catch Will's eye. He takes a sip of his wine without losing eye contact with me and I feel my neck flush.

The doorbell rings and Brandy opens it to more guests; Bernard, the bartender at the Miner's Inn, and Valerie, who owns the flower shop on the edge of town. Someone swaps Aretha for Cole Porter and I find myself dancing around the room, flirting with everyone. Well, everyone except Will. I am sure that if anyone sees me looking at him, they'll know how crazy I am about him. I've barely accepted it myself, so I avoid him. For the moment, I like to imagine it's my little secret.

The wine flows and the dinner is delicious and Will and I don't say a word to each other, but we don't take our eyes off each other much, either. I float about, trading jokes and compliments, refilling wine. At some point during the evening, someone tucks one of Valerie's orchids behind my ear, and the fragrance follows me around the room. I feel like Cinderella, like the dress has magically changed me at my core. For the first time in my life, I am completely carefree, and it is a beautiful, beautiful feeling.

Finally, toward the end of the night, Will and I end up in the kitchen together. I am wrapping up the remaining pumpkin pie and putting it in the refrigerator, and he's donning an apron and moving toward the dishes. We exchange smiles, and he speaks first.

"So," he says, "it looks like you're having a good time."

"I really am." I shut the refrigerator door and lean against it. "Are you?"

He simply smiles at me, his blue eyes twinkling at the edges. I reach for an apron as he fills the sink, but he puts his hand on my arm, and his touch sends shocks through me that immobilize me where I stand.

"Brandy said you helped cook, which means no dishes for you." He grins. "Them's the rules, kiddo."

"Kiddo? Please," I say. "I'm older than you."

His hand is still on my arm. "I'm thirty-one."

"And you dated my little sister?" I give a mock-horrified gasp. "You dirty old man."

He quirks a brow at me. "You have no idea."

He releases my arm and turns toward the dishes. I step back and start to walk away.

"Don't go," he says, so quietly that I can run away

and pretend not to have heard him, which is probably what I would have done on any other night. Instead, I lean against the butcher-block island and dip one finger in the bowl of whipped cream.

"I can keep you company for a while, I guess." I lick the cream off my finger. Will chuckles and shakes his head at me.

"Now that's just cruel," he says.

"Oh, sorry." I pick up the bowl and hold it out to him. "You want some?"

Will looks at me for a second, then laughs again. "No. Thanks."

Suddenly, I realize what he's saying, and I flush madly and roll my eyes at myself. "Oh. Sorry. I—"

"It's okay." He grabs a plate, dunks it in the soapy water, and scrubs at it a little too hard. His neck is flushed and there's a light smile on his face.

"I thought you were supposed to be in Ottawa," I say.

"I was. I am. I'm catching a red-eye back at two a.m."

I feel a rush of disappointment. "So you just came back for what, twelve hours?"

He rinses the soapy plate and sets it in the wooden dish rack. "More like fourteen. But, yeah. I haven't missed one of Brandy's Thanksgivings since I moved here, so I put myself on a standby flight just in case. I didn't say anything because I figured there was no way I'd get a flight, but . . . here I am."

"I guess it was meant to be." My voice barely registers, it's so low as I say this. Part of me hopes he didn't hear me.

But he did. He raises his eyes to mine. "I like to think so."

We stare at each other for a few moments, and then we are interrupted by Gladys and Valerie, who both flirt shamelessly with Will until Valerie pats his ass, at which point Brandy comes in and chases them off. I push away from the counter and am about to shuffle off with them when Will calls my name. I turn and look at him.

"I'm gonna have to head back to Tucson within the hour or I'm gonna miss my flight." He pauses for a moment. "If you're leaving soon, I was thinking maybe I could walk you back to your cabin."

I look at the clock. Twenty minutes to midnight. Sounds about fitting for the Cinderella theme of the evening.

"You finish up and I'll go get my things," I say.

Will smiles. "Okay."

I make my rounds, give my good-byes. The men all kiss me on the cheek and the women all hug me, and I laugh and ham it up as I make my way upstairs, sprinkling kisses from my fingers like rose petals onto an adoring public. Once in the loft, I gather my clothes and put on my Keds. As I'm about to turn around and head back down the stairs, I notice my quilt poking out from the middle of the pile on the dresser. I stop for a moment, then walk over and touch it again. I pull it out of the stack and wrap it around my shoulders, then glide down the stairs, not stumbling at all, and Will meets me at the bottom. The group heckles us as we head out. I catch Brandy's attention and touch the quilt with a questioning look. She grins and nods permission. Will puts his hand on the small of my back and leads me out. Just as we reach the stone path that winds around Brandy's and back toward the cabins, I hear Valerie yell, "Send him back when you're done with him, Carly!" out the window. Will and I laugh, and a moment later we are alone, walking down the path by moonlight.

"I'm really glad you came back today," I say.

"Me, too."

We pass by his cabin and keep on down the path. My heart rate is kicking up, and I can feel an electric zing running up and down my legs. When we get to my cabin, I step up on the stoop and turn to face him. Even with the boost, he's still a bit taller than me, but our eyes are level enough for me to see the way he's looking at me, and I like it.

"I know you have to get on your plane," I say, "but do you want to come in for a few minutes?"

"Yes," he says quickly, then releases a deep breath and shakes his head. "But it's probably not a good idea."

"Oh." It must be midnight. I'm turning back into a pumpkin. "Okay. Well. Thanks for walking me. I'll see you when you get back."

I'm about to turn and go inside when his hand grasps mine. The quilt slips from my grip and my shoulder is exposed to the chill night air, but my skin is so flushed with wine and sexual tension that it feels good.

"Don't misunderstand," he says, his voice quiet and his eyes locked on mine. "It's just that if I go in there, I'll probably miss my plane, and I can't afford to do that."

"Okay," I say. His fingers are caressing my palm and I really, really, really want him to come inside.

We are silent for a long moment. He is looking at me and I am looking at him and we're not saying anything and we're not moving closer together but we're not moving farther away.

"Well . . ." His voice sounds strained. I make a tiny move forward, then go still. His hand travels up my arm and I realize with full certainty that if he doesn't kiss me right this minute, my heart is going to burst from my chest and I'm going to die. His fingers blaze a slow trail up to my face, then slide around the back of my head and he pulls me to him, his lips gliding over mine like a whisper. Now my entire body is zinging, and his other arm wraps around my waist and pulls me up tight against him. My hands find his face and the kiss takes over my entire body until, finally, our lips separate and we look at each other, our ragged breaths mingling in hot bursts. I stumble back a bit and Will catches my arm and gives me balance, his eyes laughing.

"Your feet don't seem to like you much."

"Okay, this time is not my fault," I say. "Tyra Banks would fall over after a kiss like that."

He smiles. "Tyra Banks, huh?"

I don't say anything, just stare into his eyes, trying to work a Jedi mind trick on him. *Come inside, Will. Miss your plane, Will. You know you want to, Will.*

"I have to go," he says finally. So much for Jedi mind tricks. "Okay. Well. I'll see you on Tuesday then?"

I nod. "Mmmm-hmmm."

"Okay." He takes a step back, releases a breath. "Whew. Okay."

I watch him as he takes a few steps away, then turns back to face me.

"Is it just me, or was that kiss the kind of thing people write books about?"

I can't help but sink into a big, fat smile. "It's not just you."

"Good," he says, nodding happily into the night. "Glad we're on the same page."

He puts his hands in his pockets and heads down the path. I hug the quilt in my arms and stand with the cold air kissing my skin until he is out of sight.

I float through the next few days. Will calls me twice, just to chat, and each call makes me extraordinarily happy. His job in Ottawa is for some catalogue of kitschy kitchen items—teapots shaped like cats, Statue of Liberty pepper grinders, that sort of thing. I spend Saturday night with Brandy, and I finish my brown turd scarf. It's lumpy and a little off-looking, but I made it, and I can't help but love it despite how ugly it is. Brandy wants to get me started on another project, but I beg off, wrap my scarf around my neck, and head home.

On Sunday morning, I go to Mass at St. Cecilia's, the church on the edge of town. I don't know why. I haven't been to a church since Ella's wedding, and before that I only went when Dad dragged me on holidays. As I step into the church, I wonder what Dad would think if he knew I was going of my own volition. Then I take a whiff of the incense and am suddenly overwhelmed with missing him. I cross myself and genuflect at a pew, then take a seat as the priest does the homily. I sit through the Mass but pass on the communion since I can't even remember the last time I confessed and I'm beyond lapsed. Still, after Mass I go up to the shrine of candles, put five dollars in the box, and light five candles. One for Ella and Greg. One for Five. One for Dad. One for Will's safe travel home. The last one takes me a while to light, but finally I say a quick prayer for Mary and turn quickly to escape, smashing headfirst into the lady behind me. I blurt out a quick apology and race out the back of the church.

Will is in my living room, wearing only flannel lounge pants, drinking coffee, and staring up at *She Might Be Crying.* I watch him from the doorway of my bedroom. I love the way he looks, his skin practically glowing in the morning light.

He is beautiful.

I try to take a step toward him, but my feet won't move. I look down, trying to figure out what's holding me back. There's nothing on my feet, but they feel really heavy.

And I realize I'm dreaming.

"Oh, crap," I say. "This was a good one."

Will laughs. "It had potential."

I stare at him, trying to will him to come to me and make this a really good dream, but there's a knock at the door.

"Are you gonna get that?" he asks.

"No." I stare harder, concentrate, furrow my brow.

Maybe the Jedi mind trick will work in my dream world.

Come to me, Dream Will, I think. *You know you want to.*

Will laughs. "You have a funny look on your face."

"That's not sweet talk."

He winks at me. "I'm coming back tomorrow. Can't you wait one more day?"

I hold his eye. "No."

There's another knock. Will starts for the back door.

"Wait, where are you going?" I still can't move.

"You need to get that," he says. I whimper, and he laughs. He blows me a kiss from the back door, then leaves. I look down at my feet and curse.

"Stupid feet," I say.

The knocking continues. I open one eye, and I am in bed. The sheets are wrapped around my ankles under the bedspread and quilt, which are bunched over me in such a strange jumble that it takes me a few moments of cursing and scrambling to extricate myself. I mutter to myself as I hobble out of bed, grabbing my robe off the top of the dresser on my way to the front door.

"I don't know what time it is," I say as I answer the door, one eye open, "but it's too damn early."

I stop when I see who's there, and I start blinking to get both eyes functioning. Ella's eyes are red, like either she hasn't slept or has been crying. Looking at her, I think it's quite possibly both. She's wearing an oversized U of A sweatshirt and jeans, both wrinkled. She has no makeup on, and as her eyes meet mine, they start to brim up. Her lips tremble and the tears spill down her cheeks.

We stare at each other for a long while, and I'm not sure what to do, so I do nothing and wait for her to speak while she stares at her feet.

"I don't blame you if you don't want to let me in," she says. "I know I was really horrible to you. I've been wanting to call you and tell you how sorry I am, but I didn't know how. I didn't know if you'd want to talk to me again."

She puts her hand to her face and cries harder. Without a word, I step outside and pull her into a hug. She sobs onto my shoulder, and I run my hand over her back and make shushing sounds. She is instantly forgiven, because there's nothing in this world that I wouldn't instantly forgive her for. "It's okay, sweetie."

"No, it's not," she says. "I was so mean to you."

I smile and hug her tighter, a little surprised at how much I just don't care. "It's forgotten, babe."

She steps back from me, sniffles and wipes her nose on her sleeve. *Ew.*

"Why don't you come on in?" I say. "I have coffee. And tissues."

She wraps her arms around her middle and looks so much like she did when she was younger that I almost think I'm still dreaming. Maybe I am. I kinda hope so. Because this broken little girl in front of me is not at all like my confident, beautiful, sophisticated, and overly hygienic sister. I'm beginning to get a little worried.

"Is everyone okay?" I say. My mind rushes to conclusions, and my heart seizes. "Is Dad okay?"

Her eyes brim over, and she nods.

"He's fine," she squeaks. "I left Greg."

Wow. I have to say, I didn't see that one coming.

"Oh, sweetie." I put my hand on her arm. "What happened?"

She shrugs and a breath stutters out of her. "I don't know."

My protective-sister hackles go up. Ella rarely gets angry, and almost never holds grudges. For her to be upset enough to come all the way down here, it's got to be bad. "What did he do?"

Her face crinkles up and she starts to sob. "He . . . said . . . I . . . use too much bleach. And he doesn't like my shepherd's pie."

The sobs come harder, and I refrain from telling her that no one likes her shepherd's pie. It's really vile.

"Okay." I step back and hold the door open. "Why don't you come inside and we can talk for a while?"

She gives a little nod and steps around me into the cabin, beelining for the couch and collapsing onto it with a thud. I hold a tissue box out to her, and she takes one and blows her nose.

"Do you want some coffee?" I ask gently.

She sniffles. "Do you have real half-and-half?"

I make a sound of mock indignation. "Of course."

She smiles, and her eyes brim up more. Wow. She's really a mess, which is very unusual for Ella. Then again, it used to be fairly unusual for me, too. I start toward the kitchenette.

"How did you find me?"

She sniffles. "Christopher."

There's a dull pain in my gut at the sound of Christopher's name, but I try to keep my voice casual. "You talked to Christopher? How's he doing?"

"He's . . . a mess. We're all a mess. Everything's a mess." Ella's chin quivers. "It wasn't supposed to be like this."

"Like what?"

She stares at me, and I know she's talking about Mary. About the way she thought it would be when Mary came back. I can't relate; I never thought about what it would be like when Mary came back, because I never in a million years thought it would happen. I dump the last scoop of coffee into the filter basket, shut it, and turn on the coffeemaker, then go sit by her side.

"How did everything get to be such a mess?" she says, grabbing another tissue out of the box.

"I don't know," I say. "Do you want to tell me what happened?"

She stares at a point on the wall and shakes her head. "Being married is hard."

I nod in sympathy, although of course I can't sympathize, as I have no idea how to make it through an engagement, let alone a marriage.

"Yeah," I say finally. "That's the word on the street."

"I mean, what if we end up like Mom and Dad? What if I have a baby and freak out and run off? What if I don't have what it takes?" She turns to look at me. "Or, worse, what if he doesn't? What if he and Tami With an 'I'—she's that surgical nurse with the huge, fake boobs, Tami With an 'I'—what if they lock eyes over a rhinoplasty and end up catching stolen moments in the supply closet and he comes home and says he doesn't love me anymore?"

I'm not sure what to say. I'm still stuck on "rhinoplasty."

"That sounds like a lot of what-ifs," I say finally. Ella reaches forward and snatches a tissue and blows her nose. At least it's a step up from the sleeve. "What if you and Greg end up making it through all that and have a wonderful life together? Have you considered that?"

She gives a little shrug and stares up at the wall again.

"Who painted that picture of you?" she says. "It looks like the stuff Will used to do."

I glance up at *She Might Be Crying*. "It is Will's. But it's not of me."

"Sure it is," she says. "How did you end up being painted by Will?"

"He lives next door," I say. I get up to get the coffee. "I found it in a shop when I first got here. And it's not me."

I combine sugar, coffee, and half-and-half in two mugs, then return to Ella. She is standing in front of my fireplace, staring at *She Might Be Crying*. I hand her a mug.

"It's you," she says. "Look, the eyes have that ring of brown in the center of the green, just like yours."

I look closer. Yeah, there's a touch of brown around the iris, but . . .

"And the little curl of hair, the one that always dips down over your left eye."

I swipe absently at my hair. "No. It can't be me.

Before moving in here, we'd only met for like five minutes at your wedding." I look closer at the painting, and my heart seizes.

Holy shit. I think it might be me.

Ella sips her coffee. "Don't get wigged. Something catches his imagination, he paints it. He once did twelve paintings of a single Granny Smith apple."

I look at her. "Really?"

She sniffles. "Really. That's what got him the show in New York, actually, if you can believe it. I think they saw him as a Warhol type, without all the crazy."

"He had a show in New York?" I look back at *She Might Be Crying*. "Wow."

"Yeah," she says. "He left a little while after we broke up. But then, I guess it didn't work out or something. Next thing I know, he's back in Arizona. And now you two are neighbors." She lets out a tired little laugh. "Small world, huh?"

"Yeah." I sit down next to her and sip my coffee. "He's not, like, you know, crazy or anything, is he?"

She shrugs. "No. I don't think so. He never seemed crazy to me."

Wow. What a ringing endorsement. Then again, she just left her husband. She'd probably have trouble drumming up enthusiasm for puppies bearing chocolate right now.

"I wouldn't worry about it," she adds. "I don't think he's likely to kill you in your sleep or anything."

"Good to know." I stare at the painting for a minute. The idea that I might be the "She" in *She Might Be Crying* weirds me out a little. I'm not sure if the

Granny Smith apple thing makes me feel better or worse about it.

"So . . ." she says after a short silence, "is there something going on with you two that I should know about?"

"I don't know," I say evasively. "What should you know about?"

She shrugs. "It won't bother me, if that's what you're worried about. Will's a great guy. I really liked him, but we never really . . . connected, you know? He was one of those good-on-paper guys, the ones that there's absolutely nothing wrong with them, except that there's nothing really right either, you know?" She leans toward me with a smile. "So what's the what?"

"Nothing's the what," I say too quickly, then sigh. I'm busted. I might as well accept it. "One kiss and wondering, that's it."

"He kissed you?" She giggles. It is amazing what a little gossip can do for this girl's disposition. "Really? Wow, how was it?"

"It was . . ." I can't finish the sentence, but I can feel my face starting to heat up. Geez. For someone with two sisters, you'd think I'd be better at this kind of talk.

Ella nudges me with her elbow. "That good, huh? Well, you definitely have my blessing if that counts for anything."

I smile. "It does."

She smiles back and then breaks out with a big yawn.

"Oh, man. I'm beat." She puts her mug down on the coffee table and hugs her arms around herself. "Can I get some sleep? Do you mind? Then I don't know. Maybe we can talk later tonight? I'm just so tired."

I squeeze her hand. "Sure."

Her lower lip trembles and she walks over to me for another hug. "Thanks for not being mad at me."

I hug her tight. "You know I can't stay mad at you. You still have my angora sweater."

She gives me a hug and I send her to my room to sleep. Then I call Janesse and tell her I can't make it to work today. She takes it very well, which surprises me, since Victor used to actually require a doctor's note documenting a near-death experience if I called in to *Tucson Today*. But Janesse is cool, and gives me a laundry list of comfort food I must run out and get. She even offers to hit the bar at the Miner's Inn later for karaoke, if Ella is up for it. I thank her, leave a sticky note for Ella, and head out the door, being careful to shut it quietly behind me as I go.

Chapter Eight

When I get back from the store, Ella is in my living room, talking on her cell phone. An hour and a half has passed—the local store doesn't carry Chunky Monkey, and Janesse insisted that the breakup of a marriage requires Chunky Monkey. In that time, Ella has napped, showered, and changed. Her hair is in a ponytail, and she looks fresh and happy. She gives me a smile and a wave as I make my way across the room to put the groceries away.

"I'm sorry. I didn't mean to worry you, Greg," she says. I tense up for a moment, wondering if I should go in the other room to give them privacy. Then I decide that if Ella wants privacy, she knows where to get it, and I open up the freezer.

"I don't know. We got to talking and I'll probably

stay the night. So, I guess you can expect me back to-morrow sometime."

Wow. They made up fast. I pull the Doritos out and put them on top of the fridge.

"I told you," she says, her voice all sunshiny-happy. "Everything's fine. Nothing's bothering me, silly."

An idea about what's been happening begins to dawn on me. I chuckle to myself and put the wine in the fridge to chill.

"I love you, too," she says, then flips her phone shut.

I turn on her. "He doesn't know, does he?"

"Hmmm?" she says, grabbing a *National Geographic* off my coffee table and flipping through it.

"That you left him," I say. "He doesn't know."

"I didn't leave *him*," she says, her voice getting defensive. "I left the *house*."

I laugh. I can't help it. "You really need to work on your conflict-handling skills."

"We fought last night and he just went to bed and I slept on the couch, only I couldn't sleep, so I called Christopher and he told me about your psychic quilt-maker and I drove out here." She casually flips a page in the magazine. "Is she really psychic?"

I stare at her. Even though I've known Ella for her entire existence, she still amazes me. "Seriously? We're talking about the quiltmaker now?"

She snaps the magazine shut and dumps it back on the coffee table. "I mean, he just up and went to bed. During a fight!"

I take a moment to figure out how to say this tactfully, then give up the ghost. "Are you sure he knew you were having a fight?"

She narrows her eyes at me and I can't help but smile. We're back, me and Ella, and it feels really good.

"He knew we were having a fight." Her expression quickly brightens. "Hey, did you get Doritos?"

I grab the bag off the top of the fridge and walk it over to the couch, where she snatches it from me and rips it open.

"Ooooh, Cool Ranch," she says, and shoves one into her mouth.

"Ella, what's going on?"

"I'm fine." She grabs another chip. "I freaked out a little, but now that I've had some sleep, I'm really feeling better. I overreacted, and it's okay. I'll go back in the morning and everything with Greg will be great." She smiles brightly. "See?"

It takes me a moment to verbalize my thoughts. "Oh, my God. Is that what I sound like?"

She blinks. "What?"

"When I'm all with the 'I'm fine,' even though I'm a complete mess. Do I sound like that?" I stick my hand in the bag and nab a chip.

"Like what? And I'm not a complete mess. I'm really fine."

"All high-pitched and in denial." I take the bag of chips from her. "I mean, 'cuz if that's the case, that's just sad. And you and fine? Aren't within shouting distance, sweetheart."

"What do you want?" she says. "Do you want me to

sit here and cry and bitch and moan because my perfect husband isn't perfect enough, or because my mother—"

It's like a guillotine has come down and chopped off her speech. She stares at me for a moment, then says, "Never mind."

"It's okay," I say. "If you want to talk about her, you can talk about her."

She stares down at her hands. "No, I can't. You're just going to say 'I told you so,' and I don't want to hear it."

"I'm not going to say 'I told you so.'"

She glances at me sideways, then sighs. "She's trying so hard, you know? She's being great. She's nice, but not too pushy. She's there when I want to see her, but never asks anything of me. I canceled three dates on her in the last month, and she never said a word about it. Then, last night, we went over there for dinner and she made this great meal and it was really nice."

"Wow," I say. "Bitch."

"That's just it. She's not. She's great. But the more time I spend with her, the more I just want to yell at her, you know?"

"But you can't," I say, "so you yelled at Greg."

"He said her shepherd's pie was better than mine." Her eyes start to tear up again.

"Oh, honey," I say, putting my hand on her arm. "It probably was. But that's not the point. The thing is that she's your mother, and she hurt you. She hurt all of us. You can't just decide you're going to forgive her and it magically happens. You have to work at it."

"Why? You didn't. You freaked out and ran away. Why can't I do that?"

"Um . . . you did. Only difference is, you're going back and you're going to make it all work because you're Ella and that's what you do."

She grabs another chip and stuffs it in her mouth, chewing thoughtfully for a moment before speaking again.

"And what are you going to do?" she says finally.

"Hmmm?"

"It's not like you're really going to stay here forever, are you?" She glances around. "The walls are all different colors."

"Yeah? So what? I like my walls."

"And you like . . . what? Working in an art supply store?"

I think on that for a moment, and when I answer, I answer honestly. "Yeah, I like it."

"But what are you going to *do*? With your life? When you're done screwing around here?"

"I'm not screwing around. I'm . . ." I squinch my eyes shut and mumble, "I'm reimagining my life."

Ella stares at me, her expression frozen as though I'd just sprouted polka-dot wings and announced I was a ladybug. "You're *what*?"

Looking at her, for the first moment since coming to Bilby, I'm filled with doubt as to whether I've made the right decision. Have I gone off the deep end? Because my sister, who knows me about as well as anyone, is looking at me like I've gone off the deep end, and that can't be a good sign. Can it?

Ella leans forward and grabs her purse off the coffee table. After rummaging through it for a few moments, she pulls out a folded piece of paper and hands it to me.

"What's this?" I start unfolding it and see the name "Rob Jenkins" and a phone number scribbled in Ella's handwriting.

"It's something Christopher asked me to tell you about. I guess now that *Tucson Today* is *Tucson Yesterday*, the independent station is trying to build up a new show. They're doing a series of half-hour documentaries—full documentaries—and they need freelance producers." Her face beams at me. "It's just the kind of stuff you've always wanted to do, and they're looking for people."

Wow. This should be really good news. I should be really excited. And yet . . . I shrug and toss the paper onto the coffee table. "I'm happy where I am."

There's a long silence, and I can feel the frustration coming off Ella in waves.

"Carly. You're an award-winning television producer—"

"Oh, whatever," I say. "A couple of local press-club awards hardly make me award-winning."

"Yeah," she says. "They do, you big stupid. And you'd be perfect for this, and then you could come home and—"

"And totally mess up my life again by going back to the very thing I left? No. Thank. You."

"Wow." She stares at me, her blue eyes narrowed and evaluating. "I never realized it before, but you can be really stubborn sometimes."

"And this from the woman whose husband doesn't know she left him."

Ella opens her mouth to say something back, but stops and lets out a small laugh.

"We're a hell of a pair, Car," she says, grabbing the

bag of Doritos out of my hand and diving in. "We should take this act on the road."

Ella and I spend a quiet evening at home, eating ice cream and talking things to death. We decide that my fledgling relationship with Will is an exciting new start, and that her marriage is just going through the classic first-year bumps. Before she leaves the next morning, she promises to call me when she gets home, and makes me promise to call the guy from the independent station. We hug tightly before she takes off, and I watch her walk away until the foliage overtakes the path and she disappears. I go inside, tuck the piece of paper away in the front of my phone book, stick it in a drawer, and decide to think about it later.

Work is work. I stock shelves, I ring up customers, and I gossip with Janesse. Best of all, when I leave, I don't think about it anymore. I'm not loaded with tapes or worrying about scripts I have to write or how we're going to do in sweeps, or anything. My mind is free and clear, and I like it. Ella may not understand, but there are some great benefits to being a clerk at an art supply store. As I walk on the path back to my little cabin in the foothills, I form all my arguments about why I won't be calling the guy from the independent station, why I don't want to work in television, why I'm happy with my reimagined life. My mind is caught up in the hurricane fury of my thoughts when I emerge into the clearing, and it takes me a moment before I realize there's music playing. I look up and see lights on in Will's cabin, and my heart skips. I sneak up on the porch and peek in the front window. Will is in an apron, cooking over his stove, dancing and singing to the Jackson 5's "I Want You Back," and he's awful. Off the beat, off-key, and I've never seen anything more adorable in my life. I sneak back off the porch and go to my place, where there's a note tacked to my door that simply says, *Call me when you get home.*

I grab my cell phone from my bag and dial. After a ring or two, the music lowers and I hear Will's voice on the other end.

"You're back," I say.

"I'm back. Where are you?"

"On my porch."

He pokes his head out his front door and we look at each other for a moment.

"Nice apron," I say.

He smiles. I can see it even from my porch and it makes my insides get all zingy. "So, you coming over or what?"

"Give me five minutes."

We each hang up and go back inside our cabins. I rush around, brushing my teeth and my hair at the same time, then jump into a fresh pair of jeans and my only nice sweater, a creamy cable-knit. I do a light mascara/lip gloss touch-up and rush out the door, then turn back to grab my purse, in which I have two just-in-case condoms. It's still very early and I doubt we'll use them, but knowing they're present and ready makes me feel all tingly, and I like it.

I've barely knocked on his door when it opens. He's lost the apron, his hair is still in a thousand directions but cutely so, and he looks really good in his dark blue, long-sleeved T-shirt and jeans.

"Hey," he says.

"Hey." I'm trying to put a damper on my smile because my face is starting to ache, but I can't help it. He touches my shoulder lightly to guide me inside and then swipes his hands on his thighs as he heads toward the kitchenette.

"Um, I'm not a great cook, but I thought maybe I'd try to whip up something. It's just spaghetti. Probably inedible."

"It smells great," I say, but to be honest, I haven't noticed. Instead, I find myself watching him move with that tall, lanky grace, and I accept that I am so far gone in this crush that I'm probably never coming back.

He grabs a bottle of wine off the counter. "Can I pour you some wine?"

"Yes. Please."

He pours two glasses, puts the sauce on simmer, and we settle on the couch.

"So, did you have a good weekend?" he asks.

"Yeah," I say. "Ella stopped by."

"Ella? Really?"

"She had a fight with Greg, so she came down here and we made up and actually had a pretty nice time."

"She had a fight with Greg?" Will says. "Everything okay there?"

I roll my eyes. "Yeah, it's fine. He didn't even know she left him."

Will's eyes widen in surprise. "She left him? I thought you said they just had a fight."

"No. They did. It's a long story. It's just . . . Ella."

"Yeah, I remember."

The comment makes me feel a little tense, and I can see by his face that my internal reaction is obvious. He puts his wineglass on the coffee table. "I mean, she used to get upset with me and I would never know. She never said anything. It was crazy."

There's an awkward silence. I sip my wine. Will sighs.

"Is it going to be weird, that Ella and I used to date? Maybe we should talk about it."

"No," I say. "I think it's okay. It just takes some getting used to. It was a long time ago, and she's fine with it, so really, I think it's okay."

A small smile spreads over Will's face. "You told her about us?"

I can feel my face heating up. Crap. "Well. Kinda. I, uh . . . have this painting I bought of yours and she noticed it so I kinda mentioned . . ." I giggle like an idiot, beg myself internally to shut up, and yet keep going. "Not that there's anything to tell, really, yet, but you two dated so . . . you know. It's a little weird. But not very. She's fine with it. I'm fine with it." I meet his eye. "Are you fine with it?"

Will smiles and leans a little closer, looking into my eyes as he speaks. "Yeah. I'm fine with it. You seem a little nervous, though."

"Oh," I say. "I thought I was hiding it so well."

He reaches up and touches my chin, turning my face toward him a bit.

"If it helps, I'm a little nervous, too."

"It helps." I smile up into his eyes. "Nervousness loves company, right?"

He watches me for a moment. "I think maybe there's something we need to get out of the way so we can relax."

"Yeah, what's that?" I ask as he leans toward me. His lips whisper over mine and the kiss is sweet and light, but I still feel dizzy when he pulls away, a smile on his face as his eyes catch mine.

"Is that better?" he asks.

"Mmmm," I say, nodding.

He puts one hand on the couch behind me and lightly grazes his fingers over my hair, and then there's another kiss, this one longer and even more dizzy-making. I've been kissed a fair number of times in my life, but I've never been made dizzy before. I didn't know it was possible. When he pulls away, I emit a small, inadvertent whine.

"Sorry." He gives a self-conscious laugh. I adore it. "I was planning on feeding you before we got to this, I swear."

"It's okay," I say, although I'm not sure if I'm audible over the crazy pounding in my chest. All I want is for him to touch me again. I don't care where. The elbow's fine. But he's got a look on his face like he doesn't want me to think he's just out for sex, and I don't want him to think I'm a slut, and yet we're sitting with our faces inches apart and neither one of us is moving away.

"Maybe we should talk for a while," I say helpfully.

He nods, leans back a bit. "Sure. Talk. Good idea."

I sit up, smooth out my sweater, and reach for my wine.

"So, maybe tell me about your family?" I say, and at the same time Will says, "What painting?"

I stare at him for a moment, then realize what he's asking. "Oh. Yeah. Um, I got it the day I got here. The one with the girl with her hands over her face and you can't tell if she's laughing or crying?" I giggle nervously. Good God. I sound more like a fifteen-year-old than ever. "Ella saw it and recognized your style. She said it was of me, but that's crazy, right? Because we didn't even know each other when—"

I catch the expression on his face and stop talking.

"Oh. Wow." I take a sip of wine, then turn back to face him. "It's me?"

"Um. Well." He gives an awkward laugh. "Yeah. I went down to the Café to get it after you moved to town and it was gone, so I just figured I'd dodged the bullet, you know?" He stares at me for a minute, his expression wary. "You think I'm gonna put you in a pit and lower lotion down to you in a basket, don't you?"

"Not until you said that," I say, laughing. "It's . . . you know, sure. A little weird, but—"

He pivots on the couch to face me.

"Look, I paint things that catch my imagination. That day, at the wedding, you were . . ." He watches me for a moment, and I can see the internal debate playing in his eyes before he finally talks again. "You were so strong and in charge, and yet there was this part of you that just seemed . . . I don't know. Vulnerable. And after that I couldn't get you out of my head, so I painted you."

"And then I was out of your head?"

He laughs. "Until you showed up in my bed,

yeah. Since then . . ." He sighs and trails off. "Are you freaked out?"

I smile. "Only by my apparent narcissism."

"Good." He smiles back. "And, just so you know, your narcissism is kinda freaking me out, too."

"So, what happened in New York?" I say suddenly, and just as suddenly regret it. His face goes tight, and he leans away from me a bit.

"Ella told you about New York?"

"Well, a little," I say, suddenly very unsure of myself. "I mean, she said something about Granny Smith apples and Andy Warhol."

He is quiet for a while, just staring into his wineglass. Then he shakes his head. "Yeah. Well, it was a dumb thing to do."

"Why?"

He takes a breath to say something, then stops himself and shakes his head, saying nothing. I turn my body sideways to face him.

"Is that why you don't really paint much anymore? Because things didn't work out in New York?"

He shrugs, and his voice takes on a hint of defensiveness. "I paint. I just . . . you know, I had to make a living. You can't spend all your life chasing down some stupid dream that's never gonna pan out. There comes a point where you have to grow up."

I put my hand on his arm. "It's not stupid. You're an amazing artist."

He lets out a derisive snort. "Well. That's all a matter of opinion, isn't it?" He stares into his wineglass for a moment more, and then a cringe takes over his face.

"I'm acting like such an asshole. I'm sorry." He raises his eyes to mine. "I guess it's still a bit of a sore spot."

"No, I totally understand," I say. "It's okay."

"It's not," he says, lifting up my fingers and putting them to his lips for a quick kiss, "but it's nice of you to say. And, to answer your question, what happened is this: I had a showing in Tucson, and a moderately successful Broadway actress saw it and loved it. A week later, I got a call from New York from someone she knew, and they asked me to do a showing at a gallery in SoHo." He takes a sip of his wine, his eyes still on my fingers, which rest lazily in his hand. "Which is not the real big big time, but it was a hell of a lot bigger than Tucson. So, like an idiot, I packed up everything I could fit in a suitcase, sold everything else, and went out there like a big, dumb dog. In about three weeks I ran out of money, and the gallery showed my stuff and I sold exactly one painting, and got exactly one horrible review in a very small but exceedingly nasty weekly paper. And that was my big New York debut."

He lets out a self-deprecatory laugh and turns to look at me. I smile and entwine my fingers in his.

"The people of New York obviously have no taste," I say.

He laughs, a real one this time, and stares at me with this amazed look on his face. We hold the gaze for a while, each of our smiles widening as the moment passes. It's a good moment, and I think we're about to kiss again when his eyes suddenly widen and he snaps his fingers at me.

"I almost forgot. I got you something in Ottawa."

He hops up off the couch like a kid on Christmas morning and I follow him toward his bed, where he grabs a white box out of a paper bag and hands it to me. "I would have wrapped it up nicely, but I didn't have a whole lot of time."

I take the box and open it to find the ugliest ceramic frog I've ever seen. It's a shade of greenish-brown that is not flattering on any animal, and the back is huge and fat and hunched, while the head is disproportionately small.

"Oh. Wow. It's a hunchback frog." I turn it over and look at the lettering on the bottom, then raise one eyebrow at him. "*Quasitoado?* Are you serious?"

Will laughs. "Took me forever to get a shot of that damn thing that made it look good. I'm not sure I ever did."

I hold Quasitoado up, looking into the tiny face. "Is he smirking at me?"

"I don't know. I thought it was more an evil-plot-to-take-over-the-world kind of expression."

I tilt my head to take the frog in from another angle. "Yeah. I think you're right." I turn it over in my hands again, fascinated. "What exactly is it?"

"Ah, that's the best part." Will lifts the hunchback off to reveal a bowl underneath. "Sugar dish."

I laugh and take the top from him. My fingers graze over his and our eyes lock for a beat.

Finally, I get the presence of mind to say something. "So, you saw the ugly hunchback frog and thought of me, is that what you're trying to say?"

His smile fades a touch. "I saw everything and thought of you."

I let out a half laugh, half groan. "Oh, man, that's a bad line."

He chuckles. "It sounded better in my head." He takes a step toward me and runs one hand down my arm. "It's true, though. I was really looking forward to getting back here to see you."

"What a coincidence. I was really looking forward to being seen."

He holds my gaze for a moment longer, then takes in a sharp breath and lowers his hand.

"Hey, I'm pretty sure I've burned that sauce. How do you feel about ordering pizza?"

"I feel great," I say. He heads over to the spaghetti and tosses it in the sink, then keeps his eyes on me as he calls for pizza. I tuck Quasitoado back in his box and set it carefully by my purse where it won't get stepped on. It's positively the ugliest gift I've ever received, but already I love it with all my heart.

"Oh, my god," Janesse says the next day, leaning over the counter of Art's Desire and looking Quasitoado in the face. "That is the fugliest thing I have ever seen."

Allegra hands Janesse the coffee we've just brought over from the Café, then grabs Quasitoado and turns him to face her.

"It's not that bad," she says. "It's kinda gone so far to ugly that it's circled back to cute."

"Yeah," I say. "I think he's cute."

Janesse raises an eyebrow at me. "Would you eat sugar out of that thing?"

"Um . . ." I stare dubiously at the frog. "Probably not. But it doesn't have to be a sugar dish. It could be a paper-clip holder or something."

Allegra hops up on the counter. "Forget the damn frog. How was Will? You know, in the purely sexual sense."

Janesse doesn't encourage Allegra, but she does raise one eyebrow indicating that she wouldn't be averse to hearing the details. I scoff.

"Oh, please," I say. "I don't know."

"So, what?" Janesse says. "You just ate pizza and talked?"

"Well, no," I say. "Not *just*. But mostly, yeah. It was nice."

"Oh, man," Allegra says. "What are you waiting for? You need to hit that."

I stare at her. "*Hit that?* Are you kidding?"

"Beta males, I'm telling you. They'll make you scream."

I put one hand gently on her face. "Allegra, I love you. I do. But you have to stop. You are the same age as my little baby sister, and when you talk like that, it skeeves me out."

One side of Janesse's mouth quirks up in a smirk. "Don't be skeeved. She's just a virgin who reads too many trashy magazines and likes to talk out her ass."

I laugh, then notice that neither Allegra nor Janesse is laughing with me. I look at Allegra. "You're a virgin?"

Allegra raises one eyebrow at me. "I'm a seventeen-year-old girl who was homeschooled in Bilby, Arizona. Not exactly the land of opportunity." She motions toward Janesse with her coffee cup. "Hell, the best-looking man in town is a woman."

Janesse's face is stony for a moment as she decides

how she feels about that comment, then breaks out in a smile. "Thanks."

Allegra grins at her. "No problem, sugar."

"But . . ." I stammer. "The way you talk . . ."

"I was raised by two gay men who taught me to not be afraid of my sexuality, and I'm not. I'm also not going to be pressured out of my virginity by a culture so obsessed with sex that no one cares if it's any good or not. These knickers are staying in place until I'm sure I've found a man who'll knock my socks off on his first at bat."

I blink. Wow. That was good. I decide that I definitely want Allegra and Five to hang out.

Allegra stands up straighter, obviously proud of herself. "And, for the record, I never said I wasn't a virgin."

"You never said you were," I counter lamely.

"I never said I was a Pisces, either. That doesn't make me not a Pisces."

"You knew about this?" I say to Janesse, who shrugs and takes a sip of her coffee, then sputters. "What the hell is this?"

"Orange-coconut cappuccino," Allegra says. "What do you think?"

"I think it's vile." Janesse looks at me. "You let her make you drink this stuff?"

"She gives me what I order on Fridays," I say, taking another sip. It's not *that* bad.

Janesse walks around the counter, grabs Allegra by the hand, and starts toward the door. "Watch the store for a minute, okay, Carly? I'm gonna get me a real cappuccino."

"You hit that!" Allegra calls over her shoulder with a giggle as Janesse pulls her out of the store. They're gone for maybe two minutes when Mr. Trimble walks in. I stand awkwardly behind the counter trying to ignore him as he goes to the charcoals and picks out his regular box, then makes his way to the counter. I manage to ring him up and am giving him his change when I accidentally make eye contact. His eyes widen as though I've slapped him. I freeze with my hand holding the change over his open palm. He freezes as well.

Well. In for a penny . . .

"What's up with the charcoal?" I say before I can stop myself. "No paper. Just the charcoal. What's up with that, Mr. Trimble?"

"Fuck off," he says.

"Okay, then." I drop the change into his open palm, and he stuffs it in his pocket, snatches the bag with the charcoal off the countertop, and stalks out of the store.

"Have a nice day," I call out after him. "Come again!"

"Fuck off!" He pushes the door open and is gone from sight before the little bells stop jingling.

Something is ringing. Something is ringing. Something . . .

I open one eye, and see only a sheen of moonlight glancing off my lace curtains. The ringing stops. I am about to fall back asleep when a shot of panic causes me to open my eyes. I glance at the clock: 3:12. My mind starts piecing it together. People don't call to chat at 3:12 in the morning. It's probably an emergency. If there's an emergency, I need to get up. With some effort, I reach over and flick on my light, then grab my cell phone off the nightstand, where it's been charging. I am just about to check my missed calls list when it rings again, and I see Dad's name on the caller ID panel. I take a deep breath and flip it open.

"Is she there?" he says before I get a chance to say hello.

"Dad? What? Is who here? Ella? No."

"Not Ella. Five."

It feels like someone has stabbed a hypodermic of adrenaline into my heart, and I bolt upright in bed. "No. She's not there? Where is she? What happened?"

"There was an argument. We all went to bed, but when your mother went in to check on Five, she wasn't in her room."

I am off the bed in a shot, grabbing a pair of jeans from my dresser and dashing into them. "Where is she? How long has she been gone? Did you call Rebecca? Is she over there?"

"We called Rebecca." There is mumbling in the background; I can hear Mary's voice, and then Dad is back on the line. "We just wanted to see if she'd called you or ended up there. Will you call us if she contacts you?"

I freeze where I am. "What? Will I call you? Yeah, Dad. I'll be there in two hours. An hour and a half if I drive like a maniac."

"Go back to sleep." There's a tightness in his voice, and it stops me where I stand. "Just let us know if you hear from her, okay?"

He hangs up. I stare at the phone in my hand. Five is

gone. Five is missing. Five is seventeen and God only knows where she is. Horrible images race through my head. As soon as I banish one, there's another in its place. My heart is pounding so hard it hurts and my breathing is coming really fast.

Five is missing.

I finish getting dressed, grab my keys and purse, and head over to Will's, where I bang on the door until the lights come on and it opens, revealing Will in a rumpled T-shirt and boxer shorts.

"Five is missing," I say, staring into the Miner's Inn logo on the center of the T-shirt. "Five is missing and I'm freaking out."

Will blinks once and looks instantly awake. "She's missing? What happened?"

"I don't know," I say. He touches me on the arm and guides me inside as I babble. "Dad just called and they had a fight and she ran off and no one knows where she is and she's only seventeen and she's book-smart but she's really street-stupid and do you know what happens to street-stupid girls? Not good things. I used to work at a news station. These are exactly the kinds of things we used to freak people out about during sweeps."

He puts both hands on my shoulders and turns me to face him. His face is serious and calm and in charge, and I love him for that.

"I'm going to throw on some jeans and we'll go to Tucson and find her, okay?" He leans down a bit and looks me in the eye. "We'll find her."

I feel my eyes start to heat up, but I blink it away. "She's alone somewhere."

He tightens his hold on my shoulders, and his strength calms me. "I'm gonna go throw on a pair of jeans and we're on our way, okay?"

"Okay." I nod. "Okay."

He darts over to his bed and I wrap my arms around myself and swallow hard, chanting internally. *She'll be fine. She'll be fine. She'll be fine.* But the images in my head are graphic and horrible and I curse the day that I ever decided to work in television.

Just then, my phone rings. I jump about a half a foot and scramble to grab it out of my purse.

"Hello? Dad? Did you find her? Is she okay?"

There's a long silence. Then a wavery voice says, "Carly?"

Will is at my side, and I grab his hand and hold it tight. "Five?"

"I'm at the bus station."

I put my hand over my forehead and rub hard. "Five, I'm going to hang up and call Dad and he's going to come get you, okay? So just find a security guard and stay with him until Dad gets there. Which station are you at?"

There's another long silence, then, "I don't know. I think there's only one in Douglas."

"Douglas?" My voice cracks on the word. "Douglas? You're down here?"

Her voice is quiet and childlike. "Yeah. Can you come get me?"

"Find a security guard. We'll be there in twenty minutes," I say, and flip the phone shut.

———

Will drives us to Douglas, and I call Dad and tell him not to worry. We decide that Five can stay with me for the night, and we'll figure the rest out in the morning. As I hang up, my hands are shaking from emotions so tangled I can't tell one from the other. There's fear and relief and anger and sadness and others, all wound up tight together under cords of adrenaline. Will puts his hand over mine and the touch makes me strangely tense. I want to pull my hand away, but I don't, because I can't take any more feeling bad tonight.

Will has barely parked the car when I hop out and run into the bus station. The automatic doors don't open fast enough, and I dart sideways through them, my eyes scanning the empty space for Five. I see a security guard and run over to him.

"My sister. She's seventeen. She's here."

He nods and points to a bench that appears to be empty, but when I walk around, I see Five curled up on it, asleep. I walk over to her and kneel down in front of her, touching her shoulder lightly. "Hey, sweetie."

She opens her eyes immediately. They are swollen and red, and when she focuses on me, they fill up again. She throws her arms around my neck and starts crying into my shoulder, and I rub her back until she calms down. When her breathing starts to stabilize, I pull back and hold out a package of travel tissues. She grabs one and dabs at her face.

"I'm sorry," she says. "I just didn't know what to do."

I run one hand over her hair. "Yeah. There's a lot of that going around."

She looks up over my shoulder and gives a small wave. "Hey, Will."

Oh. God. Will. I'd completely forgotten about Will. I turn around to see him smiling down at Five.

"Hey, Fiver," he says kindly. "Thanks for scaring the shit out of us. I hear it's good for the soul."

She starts to laugh, and then her lip trembles. "I'm sorry," she squeaks. I give her shoulders a squeeze.

"You get a reprieve on the ass kicking until tomorrow morning," I say. "So live it up now, sunshine."

"Okay." She attempts a smile and blows her nose, then looks from me to Will and back again. "So . . . Um. I guess you guys are, uh . . . I mean, Ella said . . ."

"Well . . ." Will begins, but I stand up and cut him off.

"We're neighbors," I say. Will hesitates for a second, then nods.

"She just happened to rent the cabin next door." He meets my eye for the briefest flash, then smiles at Five. "Hell of a coincidence, huh?"

"Yeah." Five looks confused. "Okay."

I hold my hand out to Five. "Let's get you back to my place, kiddo."

She takes my hand and leans against me as we make our way to the car. I am vaguely aware of a weirdness with Will, but I don't want to think about it.

I'll deal with that, I decide, tomorrow.

Chapter Nine

I am woken up by the sound of my front door opening. I open my eyes, but all is a muted shade of blue, as my head is completely under the quilt. I pull it down and see Will setting a drink carrier with coffee and a white paper bag down on the table.

"Sorry," he says. "I tried to sneak in quietly. Thought you guys could use some coffee."

"Yeah. Thanks." I scratch my head. "What time is it?"

"Nine." He stands where he is for a moment, then nods toward the back door. "I'll just let you go back to sleep, then."

I throw my legs over the side of the couch. "Wait. I'm sorry. I'm still waking up. I'm slow in the morning."

He nods again, keeps his eyes on me. "Do you want to talk about it?"

I sigh and lean back on the couch. "There's not much to talk about. I guess I'll take her back today."

Will gives me a curious look. "Then there's probably plenty to talk about. You'll be seeing your dad again. And your mom. I mean, that's gotta be . . . I don't know. Something."

I shrug and get up, making a beeline for the coffee. "It is what it is. I'll bring her back, I'll make nice for a few minutes, and then I'll come home."

He smiles, but his eyes still look worried. "Okay. If you're sure you don't need to talk about it."

"I'm sure." I take a sip of the coffee. "Mmmmm. Thanks so much. This is perfect."

"Yeah." He glances at the quilt on the couch. "Hey, how'd you get Brandy to let you keep that quilt? I've been trying to get one out of her for ages."

"Actually, it's mine. She gave it to me with a reading when I came to do a story on her. I left it at her place for a while, then took it back on Thanksgiving."

Our eyes meet for a moment as we both remember Thanksgiving. I look away and take another sip of the coffee. "Did Allegra really make you just a plain cappuccino? How did you get her to do that?"

But Will isn't listening. He's heading for the couch, studying the quilt. "So, what did she tell you?"

I shrug. "I don't know. Leave the gun. Take the cannoli."

He looks at me over his shoulder. "What?"

Before I can answer, the door to my bedroom opens and Five comes out. She's wearing a pair of my sweats that come up to her midcalf, and her hair is all smooshed up on one side.

"Hey," she says, and staggers toward the coffee. "Whoever got coffee, I love you."

"It was Will."

Five looks at him and smiles. "Thanks."

"No problem." Will nods at me. "Well, I'll let you guys sort everything out."

"Don't leave on my account," Five says.

"No, I've got . . ." He motions vaguely in the direction of his cabin. "Stuff to do." He looks at me. "So, I'll . . . see you later?"

I nod. "I'll call you when I get back."

He pauses for a moment. I don't know if I'm supposed to give him a kiss or not, but considering my morning coffee breath, I stay where I am. He gives a stiff smile and a stiffer wave, and heads out the door.

"What's up with that?" Five says. "Ella said you guys were dating."

"We're not dating," I say. "We're . . . I don't know what we are. We're . . . us."

"Oh. Well. That makes it all clear." She nods toward the bag. "What'd he bring us?"

I grab it and dip my nose in. "Doughnuts."

Her eyes widen. "What kind?"

I look again. "Double-chocolate."

She sighs, dips into the bag, and pulls out a doughnut. "Oh, man. Poor Will."

"Poor Will? Why poor Will?"

She breaks the doughnut in half. "Nothing. It's just

that you know how different flowers have different meanings? Like white carnations are friendship, red roses are love, blah blah?"

I sit down across from her and reach for the bag. "Yeah?"

"Well, Rebecca and I have this theory that doughnuts have meaning, too. And double-chocolate is pretty much the red rose of the pastry set."

I freeze with my doughnut in midair. "That's ridiculous."

She shrugs and takes a bite. "Maybe."

"Hey," I say, as my brain slowly catches up with the conversation. "Why poor Will?"

"Hmmm?" She blinks. "Did I say that?"

"Yeah."

"Hmmm."

We both stare blankly at our coffee cups for a moment. Neither one of us is a morning person on our best day.

"So," I say finally, "you gonna tell me what happened with Dad and Mary?"

She lets out a heavy, dramatic sigh. "Oh, it's so stupid. I was out at this party on Saturday, and I had a little beer—not a lot, just a little. You should have seen how much everyone else was drinking. Then, anyway, Bo was driving home and we got in a little accident."

"What?" I am suddenly awake and clearheaded and filled with an all-consuming rage I'd like very much to unleash on Botox. "What the hell happened?"

"It was nothing. We were fine. The stupid cops gave

him a DUI, which was totally unfair because he was just barely over the limit and it was his first offense and we only hit, like, a mailbox, anyway. The cops would have never even known if one of them hadn't been driving down the street right at that moment."

"This is your defense?" I say.

She rolls her eyes. "So then last night Mom sits down with me and tells me she doesn't want me to see Bo anymore." Her lower lip trembles, but she sucks it up and plays tough. "Like she has the right. She hasn't even been here most of my life, and she thinks she can tell me who I can and cannot date?" She rolls her eyes upward to distribute the tears so they don't fall. "That's bullshit."

I take a moment to process the fact that Five is actually trying to get this past me. "Excuse me?"

She leans forward and grins. "Yeah, I know. You should have seen her face when I said it. She was all, 'Go to your room,' and I was all, 'You can't tell me what to do,' and then we got in a fight and I went to my room, packed my backpack, and shimmied down the drainpipe." Five leans over her coffee. Her eyes are dry. "She's such a bitch. You were totally right about her, Carly."

I am so stunned that I can't talk for a moment, but then I get my sea legs back.

"No," I say. "I wasn't."

Five's eyes dart to connect with mine, and she stares at me, uncomprehending. Meanwhile, I can't believe Five thinks I'd actually take her side on this, just because it's against Mary. I sit back in my chair and cross my arms over my stomach, giving Five my sternest, I-mean-it look.

"She's right, Five. I would have told you the same thing. As a matter of fact, I'm telling you now. You can't see that boy, ever, ever again."

Five stares at me for a moment longer, her eyes wide, and then her expression goes hard.

"He's my boyfriend," she says. "I love him."

"I don't care. He could have killed you, and he's not going to get a second swing at bat. You're going back home, and if I ever hear about that boy coming within ten yards of you, I will personally come after his sorry ass and scare him off but good."

Five throws her hands up in the air and thuds back in her chair.

"Of course you will," she says. "It's your specialty, isn't it?"

I let out a tired sigh. "This isn't about me, Five."

"Whatever," she says. "You want to know what I meant when I said poor Will? I meant that he's going to end up like the rest of them. Like Seth. Like Christopher. Just standing there with wilted flowers in his hand, looking all heartbroken and dumbfounded."

"What? What are you . . . ?" I can't get the words out, though. Five narrows her eyes at me and continues to spew her venom.

"I should have known you'd take their side. You're too damaged to be in love, so you don't want anyone else to be."

She darts up from the table, stomps across the room, and slams the bedroom door behind her.

"You'd better be in there packing your stuff, because we're leaving in fifteen minutes," I yell after her. She mutters something so low I can't hear it, but I'm pretty sure it's in language unbecoming. I drop my doughnut on the table, wipe my hands on a napkin, grab my cell phone, and dial. When Mary answers, I don't even bother to say hello.

"We'll be there in two hours," I say, then hang up. I don't feel angry. I don't feel upset. I don't feel hurt. I stare blankly down at the half-mangled doughnuts on the table, and I don't feel anything.

The ride home is long and silent. Five and I speak to each other only when absolutely necessary, and with as few words as possible. I feel strangely disconnected as I pull off I-10 and back onto the familiar streets I've known my whole life. Somehow, it doesn't feel like my life. I feel like I'm just riding through someone else's, going through the motions until I can get to a place I recognize.

I pull up in front of the house and get out of the car. Five sits in the front seat, unmoving, her arms crossed over her chest. I open the passenger-side door, and she doesn't get out. I stand there, waiting, and finally she kicks her legs out of the car and stomps up the walkway to the house. I follow a bit of a distance behind.

Mary opens the door before Five gets there, and Five just slides in past her without a word. My eyes meet with Mary's and I pause for a moment, then continue up the front walk and into the house. Mary shuts the door behind me, but doesn't move.

"Is Dad here?" I ask.

"He's on his way home from work," she says.

She gives me a look I can't read before continuing into the living room. I follow. Five is sitting on the couch, her face angry and her eyes focused on the window glass like she's trying to break it with the force of her mind.

"Five," Mary says. "We need to talk."

Five says nothing, but I can see her lower lip start to tremble. Mary takes another step closer to Five.

"Five. Honey. I know you're upset, but you can't just leave like that."

"Why not?" she says, her eyes now digging into Mary. "You did." She jerks her head toward me. "She did. Why the hell can't I just run away whenever I want to? That's what people in this family do, right?"

I say nothing, just watch Mary. Her expression falters for a slight second, and then settles into steely resolve.

"You listen to me, young lady," she says. "What I did or didn't do has nothing to do with this."

Five slams her hand down on the couch. "It has everything to do with this! First you leave, and then you come back, and you make Carly leave." Tears track down her face, and her voice cracks. "Bo is the only one who loves me enough to stay around. You have no right to take him away from me, too!" She shoots a look at me. "Either of you."

The front door opens and I step back, pressing my back against the wall. Dad comes in and stands beside Mary.

"Five, go to your room," he says quietly.

"But—"

"Go!"

The room is silent, save for the reverberation of my father's voice still rattling the walls. Five's eyes widen, and she looks genuinely scared. She gets up off the couch and goes upstairs, and we all stand in silence for a long moment.

"I hope you've nailed the windows shut," I say.

Dad doesn't look at me. Mary stares at her feet. I'm two for two.

"Well," I say quietly. "I guess my work here is done."

"Carly?" Mary takes a step toward me. "It's a long drive. Do you want maybe something to drink? Or I could make you a sandwich?"

"No, thank you," I say. "I'm fine."

Dad won't look at me, just turns and goes into his office and shuts the door behind him. Mary and I stand in silence for a moment.

"Well—" I begin, motioning toward the door, but Mary interrupts me.

"Do you need a drink?" she says. "I'll tell you, right now, I could use a fucking drink."

I look at her, and for the first time, I see her. Not as my mother, the woman who abandoned me, but as Mary, a person who can't find a glue strong enough to fix what she's broken. I can relate to that. I force on a feeble smile.

"Yeah," I say. "A fucking drink sounds just about right."

Ten minutes later, we're out on the back deck, two Irish women nursing tall scotches at high noon, the way God intended.

"So . . ." I say after a while. "How's it going?"

She chuckles and takes a drink. "Super. You?"

"Great," I say. "I'm a retail clerk in an art supply store. My boss is a transgendered woman, and my landlord is her ex-wife. They're not speaking. It's really awkward. Oh, and there's a man who comes in the store twice a week and tells me to fuck off if I make eye contact. And I have a seventeen-year-old virgin giving me advice on my sex life."

Mary laughs, although her eyes still look tentative and self-conscious. "Wow. Sounds like a fun place."

"It is," I say, taking a sip of my drink. "I like it."

"I'm glad." She takes a breath and pauses, as though she's unsure if she should say what she's thinking. Eventually, though, she does. "The therapist tells me I'm not supposed to feel guilty about what happened, that I can't keep punishing myself. That I won't be any kind of help to Five if I'm not strong, if I don't hold my ground as though I have a right to be here. But between you and me . . ." She lets out a long, slow breath. "I never thought I'd tear you guys apart. I never wanted to do that."

I swim through a sea of possible responses to this, most of them reactionary and defensive. *What the hell did you think would happen?* is one. *Since when do you care about what happens to us?* is another, followed closely by its evil twin, *I thought all you cared about was yourself.* But for the first time in my memory, I'm not furious with her, and when I do speak, it's not with accusation or anger, just genuine curiosity.

"Why'd you leave?"

There's a long silence. I stare into my glass. I can't look at her, so I can't read her face. All I can see are the toes of her shoes against the pavement, still as stone.

"I thought I was a bad mother. I thought I was being selfish by staying. I thought your dad would remarry someone who was better than me. Every day I waited for a private detective or someone to show up with divorce papers, but no one ever did." Her voice cracks and grows thick, but her feet don't move. "I thought you'd be better off. I thought that someday I'd stop missing you so much. I thought I could build a new life that would fill that empty pit inside. I thought that someday I'd be able to forgive myself." She lifts her glass, gives an embittered laugh, and takes a drink. "And then I had a scare, and I realized that you people were the only important thing I'd ever done in my life."

I look up at her and see that her eyes are a little wet, but she's not crying. She's being strong. She's forcing herself to rise above it. And I understand her; I totally get what she's doing because this apple did not fall far from that tree. For better or worse, I am my mother's daughter. This realization inspires me to look into the swirly brown surface of my whiskey and down the last bit.

"I want you to know that I don't blame you for hating me," she continues, her voice calm and steady. "I understand. Part of me hates me, too. But I love you enough to be here whether you hate me or not, and I need you to know that. There is nothing you could ever say or do that will ever change how much I love you. Ever."

There is a long silence, and I don't know what to say.

I feel ripped apart inside. Part of me wants to tell her that I forgive her, to make her feel better, but I just can't.

"So," she says finally, "you're working in an art supply store, huh?"

I am taken a bit off guard by her casual tone. It's a mom tone. An I'm-concerned-about-the-direction-your-life-is-taking tone. And rather than being annoyed by it, even though I want to be, I'm comforted, even though that makes no sense.

"Yeah." I twirl my empty glass in my hands. "I'm working in an art supply store."

"And you like it in Bilby?"

"Yeah." I look up and meet her eye. "I like it in Bilby."

"And is it temporary? Or permanent?"

"I don't know," I say. "Was New Mexico temporary or permanent?"

Our eyes lock and in some unspoken way, we seem to come to an understanding, so I decide to take it down a notch.

"I don't know," I say. "I don't think it's permanent-permanent. Like forever permanent. But . . . yeah. I'm happy there. I have friends. I have a—"

I stop there, realizing that I don't know how to define Will in my life. I'm not ready to define Will in my life. I'm not ready to wonder whether Bilby is my life derailed or on track. I'm not ready for this conversation, not with Mary or anyone else, so I do the one thing I'm always ready to do.

"I'm gonna walk this off," I say, putting my glass on

the table and standing up, "and then I've got a long drive back to Bilby."

Mary holds her hand up to shade her eyes, and smiles at me. "Okay."

I nod. "Okay."

"We're all having dinner on Sunday," she says, standing up. "I hope you'll come."

I stare at her, and I have to allow a grudging respect. Tables turned, I don't know if I'd have the nerve to ask her to dinner. "Seriously?"

"Yes, seriously." She gives me a slight smile. "Please come. Seven o'clock."

I look at her for a long moment, then nod my head. "Okay."

She reaches out and squeezes my hand. "Thank you."

I don't know what she's thanking me for, but I squeeze her hand back and release it, then walk toward the gate. I wander around the old neighborhood for a while, spending some time on the swings at my elementary school, and then, when I feel strong again, I head back and get in my car for the long drive home.

It's midafternoon when I get back to Bilby. I trudge back to my cabin and sit alone for a while, thinking about everything. And nothing. My thoughts are mixed. I worry about Five, and then wonder where Eloise Tucker ended up. I marvel at the fact that I can't remember the last time I watched television, and I wonder if Dad will ever speak to me again. My nerves are jumbled, and I want to pace, but only crazy people pace alone in their living rooms, and I've decided I don't want to be crazy anymore. I leave my cabin and knock on Will's door, but there's no answer. I am both disappointed and relieved. I want to see him, but I don't have the energy to Talk, and after the way I've treated him, I fear we need a Talk. I hop down off his porch and follow the path to Brandy's house. I ring the doorbell, and in a severe act of cosmic kindness, it doesn't zap me.

Brandy answers the door a second later, and her face is awash in sympathy.

"Will told me about your sister," she says. "Are you okay?"

"Pffft. Fine," I lie. "I was just feeling kinda antsy and I thought maybe we could . . . you know. Have some tea or something? Do you have any of that chamomile? I think I could use being knocked out by that again."

She smiles and steps back, allowing me passage into the house. I wander over to her workstation and stare quietly at her current quilt in progress, a funky piece with shards of orange and brown seeming to explode out from the center. Brandy goes into the kitchen to put the water on, then comes back with a platter full of Pepperidge Farm cookies.

"I thought we could use a treat," she says as she sets it on the coffee table.

"Mmmm," I say, then look back at the quilt. "This is really neat."

"Oh. Thanks," she says, crossing her arms over her stomach and cocking her head to the side as if trying to study it from a new angle. "It belongs to a man. Or a woman. I haven't met them yet." She crinkles her nose and levels her head. "Although I'm looking forward to it. Whoever it is is a real spitfire." Her eyes glaze over as she continues to stare. "Wanda."

"Hmmm?"

She continues to stare. "She's pregnant."

"Wow," I say. Two months ago, I would have had to fight not to roll my eyes. Now, I'm sending a small prayer to the Universe for this Wanda to have an easy pregnancy. I sit down in Brandy's rocking chair and she settles on the couch, nudging the platter of cookies at me. I reach over and take one to be polite, but end up just playing with it in my fingers. I don't really feel like eating.

"So," Brandy says. "Do you want to talk about it or talk around it? Because I'm great at both."

"Are you ever going to forgive her?" I raise my head suddenly. Looks like I'm going to do both.

Brandy sits back and takes a deep breath. She doesn't pretend she doesn't know who I'm talking about, and I respect her for that.

"I already have," she says, then raises guilty eyes to me. "Okay. Well, we both know that's a lie. Progress is slow, but I think I'm making it. I'm not angry anymore. I was, at first. I felt like, all those times he told me he loved me, that it was just a lie. I've never felt so betrayed in my life. When you trust someone with your whole heart and they give it back to you in bits and pieces, it can be really . . . upsetting."

"Yeah. I've heard that."

"You know what's strange?" she says suddenly. "I forgive him. But I don't know if I can forgive her." She stares at me as though the realization is just hitting her at this moment. "We manage to avoid each other pretty well, but every now and again I see her at the grocery store or something, and I think, 'This is the woman who took my husband away from me.' Is that crazy? It feels like he's dead and she killed him."

"Do you ever wonder what it would be like if you could forgive her? Do you think it would be like having him back, or would it be . . . ?" I can't verbalize what I'm thinking, but the curiosity within me is burning.

"I'll never have him back," she says quietly.

"But . . . do you ever wonder what it would be like? If, somehow, you could get past it and be friends? If, when you needed her, she was there?"

Brandy watches me for a long time, her brow furrowed and her eyes so sad that I can't believe she's not crying.

"No," she says finally. Then the kettle whistles and she goes into the kitchen to make the tea.

Brandy and I spend a good two hours talking around everything, and it's nice. The effects of the chamomile tea hit me quick and hard, but I'm enjoying Brandy's company so much that I push through it, and when I finally head back to my cabin, I'm wide-awake. Will's car isn't parked in his usual spot, and when I pass by his cabin, it's dark, so I head to my own cabin and flick on the lights. The first thing that catches my eye is the quilt, lying in a bundle on my couch where I left it this morning. I walk over to it and pick it up in my arms, running my hands over the images sewn in. All the little blue boxes, keeping everything separate.

I walk into my room. Five didn't bother making the bed—big surprise—so I do, pulling the sheets and bedspread up tight, then flashing the quilt out over the top. As the quilt settles over the bed, I experience a sudden understanding of how much time and energy and material and heart goes into each one of these things, and I am profoundly touched and humbled that Brandy gave this one to me. She made it twelve years ago, and saved it for me, and gave it to me without asking for anything in return. She does it because it's what she's supposed to be doing, and she knows what she's supposed to be doing. It's amazing and humbling. For a moment, I get a glimpse of what it must be like to have real faith, to trust that what's meant to be will come, and what's not won't.

"Wow," I whisper to myself. Then I get ready for bed, crawl under my quilt, and fall into a dark and restful sleep.

"Hi. My name's Carly. I'm an idiot. Can I come in?"

Will is looking at me through his screen door. He's wearing flannel lounge pants and a white T-shirt that says "Visualize World Peas" with a bunch of little Earths lined up in a pea pod. He has one eye open and his hair is going everywhere, and he's absolutely adorable.

"What time is it?"

"Eight thirty." I hold up the drink carrier and white bakery bag in my hand. "I come bearing gifts."

He smiles and steps back, holding the screen door open with one hand and running the other through his hair. I move into the cabin and set the coffee and doughnuts on his table, then turn to face him.

"Will, I'm so sorry. I know I acted like—"

He holds up his hand to stop me. "Carly, don't worry about—"

"No," I say firmly. "I practiced this speech. You're going to hear it."

A smile creeps over his face and he raises his eyebrows in surprise. "You practiced? For me?"

"I practiced," I say, pulling out a chair and motioning for him to sit. "For you."

Will laughs and sits down. I open up the bakery bag and hold it out to him.

"Double-chocolate doughnut?"

He shakes his head. "Not right now. What's for coffee, though?"

I give him a cup. "Peppermint mocha. Allegra went easy on me today."

I pull one out of the carrier and hand it to him, dramatically clearing my throat as I stand before him. He laughs and sips the coffee.

"Okay. Where was I? I'm an idiot. I'm so sorry . . . Oh. Yes." I snap my fingers, stand before him, back straight. "I acted like a big tool. I have this history of closing myself off when things get real and emotional, and I know it's wrong." I soften my stance a little, and I can feel my smile fading. "I don't want to do that with you. I want to not screw this up."

I can't believe it. I actually said sincerely what I meant. Yay me.

He puts his coffee down and reaches out to take my hands in his. "You didn't screw up. You weren't an idiot. I'm just glad you're okay."

"So, you weren't out last night getting drunk and finding an emotionally healthy woman?" He looks at me like I'm crazy. Which, I guess, is fair. I shrug and look at my hands. "I looked for you twice. You weren't here."

He laughs. "Why didn't you just call my cell phone?"

"Pffft," I say, throwing my hands up in the air. "Because then I would look pathetic and insecure, and if you were out with an emotionally healthy woman, you'd have her to compare me to and I would inevitably come up short." I pause. "That made a lot more sense in my head last night."

He tucks a finger under my chin and makes me look at him. "A slot opened up at the darkroom I use in Douglas. The guy there called me, so I went over and got some proof sheets done. I didn't get home until two."

"Oh, man," I say. "I'm sorry, and here I am waking you up at the crack of dawn . . ."

"It's okay," he says, a smile playing on his lips. "I like you waking me up at the crack of dawn."

I raise one eyebrow at him, and he laughs.

"So, are we okay?" I ask.

"I think so," he says, looking up at me with a mystified expression on his face. "Are we? I mean, are you? That was a lot to deal with. And seeing your parents . . . how was that?"

"It was great," I say, forcing a wide grin. "It was a big party. Loads of fun."

"You know, we can talk about it seriously if you want to," he says.

"Can we not talk about it seriously if I don't want to?"

Will shrugs and smiles at me. "Sure. I just want you to know that if you need a shoulder or anything . . ."

"Thank you." I lean down to kiss him lightly on the lips, but he reaches for me and pulls me onto his lap. He tastes like peppermint mocha and his touch blazes through me and we're going from zero to sixty so fast it's making me a little dizzy.

But I like it.

After a moment he pulls back, looks at me with heavy-lidded eyes.

"If you need us to slow down . . ." he begins, but I shake my head.

"I don't. Do you?"

He closes his eyes and laughs. "I don't know." He opens his eyes and touches my hair. "It's not too soon?"

"Well," I say. "We're both adults. We're both healthy. Right?"

He laughs. "Yeah."

"And I have condoms in my purse, so . . ."

"You do?" He grins. "I thought only men did that, carried condoms around."

I quirk a brow at him. "I like to be prepared."

"I like you prepared," he says, and pulls me in for another kiss. A few minutes later, he lifts me up and carries me to the bed—which, luckily, is only a few feet away—and we proceed to have a lovely morning. We laugh and tease and play, and when we get down to it, everything works pretty darn well for a first time.

The second time? It works great.

Afterward, we lie in bed together with his head on my stomach, and my heart is so full of him that there's no room for the worries I usually have at this point in my relationships about the myriad ways in which it can all go horribly, horribly wrong. All I can see right now is him, and all I can feel is how happy he has made me, and this is about as close to a perfect moment as I've ever had in my life.

Yay me.

Chapter Ten

"Mr. Trimble called for a delivery," Janesse says as I walk into the store. The bells that hang from the front door aren't even done jingling when she stuffs a box of charcoals in my hand. "He lives out on Pinewood Trail."

I glance down at the box. There's a sticky note tacked to it with the address, the total price with tax (as if I didn't have it memorized), and a smiley face that reads, "Good luck." When I look back up, Janesse is still smiling.

I hand it back to her. "Funny joke."

She gives me a massive grin. "No joke, babyface. He hurt his ankle or something, and we're going to need to deliver for a while."

"Oh," I say, laughing, "and I suppose he actually told you that?"

"He has a surprisingly nice phone manner. I think it must just be eye contact that throws him off."

My heart seizes as it begins to dawn on me that this might not be a joke. She really wants me to go to Mr. Trimble's house. She can't be serious.

She looks at me and raises one expectant eyebrow. She's serious.

"No way," I say. "It's your store. You deliver it."

"All the more reason why I don't do the deliveries," she says, turning her back on me and heading toward the counter. "Wouldn't be good for my image."

I follow her and put the box down on the counter. "I don't get paid enough to deliver."

"I'll give you an extra ten bucks," she says. "Now you get paid enough."

I stare at her, nibble at my lip. "He creeps me out."

"We don't discriminate against creepy." She raises her eyes. "You don't expect me to discriminate against creepy, do you? How would that look, me, a black woman who used to have a dick, if I start discriminating against anyone, even the creepy ones?"

"*Janeeeeessssse*," I whine, nudging the box across the counter at her. "He's gonna hack me into pieces and bury me in the yard. I know you; if he hacks me into pieces, you're gonna feel really bad."

She nudges the box back. "He's harmless. Rude, weird, and a little crazy, but harmless. He's not going to hack you into pieces. Just bring him the box, take the money, he'll tell you to fuck off, and you come back. Stop being such a baby."

I stare down at the box, then raise my eyes to hers.

"I'll rock-paper-scissors you for it. Best two out of three?"

She stares back, saying nothing. For a long moment we lock eyes across the counter. Then, finally, I snatch the box off the counter and head toward the door.

"This was starting out to be such a good day," I mutter as I push out of the shop, bells jingling behind me.

Pinewood Trail is on the very edge of Bilby, even more the middle of nowhere than regular Bilby, and Trimble's house is at the end of a long, winding driveway. When I finally get there, it looks like exactly the kind of place a Mr. Trimble-type would live. It's small, vaguely shack-like, and isolated. I step out of my car and walk the dusty trail to the house, which has beige aluminum siding and a plain, black-shingled peak roof and is not really scary so much as . . . unsettling. As I make my way to the door, I find myself thinking about the Unabomber. It's *that* kind of unsettling.

When I step up on the tiny wooden porch, I see that the door is slightly ajar, which gives me pause for knocking, because I don't want to inadvertently open it more. I search the doorframe for a bell, but, of course, there is none. Finally, I tuck the box of charcoals under my arm, hold onto the door knob and knock lightly so it doesn't open any more. I wait. Nothing. I knock again. I hear some sounds of shuffling coming from inside, and then Mr. Trimble's voice yell, "Come on in already!"

Well, it isn't his standard refrain, but I'm still convinced Janesse really isn't paying me enough. I nudge the door open a bit and poke my head in.

"Mr. Trimble? It's Carly. From Art's Desire? With the charcoals?"

My eyes adjust to the limited light. Mr. Trimble's little hovel is about as spartan as anything I've ever seen. The main room consists of a kitchenette in one corner and an easy chair in the other. That's it. Mr. Trimble isn't in the main room, which, based on the very tininess of the hovel, means he's behind one of the two doors in the east wall that I assume lead to a bedroom and a bathroom. I'm constructing my new salary demands to Janesse in my head when I notice the west wall. Unable to stop myself, I step inside, moving closer to the wall. It was white, originally, but now it's covered with a delicately shaded charcoal drawing.

It's the main drag of Bilby, as viewed through the front window of Art's Desire. There's the Café, the Town Bookie, and the post office, all drawn faithfully down to the crack in the sidewalk next to the stop sign. Allegra is serving coffee to a skeptical patron, who sniffs it with a suspicious look on his face. Sebastian and James are walking arm in arm, gossiping. Gladys is yelling at Mack. Some townspeople I recognize but whose names I don't recall are walking in front of the Art's Desire window, parts of their bodies obscured by the hand-painted Art's Desire logo, reading backward the way it does when you're inside the store.

Outside of the front door of Art's Desire is Janesse, who appears to be showing a little boy how to dance. Brandy watches her, and Janesse doesn't notice. I am standing next to Brandy, my head resting on her shoulder as I comfort her. Down on the corner, Will stands at an easel, watching me slyly while he paints.

Mr. Trimble is nowhere in the picture. And yet, he's everywhere. This is how he sees us, and he sees so much. He sees Janesse's incredible spirit. He sees Brandy's heartbreak. He sees Allegra forcing weird coffee concoctions on people, and he sees Will and me.

I step back to take it all in. The drawing is sad and evocative, yet oddly hopeful and loving. It says so much about this man, and yet I'm besieged by a thousand questions. How does this happen? How does a man whose entire social vocabulary consists of "fuck" and "off" draw something so sensitive and insightful? And why on the wall? Where did he come from? How did he end up here? What happened to him to bring him to this place in life? Was he ever young, and hopeful, and imagining great things for his future? Who is he, and what does this town mean to him?

This would make a great documentary is the thought trailing in my head as I hear a door open behind me. Mr. Trimble is on crutches, and his left ankle is in a cast.

"Mr. Trimble," I say. "Oh, my God. What happened?"

He reaches into his pocket and pulls out a small envelope. I walk over to him and he stuffs the envelope in my hand. I can hear the change rattling inside, and I know without checking that it's exactly four dollars and eighty-six cents. I look at him, those beady eyes under the tremendous, bushy gray eyebrows, and see him for the first time as a person. A fascinating, full, complete, really unusual person.

And I want to tell his story. I want to get a camera

crew and a laptop with editing equipment. I want to talk to the guy at the independent station and get that job. I am filled with excitement and purpose, and I can't help but smile.

"This is amazing," I say, pointing behind me to the wall. "How long have you been working on it?"

He stares at me for a while, his eyes boring into mine, as if evaluating whether I'm worth talking to or not. Then, finally, he snatches the box of charcoals from my hand.

"Fuck off!" He turns around, hobbles back into what I presume to be his bedroom, and slams the door, leaving me speechless in his living room, clutching his four dollars and eighty-six cents in my hand.

"Well," I say to myself as I turn to leave. "Might have to be a documentary for a cable network."

When I get home that night, Will is at his car, loading his trunk with a duffel bag and his photography equipment. I sigh, and step out of my car.

"Going somewhere?" I call out to him as I shut my door.

He smiles, slams his trunk shut, and walks over to me.

"Hey," he says. "I was waiting for you to come home."

I raise an eyebrow toward his packed car. "So you could leave?"

He throws a regretful glance back at his car, then reaches for my hand. "So I could talk to you before I leave. I didn't want you to come home to a note on your door. Not after this morning." He raises my hand to his lips and kisses it. "I got a call from an old friend who needs me to do her wedding. She's getting married up in Flagstaff on Saturday and her photographer punked out on her and she's freaking out, so I'm going up there for the weekend."

"Oh, so it's not that this morning was so terrifying that you're running away, then?"

He shakes his head, keeping his eyes on mine. "No. It's not that at all."

"Good to know."

He leans down and gives me a sweet, lingering kiss, and when he pulls back, he looks a little nervous.

"Actually . . ." he begins, then laughs. "It might be too early for this, so feel free to say no if you're not comfortable, but I was thinking it might be fun if you came with me. Esther is putting me up at her bed-and-breakfast, and it's beautiful up there—"

I quirk a brow at him. "Esther? Esther's the bride?"

"She's sixty-seven. Used to run the restaurant where I worked when I was going to NAU. It's her fourth wedding." He reaches up and tucks a bit of hair behind my ear. "So, what do you think?"

"I'm not going to judge her," I say. "I hear the fourth time's a charm."

"No, I mean . . . I was trying to ask you if you'd come with me. For the weekend."

I stare at him for a moment. A long moment. I can't say anything, I'm totally frozen, although I don't know why. Part of me is screaming, "Hell, yes!" and the rest of me is hesitant and all that shows is the hesitation. Will smiles and squeezes my hand.

"You're right. It's too early. I totally understand."

"No," I say finally. "It's just that . . . my mother invited me to dinner with the family on Sunday, and I kind of think I should go to that."

That's not the real reason I'm hesitating, but since I don't know what the real reason is, I figure this will do. Will's face washes over with understanding, and he reaches up to touch my face.

"Wow," he says. "That's a big deal. Yeah, you should definitely do that." He puts his hands on my shoulders, his fingers cradling my face, gives me a soft kiss, then rests his forehead against mine.

"So, I'll see you again when? Monday?"

"Yeah," I say. "I'll probably stay overnight in Tucson and come back Monday."

He pulls back and looks in my eyes. "Let's do something Monday, then. I have a job next week, leaving Tuesday afternoon, so we'll have to make the most of Monday."

He kisses me again, a kiss with intent, a kiss that means there will be many, many more where this one came from, then pulls back.

"I have to go," he says.

"Okay," I say.

He gives me one more swift kiss, and then heads to his car. I watch him drive off, waving as he turns out of sight just in case he's looking back at me in his rearview. Then I head down the path to my cabin, find the paper with the name and phone number of the guy from the independent station. To my surprise, he's there. To my greater surprise, he books an interview with me for Monday morning.

———

My alarm goes off on Saturday morning, and I get up and trudge out to the coffeemaker, just like every other morning. What's not like every other morning is the movement on my couch, which I catch out of the corner of my eye. I scream and my heart does a break dance as I lose my footing and fall backward, knocking over my hall table and sending the Cochise County phone book skidding across the room.

Brandy sits on my couch, staring at me, patiently waiting for me to be done with my little display.

"Good morning," she says.

"Good . . . good . . . good *morning*?" I say, pushing myself up from the floor. "Hey, Brandy, do you even *have* boundaries, because—"

"I'm going to forgive him." She takes a deep breath and meets my eyes, and I can see how serious she is, that this is a big moment for her, and I give her a gentle smile.

"I'll make some coffee." I set the hall table upright, put the phone book back, and continue on to the coffee-maker. We are silent for a few moments while I putter, and then I settle into my ugly orange easy chair, and Brandy starts talking.

"I woke up last night," she says, her eyes still on her hands. "It was, I don't know. Two, maybe? And I couldn't get back to sleep. I had this pattern in my head. It was kind of wild; all these bright colors, waving around like ribbons over a deep purple background. Weird. So, I started to sketch it, and as I was sketching it, I started to get these impressions. Images. And I realized." She raises her head. "It's for him."

"Oh." I am unsure of what to say, so I continue with the equally insightful, "Wow."

"I've never had a quilt come to me for anyone I already knew," she says. "It's always strangers. Always. I can't do one for myself or anyone I love because I'm too close. But this was so clear. I don't want it to be for him, but it is." She blinks hard. "And I think maybe it's a little for me, too."

"Wow," I say again. "Okay. Brandy, I think that's great. Maybe you should call her and tell her?"

"No." She stands up. "I have a process. I have to go with that. You probably won't be seeing me much in the next week. I'm going to try and push through this as fast as I can. But I was wondering if . . ." She pauses, staring at some point in space for a moment before returning her eyes to me. "I was wondering if you wouldn't mind being there? When I do the reading for him?"

I stand up and walk with her to the door. "Um. Yeah. Sure, Brandy. If you need me. But . . . isn't that kind of personal? Shouldn't you two be alone so you can talk?"

She shakes her head, then shrugs. "Maybe. But I don't know if I can do this without someone there to make me see it through, you know?"

"Yep." I smile and reach out to squeeze her hand. "I'll be there."

Brandy starts for the door, then turns back to me. "Don't say anything to him." She rolls her eyes at herself. "*Her.* I still might chicken out, and if I do . . ."

"You got it."

She smiles and then goes out the door. My coffee-maker gurgles in the background as I poke my head out of my cabin and watch her make her way along the rock path, then disappear into the foliage.

I almost turn around and go back to Bilby four times on my way to Tucson. After I check into the hotel, I twice pick up the phone to call my family and cancel. And twice I hang up without dialing. It occurs to me that it's probably situations like these that turn regular people into Mr. Trimbles, and if I don't face it head-on, I will just be a hop, skip, and a shack away from being some small town's "fuck off" lady. This motivation gets me all the way to my father's front door. I'm deciding between knocking on the door and running away when it opens, and Mary smiles down at me.

"Your car's been out there for a while," she says. "I thought you might be getting cold."

"No, I'm fine," I say, although my voice is a little shaky and I feel just a bit like I'm going to fall over.

"Well, as long as you're here, why don't you come inside?"

She steps back to allow me passage. I hand her the bottle of wine I've been clutching in my hand. She takes it and smiles.

"This will go perfectly with the roast," she says. "Thank you."

"No problem." I clear my throat. "So. Where are Ella and Five?"

"They ran out to get some whipped cream for the pie," she says. "I was going to whip my own, but then the beater broke, so . . ." She trails off. "Well."

"Yeah."

There's a long silence. Then Mary lifts up the bottle. "I'm going to open this and let it breathe a bit." She motions vaguely toward Dad's office door. "Your father is in there. Maybe you could . . . ?"

She lets the question hang in the air. My heart clutches in my chest.

"Yeah," I say. "Okay."

She puts her hand on my shoulder, gives a small squeeze, and then heads for the kitchen. I swallow hard and will my feet to carry me to Dad's office. They resist for a while, but finally give in. I knock gently on the door.

"Dad?"

There's a long pause, then a gruff, "Come in."

I push the door open to find Dad sitting on his brown leather sofa, staring into a glass of scotch. I step inside and close the door gently behind me, leaning against it. My heart is beating wildly against my chest and my face is hot, and I know that neither one of us is leaving this room until this whole thing between us is resolved. Which, when you consider the fact that we're both Irish, could take a while.

He clears his throat, holds up the scotch, and glances in my direction, but not directly at me.

"Can I get you something to drink?"

"No, thanks."

He nods, continues to stare into his scotch. It's a long time before he starts talking, but when he does, his voice is strong and clear.

"When your mother left . . ." There is a long pause. I can see that this is hard for him, so I wait silently until he starts up again. "When all that happened, I was a lost man. My life had been pulled out from under me, and I was left flat on my back, thinking, 'What the hell just happened?'" He pauses again and I wonder if I'm supposed to say something. I hope not, because I have no idea what I should say. Eventually, he starts talking again. "I felt like I had failed, because I didn't know how badly she was hurting. I thought it was just a phase, just a typical postpartum thing, and she'd snap out of it. I didn't know. A better husband, he would have known."

He takes a drink, and we both breathe for a bit before he goes on.

"My whole life, I've only ever loved one woman. I know you think I shouldn't forgive her, that I should turn her away. Maybe you're right. Maybe, because of you kids, maybe that's my responsibility, that's what I should do to protect you." He raises his eyes to mine. They look tired, and sad, but at the same time there's something new, some brand of contentment that wasn't there before. "But the fact is, Carly, if she left tomorrow, I'd wait another seventeen years for her to come back, and when she did, I'd be glad to have her. You can call me stupid, and you'd be right, but that's what I'd do. I can't explain it, and I can't justify it. It's just the way it is. I'd forgive her anything, and if that makes me a stupid man, then I guess I'm a stupid man."

I take a deep breath to clear the emotion choking me before I speak. "You're not stupid."

He makes a dismissive sound, waves his hand at me, and looks at the wall.

"I'm sorry you had to grow up so fast. I'm sorry that I put you through that, and I'm sorry that I can't make this easy and choose between you." He turns his face to me and his voice grows hoarse. "But I can't."

I can feel myself in the eye of a hurricane of emotion. I know that I have a choice. I can either stay where I am and remain in the middle of it, calm and strong and un-bowed, or I can step into it and let the storm hit. I take one step toward my father and I feel a sob punch through me, but I keep walking.

"You don't have to choose," I squeak out. "I'm sorry, Daddy. I don't want to make you choose."

"You have always been such a strong little thing," he says quietly. "I always wondered where you got that from."

"I think," I say slowly, "it was my dad."

He raises his eyes to mine, and I can see the hurt and sadness there, and I realize that he has no idea what kind of man he really is. He thinks he's weak, and merely human, like the rest of us.

He has no idea.

"Remember when Aunt Kathy wanted to move in?"

He looks at me, his eyebrows quirking a bit. "No."

I laugh. "I do. It was right after Mom left, and she came down and gave you this big speech about how we needed a woman in the house and you couldn't do it alone. And you said, 'These are my girls.' " I swallow hard and smile at him. "That's it. 'These are my girls.' And when you said that, I knew that you would jump in front of a train before you'd ever let anyone take us from you."

I am unable to say anything else. I am unable to tell him how much that one moment meant to me, how the certainty of his devotion to us made it so much easier to go on without her. He reaches out for my hand, and I give it to him, settling next to him on the couch. I understand now that he's not mad at me. He was never mad at me. He was just confused and hurt, like the rest of us.

"I love you, Angel," he says. "You know that. Always."

"I know, Daddy."

He pulls me into a hug and I smoosh my face against his strong shoulder, the way I did when I was a little girl. There's a light knock on the door, and we break apart, both of us swiping at our faces. Mary steps in, and her eyes widen when she sees us.

"I'm sorry," she says, starting to back out.

"It's okay," I say. She steps back into the room and looks at me questioningly, then smiles at my father. There's more than kindness there, more than guilt or a desire for redemption. There's some kind of connection in their eyes as they look at each other that I don't understand, but I think I'd very much like to.

Someday.

"The roast ready?" I ask.

She turns her smile on me. "When you are. Five and Ella are back. But we can wait . . ."

"No." I smile at Dad. "We're ready."

We follow out behind her, arm in arm, and find Ella and Five in the dining room. When Five sees me, she jumps up from the table and gives me a hug.

"I dumped Botox," she says.

I pull back from the hug. "Really?"

She nods and rolls her eyes. "He was a jerk anyway."

I smile. "I'll get that story later?"

She nods, and we all take our seats. Dad is at the head of the table, Mary next to him, and I am next to Mary. We have just finished saying grace when I shoot a look across the table to Ella.

"So, where's Greg tonight?" I ask casually.

She smiles. "He had an emergency."

Five raises an eyebrow as she passes the potatoes to Ella. "They have emergency eye lifts?"

"No." Ella gives Five an unamused look. "It's a pro bono thing. He's on call this week for Tucson General. There was a woman who got in a car accident, and he's helping put her face back all nice and pretty."

"Oh," I say. "Good for him."

"Yeah, but . . ." She pauses, bites her lip, and smiles. "We had something we wanted to tell you tonight."

Mary claps her hands together. "You're buying that house down the street!" She puts her hand on Dad's arm. "I told you they were going to buy it."

Ella opens her mouth, but Dad holds up his hand. "No. It's that Greg's finally opening up his own practice, isn't it? He was asking me about potential office space last week."

Five and I exchange a glance and she pushes back from the table. "I'll get the kitty."

Dad reaches into his pocket and puts a ten on the table. Mary gets up.

"My purse is in the hallway," she says, calling behind her. "Don't say a word until I get back."

Ella lets out a big sigh. "Telling this family anything is never a simple process."

"Yeah," I say, forking a slice of roast, "but it's always lucrative."

Five and Mary return to the table. Dad sticks his ten in the kitty and hands it to Mary, who puts a twenty in. I reach into my pocket and pull out a five.

"You're knocked up," I say.

Ella stares at me in total disbelief and I laugh.

"Holy shit," I say. "You're knocked up?"

"Don't say 'holy shit' at the table," Dad admonishes.

"Goddamn it," Five says, tossing a handful of ones on the table. "I didn't even get a chance to guess!"

Dad turns to Mary. "I swear, I didn't raise them to talk like that at the table."

I reach over and grab Ella's wineglass. "What are you doing drinking wine, Preggo Girl?"

"I didn't drink any, but if I didn't let Mom pour it, you all would have gotten suspicious and I wanted it to be a surprise, which it would have been if Carly hadn't ruined it!"

"I didn't ruin anything," I say. "I was totally kidding. What happened to your whole 'at least a year before babies' thing?"

Ella rolls her eyes and sips her water. "You know. Things . . . happen. And it's still early. I peed on the stick this morning and it was just barely two lines but . . ." A grin takes over her face. "I'm pretty sure."

"Wow," I say, and we all fall into silence.

Then Dad raises his glass.

"Well," he says, "I think this calls for a toast."

Four hours later, I say good-bye to my family with a promise to come back the following week for Christmas, and the following month to help Ella shop for baby things. As I head toward my car, my winnings tucked in my pocket, I feel happy and at peace.

There's going to be a new generation. God help the little monkey.

Chapter Eleven

The independent station in Tucson is a small outfit, tucked in the middle of a nondescript industrial park on the north side. The interior is nice—pink walls, funky plants in the corners, and sconces lighting the hallway down which Robert Jenkins leads me to his office, which is a mess. Which is good. I learned a long time ago that anyone with a neat office was not to be trusted. He clears off some space on his desk to put a notepad, and I sit across from him. He explains that the position is freelance at this time, but they're working on securing a grant to produce a regular show covering all of Arizona. He tells me that the current working title is *Inside Arizona*, and I get a tingle when he says it. I spontaneously start talking about Bilby, about the artists, and the concept of being Towered, and how the whole town was Towered when the mines dried up, and it rebuilt itself into this thriving artist community. He leans forward with animation as I talk, and he says it's exactly the kind of thing they're looking for. He takes my resume and my tape, and tells me he'll give me a call soon.

I head down the hall after our interview with a huge smile on my face. I can't help but feel like I'm exactly where I need to be, exactly when I need to be there. I like the feeling. It's peaceful, yet a little buzzy.

"Carly!"

My hand is on the front door when I hear my name, and I turn to see Christopher heading toward me. I am surprised by how happy I am to see him, and I run to him, throwing my arms around his neck as he lifts me up into a big hug.

"What are you doing here?" I ask as he lands me on my feet again.

"I started last week. Had to take a pay cut, but it beats news by a mile." We share an eye roll: *News.* "Rob told me you'd be coming in today. I'm glad I didn't miss you."

"Yeah," I say. "Me, too. How are you?"

He thinks on this for a second, then gives me a smiling nod. "I'm good. You?"

I smile back. "I'm good."

"Good." He raises one eyebrow. "How about hungry? You hungry?"

Going to the Taco Shack with Christopher is both so familiar and so surreal that, as I sit at the white outdoor picnic bench waiting for him to return with my carne asada, I almost feel as though we've gone back in time, as if nothing ever happened or changed between us.

Christopher puts our food on the table and sits down across from me.

"So," he says. "Word on the street is you've got someone now. Someone you're seeing."

There's no tension or conflict in his face, so I pretend it is six months ago.

"Don't mess around, Christopher," I say, smiling. "Get right to it, there's no need for small talk."

He laughs and picks at his burrito, then looks up at me.

"No, it's good. I'm happy for you. If you're happy, I'm happy." He shrugs and casually sips his soda. "Besides, I'm totally over you."

"Oh," I say. "Well, good."

"Yeah. I'm lying."

I give him an exasperated look, and he laughs.

"I'm getting over it," he says. "I'm moving past it. I'll admit, when I found out you were coming in for an interview, I had a minor freak-out. Then I thought, it's not worth it. It's not worth not being friends with you. So I'm thinking: do-over."

I quirk an eyebrow at him. "Do-over?"

He raises his eyes to mine. "Yeah. You know. Like in kickball when you're a kid. You kick at the ball, you miss or break a window or something, you call do-over, and it's like it never happened. Everything goes back to the way it was." He squints in the sunlight and cocks his head to the side as he looks at me. "So, you know, if you're up for it, I'm thinking do-over."

I feel a smile spread over my face. "Yeah. I'm up for it."

"Good." He smiles and holds up his index finger. "But not yet. I have something to take care of first." He reaches into his coat and pulls out the *Jane Eyre*. He sets it on the table, takes a deep breath, and slides it across the table at me. "You should have this. I know it's weird, I know I've put seven years of angst and meaning into it, but I want it to just be . . . you know. A present. A little token. No big deal."

I put my hand on the book and draw it toward me, my mind suddenly flashing back to that first day at Brandy's. I see her kneeling over my quilt, hear her voice in my head.

Accept the book with the amber spine.

"Wow," I whisper. I can feel tears forming in my eyes, but I don't bother blinking them away. "Thank you."

"Okay." He holds up his wrist, checking his watch. "All right. The do-over officially starts . . . now."

He puts his wrist down.

"So, Car, that's a very cool book. Where'd you get it?"

I run my fingers over the cover, then look up and smile at him. "My best friend gave it to me."

He raises his eyebrows and takes a bite of his burrito.

"You're a lucky girl," he says, his mouth full.

I laugh. "That depends on who you talk to."

He swallows and laughs. *"Ba-doo-boom-chaaa."*

"Ba-doo-boom-chaaa," I say back.

On the drive back to Bilby, I am feeling strong and happy. I feel like even though things aren't perfect, they're right. Exactly how they're supposed to be. I am full of this feeling when my phone rings, and it's Rob Jenkins asking me if I'm interested in taking on an assignment about a herpetologist from the U of A who's doing a study on bullfrogs.

"Then, when that's done, I think we should sit down and talk about that Bilby idea," he says.

"And I was thinking that maybe I could feature you in the piece, you know, if we move forward with it?"

Will and I are naked, lying in my bed. My head is resting on his shoulder and we're both staring up at the ceiling.

"Why would you want to do that?" he asks. "I mean, isn't that a conflict of interest?"

"Not really," I say. "We could do a disclosure or something. Somehow. Anyway." I roll over and push up on my elbows and look down at him. "I think people should see your work. See what you do. It's so amazing. You're so talented. Maybe it'll open something up for you."

Will's eyebrows knit. "Like what?"

"Like . . . I don't know. Maybe get you a showing in a gallery, or something."

He sighs and pushes up off the bed, reaching around on the floor for his boxers. "I don't think so."

I sit up in bed, still giddy from the job and the day and the good sex. "But you're so good. Your work should be somewhere else, somewhere aside from the Café. Somewhere where people can see it, you know?"

Will shrugs and pulls on his jeans. "I'm not really into that anymore."

"But . . . why not? I mean, the exposure could be great. Why wouldn't you want that?"

He runs his hand through his hair. I can see the tension on his face, but I don't understand it until he speaks.

"Because I had that, Carly. I had it, and I failed, and that's it. It's done. I'm a photographer who paints a bit, not the other way around, and I'd like to just drop it, okay?"

He says it less like a question and more like a command. I deflate back onto the bed.

"Yeah," I say. "Sure. Okay. I'm sorry."

He sits quietly for a moment, then releases a long sigh. "No." He walks around to my side of the bed and sits next to me. "I'm sorry. And thank you. I love that you see all that potential in me." He leans down and kisses the tip of my nose. "I'm really happy for you, that you're getting this job. It's great to see you so excited about something."

He smiles, but there's a tinge of sadness in his eyes. I take his hand in mine.

"Am I missing something? Does one of us have cancer? What's with the gloom?"

"Nothing. I just . . . I'll miss you when you go back."

I feel my stomach wrench into a knot. I hadn't brought that up yet.

Will looks at his hands. "So, you are going."

"Well," I say. "It's a lot of work, a lot of long days. It's just . . . it's a really long commute. And Christopher told me about one of the girls in traffic who has an extra room in her house she'd rent me for a while. And, you know, Christmas is a week from Thursday and I'd kind of like to be with my family for that."

"Yeah. It makes sense." Will pulls on a smile and looks at me, his blue eyes digging into mine, looking for something and apparently not finding it. "I'm happy for you, you know. I think it's great that you're working things out with your family, and you're back together with your friend."

There's something strange in his expression, and I grab his hand. "Wait. Christopher and I aren't *together* together. You know it's not like that, right?"

"I know." He leans over and kisses me on the forehead. "I'm beat. It was a long weekend. I think I'm gonna go back to my place and get some sleep, okay?"

"Yeah," I say. "Okay."

I watch him as he puts on his T-shirt and jacket. Before he leaves, he leans over me and gives me a sweet, long, lingering kiss, and even though I try not to read too much into it, it feels a lot like a good-bye kiss.

The next morning, I call the girl in traffic and she says I can move in on Friday. I call Rob Jenkins, and we decide I'll report to the station first thing Monday morning for a quick confab before the holiday. He asks if I have a preference for a photog, and I say that Christopher and I always made a good team. When I hang up the phone, I feel weird. Conflicted. I'm happy to be getting my life back, but the thought of telling Will makes me tense and nervous and stressed.

So, I don't tell Will. I head straight to Janesse's and give her my notice, effective immediately. She closes the store and takes me to the Café, where Allegra allows us to order whatever we want. James and Sebastian hug me and order me to come back and visit. They invite me to Brandy's New Year's Eve party, and I say I'll try to make it. Allegra hugs me, and Janesse tears up a bit. I get in my car and watch as Janesse heads back over to the shop. A few moments later, I see the hand-painted "Help Wanted" sign go back up in the window. I stare at it for a few moments, then drive back to the cabin. I knock on Brandy's door, but she's not home, so I sneak past Will's back to my cabin, where I settle on the couch in depressed silence. I sit back and rest my head against the back of the couch, closing my eyes. I've been sitting there for a few minutes when there's a knock at my door.

"Hey, there, stranger," I say, stepping back to let Will in. My heart is racing, and I feel a cool sheen of sweat forming on the back of my neck. "I was just going to come see you."

He smiles, but it's weak.

"I hear you're leaving on Friday," he says. "That true?"

"Yeah." News travels fast in Bilby, I guess. "I was just going to tell you. Um, Maya, the girl with the extra room? She said I could move in. How did you . . . ? I mean, I was just going to come tell you—"

"James," he says. "He just called me to tell me to lock you in your cabin so you couldn't leave."

"Oh." I am awash with guilt. "Yeah. I was there this morning, with Janesse. I had to give her notice and then Allegra was there . . ."

I trail off. Even to my own ears, I sound lame. I should

have told him first. I should have and I didn't and I'm just going to have to suck it up and face the consequences.

"Yeah. No. I understand," he says. "When do you start your job?"

"We're gonna meet on Monday, and then I start work after the holidays. I was actually hoping that we could spend some time together—"

"I have that job in San Diego," he says, motioning vaguely in the direction of his cabin. "I'm leaving to-night."

"Oh." *This is good-bye*, I think, and even while part of me tries to deny it, I can feel it falling over me like a heavy blanket. "When will you be back?"

His eyes meet mine. "Saturday."

"Oh."

Yep. This is definitely good-bye. I can smell it, like the stench of death. *Here's another potentially good thing you've managed to squash into the ground, Car. Go you.*

"Is there anything . . . ?" He trails off, looks to the door, then looks back at me. "Is there anything else we should say here?"

I think about that. Is there anything I can say here to salvage this train wreck? Should I say anything? I don't know. I don't know what I should do, what I should say. I don't know how normal, emotionally functional people handle situations like this. I feel like I'm in a wheelchair and he's asking me to walk and I just don't know how.

"Okay," he says after a moment. But I'm not ready for him to say okay. I'm still trying to figure out how to walk. He leans over and kisses me on the forehead, then turns and leaves. I stand where I am, staring at my feet, for what feels like hours before I finally go into my room and fall into my bed and cry until I fall asleep.

When I wake up, it's dusk. Or, possibly, dawn. I look at my clock; it reads 5:39.

Dusk.

I push myself up on my elbows and stare at my yellow walls. I start to cry again.

I love my yellow walls. If I could pick up this cabin and relocate it in Tucson, everything would be perfect. If I could take Brandy and Allegra and Janesse and James and Sebastian with me, I would.

And Will . . . But that's over. Will has broken up with me. At least I think he has. I'm pretty sure he has. And who can blame him? He gave me a chance to tell him I still wanted this, wanted us, and I didn't do it.

"He's better off," I mutter to myself, but then my lower lip starts to tremble and I stare at my yellow walls. I wonder if Maya will let me paint the walls yellow in her extra room?

I sniffle and get up, wandering randomly through the cabin. Today is Tuesday. I'm leaving in three days. Is it too early to pack? Maybe I should just leave now, save myself the misery of extending the pain. I stop at my tiny little sink with my regular-sized dishes in it and weep for a few minutes. Then I swipe at my face and go to my tiny baby refrigerator and grab my big bottle of wine. I pull the cork out with my teeth and spit it onto the counter. I pour a very full glass and start drinking. Tonight is definitely an occasion for drinking alone.

Accept the book with the amber spine. Brandy's voice is

so clear in my head that I actually look around the cabin for her. It takes me a moment to realize that I'm just remembering what she said in the reading.

"Oh, my God," I say out loud. The reading. The tape. I have that tape somewhere. Maybe there's something there, some instruction, some magical answer that will tell me what I'm supposed to do. I put the wineglass down and head into my room, diving into the closet. I pull out the stool and climb up until I can reach the big cardboard box I packed the night I left Dad's. I haven't looked in it since I moved in, as most of the stuff is totally random and useless. I dump it on my bed and start pawing through it. A sample of items include a mouse from my old computer, an ugly yellow monkey that Seth won for me at the U of A Spring Fling a few years back, and a package of six toothbrushes that I got at Price Club once, and which I always forget I have when I need a new toothbrush. Finally, at the bottom of the pile, I find the tape that Brandy made for me the day she gave me the reading. I pull it out and jam it into my tape player. I hit rewind, wait impatiently for a few seconds, and just hit play. I catch Brandy in midsentence, her voice hushed and low.

"*. . . emotional center is jagged. You keep everything in separate boxes.*"

I glance over at the quilt, with all the pretty images kept separate from each other, in the boxes. I don't know why, but this makes me incredibly sad.

"*Pay attention to the paintbrushes.*"

I can hear my own snicker in the background, and

I'm so annoyed with myself that I wish I could go back in time and smack that girl.

"Return the frog."

All my muscles go stiff.

"Um, what?" I hear myself saying on the tape.

"Accept the book with—"

I hit stop, rewind, play.

"Return the frog."

"Um, what?"

"Accept the book with the amber spine. Take the cab."

"No," I say, over my old self saying, *"Is that like 'leave the gun, take the cannoli'?"*

I hit stop on the tape machine.

Rewind.

Play.

"Return the frog."

"No." I glance over at Quasitoado, sitting on my dresser, and I feel a tear track down my cheek. "No."

"Is that like 'leave the gun, take the cannoli'?"

That can't be what I'm supposed to do. I can't give back Quasitoado. I might have to go through the rest of my life without Will, but I'm not giving up Quasitoado.

"No," I say, my voice all high-pitched and cracking. "I love him."

"Everything's about to change," Brandy's voice says. I reach out and shut off the tape, then settle back down on my bed.

No, I think. *I don't want to give up Quasitoado. I love Quasitoado. Quasitoado makes me happy. He understands me. He doesn't judge me.*

He's already gone, says a voice in my head. *You've blown it. It's too late. He's gone.*

"Maybe he hasn't left yet," I say out loud. "Maybe . . ."

That's it. That's my answer. I'll go over to Will's. If he's still there, then we're meant to be, and I can keep Quasitoado. If he's not, then . . .

But he will be there. He has to be. We're meant to be together, I know it. I know it as I stuff my feet into my sneakers. I know it as I shrug into my jacket. I know it as I run to Will's cabin, as sure as I've ever been about anything. I'm finally getting up out of that stupid fucking wheelchair. I'm walking.

I'm walking.

He's not in his cabin. It takes my jiggling the chintzy back door lock free and entering his cabin before I accept that he's gone. He's not in the shower, where he can't hear me knocking. He's not in the bundle of blankets on his unmade bed where I thought he might be taking a postbreakup nap of his own. He is gone, on his way to wherever.

He's gone. I could call him on his cell phone but what would be the point? He's gone. Fate has spoken.

It's over.

I don't even realize I'm going to Brandy's until I find myself at her door. I ring the doorbell. It zaps me, but I don't care.

"Come in," she calls, and I open the door and step inside. It's dark, and I start talking as my eyes adjust.

"Will's back door lock is broken. I'll pay for it. But

I'm moving out, so I can't fix it myself, or I would. But I'll pay for it. And I'll pay next month's rent, too, so you have thirty days' notice. I just won't be here for it. I hope that's okay. I got a job in Tucson. I'm leaving Friday."

I stop rambling and look up to see Brandy sitting on her living room floor, kneeling before a tremendous quilt made of vibrant colors swirling over a dark purple background. It looks almost like one of those hurricane graphics they put on the Weather Channel, except prettier.

"Wow," I say.

"It's done," she says, and looks up at me. Her hair's a mess, and it looks like she hasn't slept in a while. "Will you go get him for me?"

"Sure," I say quietly. "Yeah. Of course. Right now?"

She nods and swipes at her face. "I might lose my nerve if it's not now."

"Okay." I turn around and head out the door, fumbling in my pocket for my keys.

"So, she's really got a quilt for me?" Janesse says as I pull the car to a stop in front of Brandy's house. I remove the keys from the ignition, but she doesn't move, just stares out the window at Brandy's house.

"We bought this place together," she says, but stops there, reliving her memories on her own. I wait for a minute, then follow her lead as she unhooks her seat belt and gets out of the car.

Brandy is exactly as I left her, kneeling before the quilt on the floor.

"Brandy?" I say. "I've got Janesse here."

Brandy's eyes lock on me, then drift upward and to my left. I step aside and sit on the stairs, trying to be present but out of the way at the same time.

Janesse stands frozen in the doorway for a long moment, then finally steps in and closes the door behind her. They stare at each other for a while. Brandy's eyes glisten with tears in the low light, and Janesse gives a small nod. Then Brandy smiles and holds out her hand. Janesse walks over and takes it, sitting next to Brandy. Brandy smiles, and a tear bops down her cheek as she hits the record button on the tape player at her side.

"This," she says, motioning with her free hand while still holding Janesse's hand in the other, "represents your emotional center. It's vibrant and powerful. And beautiful."

Janesse sniffles and swipes at her face. Brandy watches her, waiting, and when Janesse looks at her again, Brandy smiles before turning her eyes back to the quilt. "You are a person who brings others to their paths. You have a heart that loves unconditionally. You are . . ."

I stay because Brandy asked me to stay, but I stare at my feet and let Brandy's words fade out under a blanket of my own thoughts. The reading takes about thirty minutes, and when it's over, the three of us break out a bottle of wine and toast the upcoming new year.

Allegra, Janesse, and Brandy are sitting on my couch. I'm in the orange easy chair. The packing party lasted all of two hours. I really didn't have that much stuff. On the coffee table before us are two items: *She Might Be Crying* and Quasitoado.

"I really said, 'Return the frog'?" Brandy asks. "Maybe I didn't mean this frog. Besides, isn't this technically a toad?"

"Technically, it's ceramic," I say. "And I've listened to the tape. You said it. 'Accept the book with the amber spine. Return the frog.' "

Janesse sighs. "Then you need to return the frog."

Allegra hits Janesse. "No, she doesn't. It was a stupid reading. It doesn't mean anything." She leans forward and smiles at Brandy. "No offense, Bran."

"None taken." Brandy looks at me and sighs. "Well, what do you want to do?"

I stare at the coffee table. "I want to wrap them both up and bring them with me. I want to find Will and tell him that I want to make this work. I want to do a lot of things, but if it's not the right thing . . ." I flash back to Seth at Ella's wedding. "I don't want to put him through that."

Allegra sighs. "At least keep the painting. You paid for it. It's yours. If you don't keep that, it'll hurt his feelings."

I nod, still staring at the painting. "Yeah. Okay."

Out of the corner of my vision, I see Brandy nudge Janesse, who grabs the painting in one hand and Allegra's arm in the other.

"We'll go wrap it up for you at Brandy's and get it in your car."

I sit back, wait for them to leave, and then lock eyes on Brandy. "Okay. What's up?"

Brandy leans forward. "I'm really proud of you."

I can't stop myself from snorting in derision. "Yeah. I'm a real prize."

"You are. Look at you. I'm amazed by you, by your faith."

My head jerks up at this. "My what?"

"When I first met you, I didn't think you were that kind of girl. I thought you were one of those people who forced life to be what they thought they wanted, instead of embracing what it was meant to be."

"Hmm," I say. "That's supposed to be a compliment, right? Supposed to make me feel better?"

She smiles. "It takes a tremendous amount of courage to do what you know is right, even when it's not what you want. Even when you can rationally explain why you shouldn't. And, you know, sometimes you get what you really want by doing the very thing you don't want to do."

I rub my eyes. "Will it lower your opinion of me at all if I tell you I have no idea what the hell you're talking about?"

"Not in the least." She kneels in front of the frog. "Good-bye, Quasitoado." She stands up and brushes her knees off. "I'll wait for you at the house. You come in and say good-bye before you leave, okay?"

I nod, still staring at the frog as she leaves.

"So, this is about faith, is it?" I ask Quasitoado. "So, what? If I give you back to Will, you'll bring him back to me? Do you think you can do that?"

Quasitoado stares back at me, his mutantish, tiny face giving me no answers. I close my eyes and sit back in the chair, letting the silence wash over me. I'm so tired that my mind goes instantly blank, and I'm grateful for it.

And then, like an almost imperceptible breeze, I feel a surge of certainty pulse through me, and I open my eyes.

I know what to do. I grab Quasitoado and hold him in my arms, heading out of the cabin. I start down the path, hitching a left at Will's cabin. I set Quasi down on the little outdoor table on his porch, and I give the ugly ceramic frog a quick kiss on the nose.

I step back, swipe my face, and turn my back, knowing I've done the right thing despite the fact that I hate every minute of it.

I now know why I never had any faith before. It's because faith sucks.

Chapter Twelve

My father's annual New Year's Eve party is as crazy this year as it always is. The house is filled wall-to-wall with coworkers from his architecture firm, old friends we only see at New Year's, and, of course, our screwed-up but lovable little family. After much hesitation, I wear the brown chiffon dress to the party, and I get hit on by the guy who does Dad's payroll and the guy who delivers the champagne. They're both cute, and I'm flattered, but I'm not interested.

They're not Will.

It's been almost two weeks since I left Bilby, and Will still hasn't called. Part of me was hoping that the purpose of leaving Quasitoado behind was so that Will would realize how much I meant to him and chase me to Tucson. But that didn't happen. I've given myself until New Year's Eve to finally accept that it's over, and midnight is mere hours away, so it's time to start accepting.

We're just not meant to be.

The party is fun, but as it turns out I'm in no mood for a fun party. At nine-thirty, I make my escape to the backyard, where it's cold and quiet and matching my mood.

I sit in one of the cold, metal chairs next to the porch table and stare up at the stars. I wonder what Will's doing right now, and internally resolve that I will stop thinking about Will in the new year. I give myself two and a half more hours to indulge this crap, and then, that's it.

I'm going cold turkey.

"Care for some company?"

I turn and see Mary standing behind me, holding two fleece throw blankets in her arms. She wraps one over my shoulders and puts the other over her own, then sits down across from me, staring up at the stars. We sit in silence for a long while before she starts talking.

"When you were a little girl, about six years old or so," she says, "you came into our room, really early in the morning. You tapped me on the shoulder, and when I asked you what you wanted, you just put your finger to your lips and said 'Shhhhh.' Then you took my hand and led me outside, to this very spot." She looks at me and smiles. "It was snowing. It was amazing. It was like magic, because it was April. Right after Easter. I mean, you know it rarely ever snows here, but in April? It was crazy. We just stood out here together for a long time, catching the snow on our tongues. You looked so happy." She lets out a small laugh. "Wow. I don't know why I just remembered that. I haven't thought about that day in ages."

I'm still staring at the sky when I hear her sniffle, and when I look at her, there are tears on her face. She swipes at them hastily.

"I'm sorry," she says. "I've obviously had too much champagne." She straightens up in her seat, swipes at her face one last time, and smiles at me. "I'm sorry."

I look away. "Yeah. Me, too."

There's a long moment of silence, and then she finally speaks. "You have nothing to be sorry about."

"That's debatable," I say, still not looking at her. "No matter what you did, the fact is, you came back to try and make it right. And that takes a lot of courage. I have to give you credit for that. I don't know if I would have had that kind of courage."

"Maybe," she says, leaning back in her chair and staring up at the sky. "But I don't know if that counts for much with your sisters. At least you came out and told me how you felt. I can deal with that. Ella hides it all under this veneer of sunshine, and Five . . . Five's just all over the place. She's fine one minute, and the next, I don't know what I'm dealing with."

"Well," I say, "the secret with Ella is to just get in her face and don't let her pretend everything's fine. She'll resist for a while, but eventually she'll blow up all over you and then you can start working it out. As for Five . . ." I shake my head. "She's seventeen. My vote is, it'd be hell right now even if you'd been here all along. Just keep your liquor cabinet stocked and pray."

She lifts her glass and we toast. I watch her as she stares up into the sky and I feel a flash of genuine affection. It's not much more than a flash, nowhere near total forgiveness, but it's a promising place to start.

"You know what I think we need?" I say finally. "A do-over."

She lets out a small laugh. "A what-over?"

I open my mouth to explain when the back door creaks behind us and Five pokes her head out. "Carly, did you call a cab?"

"Um, no. I don't think so. Why?"

She lets out a huff of frustrated air. "Oh, nothing. There's a cab out front and the guy insists he was given this address and . . . whatever. I'll just tell him to leave."

"Okay," I say, but then take in a sharp breath of air as I hear Brandy's voice in my head.

Take the cab.

"Oh, my God," I say, putting my hand over my mouth. My heart starts to race.

"Carly?" Mary says as I push up from my chair.

Return the frog. Accept the book with the amber spine.

Take the cab.

"Wait, Five!" I can't believe I'm doing this. "It's mine. The cab is mine. Can you grab my coat and my purse for me, please?"

"Um. Okay." Five shrugs and disappears into the house. I turn to Mary.

"I'm sorry. I need to go. I think. I think I need to go."

Mary stands up. "It's not even midnight," she says. "Where are you going?"

I smile. "I'm not sure. But I think . . . I think the cab is for me. Does that sound crazy?"

"You're asking me about crazy?" she says.

I take the throw off my shoulders and give it back to her. "Can we continue this next week, maybe? Have lunch or something? We'll talk."

She nods. "Yeah. Sure. That'll be nice."

We exchange a brief smile and I rush toward the back door, where Five is waiting with my coat and purse.

"Where are you going?" she asks as she rushes behind me to the front door.

"I don't know." I laugh and give her a quick kiss on the cheek. "Tell everyone Happy New Year for me, okay?"

"Okay," she says, eyeing my half-empty flute of champagne. "Can I have that?"

I hand it to her. "Don't tell Dad I gave it to you."

The cab is still waiting by the curb. I run toward it, shrugging into my coat as I go.

"Where are we going?" the cabbie sighs, obviously annoyed, when I hop into the backseat.

"I don't know," I say. "Didn't they—I mean, I—give you a destination when I called?"

He shoots a look over his shoulder that shows me he is definitely not amused. But I need a sign; I need him to give me a sign that this cab is actually for me. I was hoping that sign would be him taking me straight to Bilby, although that is kind of ridiculous. I mean, coincidence is only going to take me so far, right? I feel my heart start to race and I take a deep breath.

"How much for you to take me to Bilby?"

He looks at me like I'm nuts. Which, arguably . . .

"Bilby?" he says. "I'm not taking you to Bilby, lady. This cab is city limits only."

I sit back, deflated. This isn't the way this is supposed to go. I was supposed to hop in the cab, and he was supposed to have my answer. He was supposed to take me to Bilby.

He was supposed to take me to Will.

"What if I paid you extra?" I say. "Do you take credit cards?"

He reaches over and hits the button on his meter, printing out a receipt. "That'll be four eighty-six."

"For what?" I say. "You didn't take me anywhere."

"That's the meter cost for making me sit here for nothing. Four dollars and eighty-six cents."

He hands me the receipt, and I look at it. Four dollars and eighty-six cents. The exact amount Mr. Trimble always paid for his charcoals.

"It's a sign," I mumble.

"What?" he says.

"Oh, shut up. It could be a sign." I dig into my purse and shove a twenty at him. "Keep the change."

He thanks me perfunctorily and takes the twenty. I hop out of the cab, watch him drive off, and glance at the receipt one more time before hopping into my own car.

My car clock reads 11:38 when I arrive in front of Brandy's house. Through the windows, I see James and Sebastian dancing. I see Janesse wearing a brilliant yellow dress and looking typically stunning. I watch for a while longer, catching flashes of Allegra's pink hair, Brandy's long ponytail, and Gladys's and Mack's matching holiday sweaters.

No Will. He can't be on assignment, can he? On New Year's Eve?

Maybe. I don't know. And I won't know until I get myself up out of this car and go find out. I step out of the car and stumble in my heels on the rock path that leads past Brandy's house. After a few steps, I get my footing, although I'm pretty sure my ankles are going to hate me in the morning.

I hug my coat around me as I walk through the foliage to the clearing. The night is crisp and clear, with the moon and the stars casting everything in a blue glow. My heart jumps in my chest as I see the light coming from Will's windows.

He's home.

I pause for a moment, take a deep breath, and make my way to his cabin. My hand shakes as I knock on the door. Despite the two-hour drive, I have no idea what I'm going to say. It takes him a moment, but eventually the door opens, and there he is. His hair's a mess, his shirt is splattered with paint, and he's as gorgeous as ever.

"Hey," I say.

He stares at me. It seems to take him a moment to form a response. Then he smiles. "Hey."

"I was just in the neighborhood," I say. "I thought I'd stop in and say hi."

"Yeah." He gives a confused little laugh. "Hi."

"Hi."

There's a long moment in which we just look at each other, and then he gives his head a little shake and steps back, holding the door open to let me inside. "I'm sorry. Come in. You've gotta be freezing."

"I'm fine," I say, but walk inside at his invitation. As he closes the door behind me, the room catches my attention. Well, not the room so much as what's in it.

Paintings. New ones. Everywhere. On the couch. On the floor, leaning against the walls, on the kitchen counter. What's as interesting as the fact that there are so many new paintings is the subject matter.

Quasitoado. Well, not *all* Quasitoado. There are two leaning against the wall that are definitely Quasi, all hunchbacked and mutant-faced and cute as hell. The rest seem to be Quasi evolving from an ugly sugar dish into a real frog. The settings around him are all familiar, though. I recognize Brandy's couch, the counter at Art's Desire, the mosaic table outside the Café. Individually, the paintings are neat. Quirky. But together, there's something really touching about seeing fugly Quasi grow into a beautiful frog. A real frog.

"Wow," I say, unable to tear my eyes away from the paintings.

"Yeah," he says with a laugh. "I've been working out some issues, I think."

"So . . ." I work for a minute, trying to put my thoughts into words. "Quasi was your inspiration?"

"Well . . ." He looks at his shoes, the paintings, the coffee table. Everything but me. "He kind of represented a lot for me." He finally meets my eyes. "I, uh, I've been working on the last of the series. There's a gallery in Tucson that might be interested, actually. I sent them some pictures, and they asked me to come up next week."

"That's great!" I smile up at him. "Your work should be seen. It's incredible."

"Thanks." We just stand there, our eyes locked for a long moment, then Will breaks the silence. "So. Um. Happy New Year."

"Happy New Year." I take a deep breath and laugh nervously. "You're probably wondering what I'm doing here."

He keeps his eyes on mine. "Little bit."

I blink hard against the tears blurring my vision, and my breath comes out in a hitch. "I miss my frog."

His eyebrows knit. "You miss . . . what? Quasitoado?"

I sniffle and nod. "The reading that Brandy gave me? It said to accept the book, return the frog, take the cab. And I did it, I did everything just the way the reading told me. I tried to have faith, Will, I really tried, but you didn't come back to me." I swipe at my face. "I thought that if I did it all, my life would work out right, but it didn't, because I don't think it can be right without you. And maybe you don't want me and maybe I'm just supposed to let you go. I don't know. But if it comes down to having faith or knowing I did everything in my power to keep you in my life, then I'm just gonna have to be one of those people with no faith, because I don't have it in me to want something this much and not try to make it work."

I keep my eyes on the floor, biting the inside of my cheek to stop the crying, but it's useless. Then Will puts his fingers under my chin and raises my face up to look at him.

"I was coming," he says.

I blink at him. "What?"

He smiles and swipes a tear from my cheek. "My plan was to go to Tucson. Get the showing. Send you an invite. Then, when you showed up at the gallery, I was going to be all dressed up and smelling so good that you wouldn't be able to tell me to get lost."

I laugh. "I wouldn't tell you to get lost."

"Well," he says, smiling dreamily down at me. Then he takes in a breath. "Oh, and I was going to ply you with wine. You know. Hedge my bets."

"Oh," I say, my voice squeaky under the tears. "That would have been really nice."

He moves his hand to my shoulder and steps closer. "That's okay. I like this way, too."

He leans down and kisses me, then pulls me into a hug. We start to sway to the muted music coming from Brandy's house, and I rest my head against his chest, listening to his heart beat. It's a good moment for me, one of my better ones, and I close my eyes to properly enjoy it.

"I'm not giving up the frog, you know," he says. I pull my head back and look up to see him smiling down at me. "We're a package deal."

"I see." I wrap my arms tighter around his waist. "So, what? Are we going to have to work out some shared custody deal?"

"I'm thinking, maybe, you know, if things work out, I can find an apartment up in Tucson. You know, so Quasi doesn't have to travel so far to see you. It's really not good for him. He gets impatient."

I grin. "Yeah. I can understand that."

"Then . . ." He leans his face down and kisses my neck. "Maybe I can have him when I'm in town, and you can keep him when I'm on assignment."

"Mmmm," I say as Will's hands slide under my coat, slipping it off my shoulders. "Yeah, I think that would definitely be the best solution."

He puts one hand on my face and we kiss for a long time, only breaking when we hear an explosion of cheers coming from Brandy's house.

Will laughs. "So, are you ready to ring in the new year?"

I take my coat from him and toss it over Quasi, who was watching us from his perch on the coffee table.

"Now I am," I say.

About the Author

Lani Diane Rich is a former television producer who lives in upstate New York with her husband and two daughters. You can find her at her Web site, www.lani dianerich.com, or at the group blog Literary Chicks, www.literarychicks.com.